ℊET A̶ __ __

WITH JUST O̶ __

$50 VALUE

◆ **Hotel Discounts**
up to 60%
at home
and abroad
◆ **Travel Service -**
Guaranteed lowest published
airfares plus 5% cash back on
tickets ◆ **$25 Travel Voucher**
◆ **Sensuous Petite Parfumerie**
collection ◆ **Insider
Tips Letter** with
sneak previews of
upcoming books

*𝒴ou'll get a FREE personal card, too.
It's your passport to all these benefits– and to
even more great gifts & benefits to come!*

There's no club to join. No purchase commitment. No obligation.

HS-PP6A

Enrollment Form

☐ **Yes!** I WANT TO BE A *PRIVILEGED WOMAN*.
Enclosed is one *PAGES & PRIVILEGES*™ Proof of
Purchase from any Harlequin or Silhouette book currently for
sale in stores (Proofs of Purchase are found on the back pages
of books) and the store cash register receipt. Please enroll me
in *PAGES & PRIVILEGES*™. Send my Welcome Kit and FREE
Gifts -- and activate my FREE benefits -- immediately.
More great gifts and benefits to come.

NAME (please print)

ADDRESS   APT. NO

CITY   STATE   ZIP/POSTAL CODE

PROOF OF PURCHASE ONLY

NO CLUB!
NO COMMITMENT!
*Just one purchase brings
you great Free Gifts and
Benefits!*

Please allow 6-8 weeks for delivery. Quantities are limited. We reserve the right to
substitute items. Enroll before October 31, 1995 and receive one full year of benefits.

Name of store where this book was purchased_____
Date of purchase_____
Type of store:
  ☐ Bookstore   ☐ Supermarket   ☐ Drugstore
  ☐ Dept. or discount store (e.g. K-Mart or Walmart)
  ☐ Other (specify)_____
Which Harlequin or Silhouette series do you usually read?

Complete and mail with one Proof of Purchase and store receipt to:
U.S.: *PAGES & PRIVILEGES*™, P.O. Box 1960, Danbury, CT 06813-1960
Canada: *PAGES & PRIVILEGES*™, 49-6A The Donway West, P.O. 813,
North York, ON M3C 2E8

HS-PP6B

▶ DETACH HERE AND MAIL TODAY! ▶

DUNLEAVY FARM
KENTUCKY

Dear Seth,

Permit me to introduce myself. I am your maternal grandmother, Octavia Whitworth Dunleavy.

When I think of the bitter circumstances under which your mother and I parted company, I feel safe in guessing that you've probably never heard of me. So I imagine this letter will come as quite a shock, but please bear with me.

My dear grandson, I need to see you. I have a proposition to discuss that I hope you will find most interesting....

Looking forward to hearing from you, I remain,

Yours affectionately,

Octavia Whitworth Dunleavy

ABOUT THE AUTHOR

Janis Flores has had a wide and varied publishing career. She's written several mainstream novels and more than fifteen romance novels. The Dunleavy Legacy, of which *Never Done Dreamin'* is the final title, is her first trilogy. Janis says it's been a real joy to write books about two of her favorite topics—romance, of course, and the thrill of raising and racing the finest, fleetest creatures on earth.

She hopes readers enjoy these stories. "The races are over now, but my wish is that romance will always linger in your heart."

Janis Flores

NEVER DONE DREAMIN'

Harlequin Books

TORONTO • NEW YORK • LONDON
AMSTERDAM • PARIS • SYDNEY • HAMBURG
STOCKHOLM • ATHENS • TOKYO • MILAN
MADRID • WARSAW • BUDAPEST • AUCKLAND

ISBN 0-373-70662-6

NEVER DONE DREAMIN'

NEVER DONE
DREAMIN'

Printed in the United States. ...and Trademark Office, the
® Trade Mark Office and in other countries.

in U.S.A.

CHAPTER ONE

Dunleavy Farm, Kentucky: April 1995

HOW ON EARTH was she going to explain her husband's absence?

Honey Dunleavy was very aware of the three women watching her and waiting for her to continue. "Seth really wanted to accept your kind invitation, but—" She stopped and looked at Seth's grandmother and his two cousins. She couldn't tell them the truth—that Seth wanted nothing to do with the family he'd never met. She was beginning to wish she'd listened to him and stayed far away from Dunleavy Farm herself, but the invitation had been so tempting.

Octavia Dunleavy, matriarch of the Dunleavy family obviously recognized Honey's discomfort. "I'm very glad *you* came," she said. "And I'd like you to call me grandmother if you're comfortable with that."

"I've never had a grandmother—not one I recall, anyway," Honey said. "For as long as I can remember—until I met Seth, that is—it was really just Pop and me."

"That sounds familiar," Nan said. Seth's cousin was perched on the chair to Honey's right. Honey had been surprised when they'd finally met face-to-face. She'd only talked to Nan over the phone, and had imagined that she'd look completely different. Taller, for one thing, Honey thought, hiding a smile.

Now that she was at Dunleavy Farm, Honey wanted to know all there was about Seth's cousins. They were both so lovely, she thought, yet so different from each other. Nan, small and dark-haired, with a no-nonsense manner and an air of being in motion even when she was sitting still, was the barn manager here; Carla, regal and elegantly tall, with shoulder-length chestnut hair and an unconscious grace, managed the books. They both had striking green eyes—as did Octavia, Honey realized with a start. Seth's eyes were the same color; it was obviously a family trait.

"It was the same with me," Nan went on. "My mother died when I was a child, and my dad raised me on a ranch in Montana."

"A ranch!" Honey exclaimed. "Oh, that sounds wonderful."

Nan laughed, showing even, white teeth. "It's not the kind of ranch you're thinking about. It was a dude ranch."

"That sounds even more exciting."

"Oh, it was," Nan said dryly. "Especially when we couldn't pay the bills."

"Still, it was home."

"Yes, it was. But then hard times came, and when my father died, I had to sell the place."

"Oh, I'm sorry," Honey said. There were moments when her own father's carousing and his habit of showing up at the wrong time made her angry—and drove Seth wild—but even though her husband couldn't understand, she loved her father. No matter how Seth ranted, she just couldn't ban Davey LaRue from her life for longer than a few months at a time.

"He needs me!" she tried to tell Seth.

But Seth, who had once been so protective of her, would reply coldly, "He needs whatever money you give him. He'll gamble it away and be back when it's gone. Why do you give in every time? He knows he can come to you when he's in trouble."

Seth just didn't understand, Honey would think. But as time went on, she began to wonder if perhaps he was a little jealous of her relationship with her father. After all, Seth had no family—or so she'd always believed. But then the letter from Octavia Dunleavy had come, and she'd decided that it might be good for their marriage to search them out. Maybe if he had some family of his own, he wouldn't feel so... alone, and they could get back on track again.

At the moment, she didn't want to think about how things between them had rapidly gone from bad to worse, so she tried to concentrate on the conversation and put Seth from her mind.

Nan was saying, "I didn't know where to turn at that point, but then Grandmother sent that letter, and when I came, she made me feel so welcome. I can't imagine being anywhere else now."

"Not even at ChangeOver Farm?" Carla asked slyly.

"That's different," Nan said with an attractive blush. "And besides, it's right next door."

"ChangeOver Farm?" Honey asked.

Carla winked at her. "Oh, it's a little place over the hill where a very handsome man named Trent Spencer lives."

"Trent Spencer?"

Carla leaned toward her conspiratorially and stage-whispered, "He's the guy Nan finally managed to cajole into marrying her."

"Cajole!" Nan said indignantly. "You make it sound like I *sweet-talked* him into proposing!"

Carla laughed. "With your temper? I'm sorry, dear, but I don't think that word is in your vocabulary."

"*You* should talk."

"*I?* Why, whatever do you mean?"

Honey loved to listen to Carla's voice. Seth's other cousin had a trace of a British accent that suited her. With Carla's coloring and her smooth, creamy complexion, she looked like a lovely English rose.

As though reading Honey's mind, Nan said, "No doubt you've noticed Carla's finishing-school tones. She's the aristocrat among us, isn't she, Grandmother? I'm just a poor old Montana girl, while Carla has been to the best schools in England." She paused to give Honey a knowing look. "Why, do you know, she even had tea with the queen?"

"Only once," Carla said, smiling.

"Oh, my," Honey said, impressed. "Wasn't that enough?"

Nan laughed, then confided, "You know, Carla terrified me when I first came—"

"What? I did not!"

"You certainly did," Nan said. She grinned at Honey again. "But don't worry. I learned that she might come on strong, but underneath she's all marshmallow. Just ask Wade."

"Wade?" Honey said, confused. They were throwing so many names at her, she wondered if she'd ever get them all straight.

Carla blushed, the way Nan had a short while ago. When Honey saw those telltale pink cheeks, she couldn't help thinking of Seth once more. She used to blush like that when he was mentioned. Would she ever feel that way again?

"Wade is my fiancé," Carla said. "You'll meet him later."

"And you'll meet Trent and his son, Derry, too," Nan said. "In the meantime, tell us about *you*. We're dying to know everything!"

"Well, not *everything*," Octavia interjected. "Just what you want to tell us, dear. For instance, you were saying something about being raised by your father?"

Honey was amazed at herself. Normally, she was a private person, but already she trusted these kind women enough to say, "I wish I could tell you that my dad was responsible for my care, but the truth is, every spring and summer when we went on the fair circuit, just about everyone *but* Pop helped to raise me."

Nan and Carla looked surprised, so she hastened to add, "It wasn't his fault, really. He just wasn't prepared to be a single parent, or maybe a parent at all. I was only about ten when my mother decided she'd had enough. One night, she just . . . left."

"How awful for you!" Nan exclaimed.

"Indeed," Carla murmured. "I admit there are times when I wish my mother would take the first plane to the nearest planet, but I can't imagine her just . . . leaving."

Octavia was equally as sympathetic. "It must have been difficult for your father."

"He didn't take it well," Honey said in a sweeping understatement. Remembering that time, she tried not to grimace. "When he realized my mother was gone for good, he disappeared for a few days. Someone finally found him sleeping it off in one of the tack rooms on a deserted shedrow."

"You were so young, my dear," Octavia said. "What did you do?"

"Well, one of the benefits of being raised by a big 'family' at the track, is that there's always someone around. One of the trainer's wives took me in until Pop pulled himself together."

She made it sound matter-of-fact, but the truth was Davey had never gotten over Amber LaRue's desertion. Until then, he'd been a top-winning jockey. But after his wife left, he couldn't seem to do anything right. Soon the best trainers stopped asking him to ride. After that, it was one long slide downhill until the only work he could get was exercising horses during morning workouts, or signing on as a groom.

Still, Honey had to be fair. The circuit was the only life her father knew. He sensed he'd never make it in the outside world, and he didn't even try. Honey remembered her father always scrambling to make a buck. Too many times to count, they'd lived hand-to-mouth, Honey always worrying about how they were going to make out.

Davey never worried; it wasn't in his nature. "Something will come along, Puddin'," he would say. "Don't you worry, something will come along."

And to her amazement, something always had. Out of thin air, it seemed, Davey would conjure up a few dollars for clothes, or for school, or for groceries, and they'd be okay until the next time the money ran out. Honey knew now she'd been naive. She hadn't realized for the longest time—perhaps because she didn't want to know—that her father was not only a gambler, but a minor con artist who wasn't above pulling the wool over people's eyes if the price was right. He'd never actually *hurt* anyone, she thought hastily, but still, the truth wasn't pleasant to think about.

Fortunately for her, she had known from an early age that she could always knock on the trailer next door if she needed anything. With the nomadic existence they all shared, there weren't too many kids on the backside, so she'd been adopted by almost everyone.

But even that had had its positives and negatives, she recalled. On the one hand, she'd been free to do just about anything she wanted; on the other hand, Davey had heard instantly about even her most minor transgression. It was a good thing for her that he'd been so... relaxed about fatherhood, especially when she'd started to discover boys.

But she didn't want to think about *that* or she'd start to dwell on Seth again—Seth, whom she'd adored the instant they met. She couldn't think about Seth, or she might start to cry. Then she'd have to explain why, and she just didn't have the strength for it now.

So in answer to Octavia's question about her mother, she said, "We got over it, Pop and I. You have to, I guess, or you can drive yourself crazy wondering and worrying about the possibilities."

Octavia leaned forward. "And you never heard from your mother again?"

"Once, about six years after she left. She said she was about to make it big in Hollywood, and that when she had enough money, she'd send for me. She never did, of course, but that's all right. Pop and I had our own lives, and then, of course, not long after that, I met Seth."

Honey came to a stop, wondering how long she could carry on the pretense. She hated pretending that everything was all right when it wasn't. But she couldn't just walk in and fall apart, not when these women had welcomed her as if she really *was* one of the family, and not related by marriage only.

In fact, she still couldn't believe she was actually here. Until the taxi had brought her through the gates not thirty minutes ago, she had only seen pictures of the renowned Dunleavy Farm. Now she was actually sitting in the front room—the room that held mementos of the Triple Crown win of the farm's famous stallion, Done Roamin'. Never in her wildest dreams had she imagined this. The only thing that would have made it better was if Seth were here to share it.

But Seth was back in Arizona, sulking in the cramped little house trailer that had been their home for the six years they'd been married. And he wasn't busy taking care of horses, as she'd implied. The truth was that they didn't have that many to take care of, not anymore. Soon after the accident, most of their clients had gone to other trainers.

She couldn't blame the owners, she thought wearily. Even on the state and county fair circuits, far removed from the major tracks like Churchill Downs, racehorses were expensive to run and maintain. She'd worked harder than she'd ever worked in her life, but with Seth hobbling around on crutches from the sidelines, and only one groom to help out, she couldn't keep up with the demands of the horses and travel from one fair to the other, too. It wasn't long before first one owner, then another, had asked for a final bill. They were all sorry, they said; they'd stay if they could. Maybe when Seth got better... They hoped she understood.

But Seth wasn't getting better, Honey thought. It had been six months since the aptly named Twisted Fate had fallen over backward in the cross-ties, taking Seth with him. All that time, and her husband was still on crutches, his leg in a cast. The broken bone simply wouldn't heal. Sometimes she didn't know who was more frustrated—she, or Seth, or the doctor, who kept taking X rays and shaking his head.

The miracle was that they'd had medical insurance. She hated to think what would have happened to them if she hadn't insisted on paying that premium every month. She'd seen firsthand just how quickly—and sometimes irrevocably—lives could change in the blink of an eye, and she had learned that some things were nonnegotiable. Now, Seth, who had complained constantly about the payment, was glad she'd been adamant. With other expenses mounting and no way to meet them, at least they didn't have to worry about medical bills.

But that was the only thing she didn't have to worry about, Honey thought. Now that she was in Kentucky and Seth was still in Arizona, the situation between them was even more tense. Seth had been angry with her for questioning him about not accepting Octavia Dunleavy's invitation to come here, but he had been absolutely furious that she had decided to go without him. She'd tried to convince him that he should meet his family, but he wouldn't listen. It was only, she thought wearily, one more thing about which they'd quarreled.

Nan brought her out of her depressing thoughts by asking, "How did you and Seth meet?"

Carla laughed. "She just wants to know so she can tell if it was more bizarre than how she and her fiancé were introduced."

Nan crossed her arms. "You stop that, Carla Dunleavy. You're going to give Honey the idea that I'm a complete flake!"

Deciding that she could never think that of sensible Nan, Honey laughed, too, and asked, "How did you meet . . . Trent, is it?"

"It is," Nan said, and quickly assured her, "And it wasn't my fault."

"Oh, that's right," Carla teased. "It was *Derry's* fault. He's the one who ran his bike under your truck—and then fainted right into your arms at the sight of a little blood."

Honey was wide-eyed. "Is that true?"

"Oh, Carla's exaggerating," Nan said with a mock glare in her cousin's direction. "The truth is that I was sitting there minding my own business, when Derry— he's Trent's sixteen-year-old son—came barreling down the road on his bicycle without watching where he was going. By the time he looked up and saw my truck, he couldn't stop. To my horror, he slid right under it."

Honey gasped. "Was he hurt? You said something about blood."

"From a little cut on his forehead," Nan explained. "Actually, his bike was wounded worse than he was—except maybe his pride. You know how boys are."

"But what about Trent?"

"Oh, *he* came roaring along in his big black Jaguar," Carla filled in before Nan could reply, "trying to find Derry before the boy killed himself. They'd had a fight, you see, and when he saw Derry's mangled bike under this beat-up old truck, and his teenage son passed out on Nan's front seat, well, you can imagine what he thought.''

"It was all a big misunderstanding," Nan said quickly. "We worked it out later."

"I'll say," Carla commented. She reached for Nan's hand and pointed at the square-cut emerald engagement ring she wore. "Imagine what that ring would look like if they'd met in a more conventional way."

Nan laughed again. "You should talk. You and Wade didn't get along any better than Trent and I at first. In fact, as I recall, you treated him pretty much like a lowly servant."

Carla blushed. "I certainly—"

Octavia gently cleared her throat. "Perhaps we can save that story for another time, dears. I believe Honey was about to tell us how she and Seth met."

"Oh, it was nothing as dramatic as Nan's introduction to Trent, believe me," Honey said. "We met— where else? At the track."

Carla must have seen something in Honey's face, for she said, "Somehow, I think there's more to it than that."

"Tell us," Nan commanded.

Honey obeyed. "Well, from the time I first saw him at the track in Fresno, leading a horse to a race, I was in love. I was sixteen, Seth a vastly more experienced twenty-one, and I thought he was the handsomest, sexiest, funniest, cleverest man on earth."

"And that was before you'd even talked to him," Carla joked.

Honey laughed. "That's true."

And it was still true, Honey thought wistfully. Whenever she pictured her handsome husband, with his sun-bleached blond hair and his startling green eyes—not to mention that long, lean, muscular body that never failed to make her feel weak inside—she would have had to be made of stone *not* to react to him. Even so...

She realized that the three were waiting for her to continue, so she went on, "Of course, it wasn't just his undeniable good looks that drew me to him—"

"Oh, of *course* not," Carla murmured.

"Shh!" Nan said. "Go on, Honey."

"Even when he made it very obvious that he wanted to be left alone, I couldn't do it," Honey said shyly. "I know it sounds silly, but there was something in his eyes...I don't know, a look of loneliness, something that I felt myself. It was—don't laugh now—as though I'd found a soul mate. I didn't care that he ignored me. I saw him a lot, since he was on the same fair circuit that Pop and I followed, and I did everything—short of walking down the shedrow naked—to make him notice me."

"And he did," Nan said.

"Well, it took me two years to wear him down," Honey said ruefully, "but in the end, I guess persistence paid off. Finally, one day, in complete exasperation, he asked me just what I wanted."

"And what did you say?" Nan asked.

Honey smiled at the memory. "Well, I *meant* to ask him about going out on a date, or to come over for dinner, or maybe meet somewhere for coffee, but what I actually *said* was that I wanted to marry him."

Even Carla abandoned her blasé pose and leaned forward. "And what did he say?"

"Well, he should have said that I was out of my mind, or that he had no intention of getting married, at least to me, or that he'd already had six wives, and none of them had worked out. What he actually said was, 'When?'"

Nan sighed. "How romantic!"

It had been, Honey thought. She and Seth had been married six weeks later. Proud as punch, her father had given the bride away, whispering to her at the last second that he was sure Seth was destined for the big tracks.

So happy that day, secure in her love, proud of her handsome new husband, she'd whispered back, "I think so, too, Pop."

But it hadn't worked out that way, she thought now, six years later. In fact, when she looked back on it, nothing had turned out the way she'd hoped.

"I believe you were going to tell us why Seth didn't come with you," Octavia said.

Honey knew the time had come. She couldn't lie outright to these lovely women, but she couldn't tell them that she and Seth had been on the verge of separating. She'd just have to skirt the truth and pray that Seth would soon come to his senses. Hoping to avoid Octavia's sharp eyes, she said, "Well, as I started to say, Seth had to stay behind to take care of the horses we still have left. But he'll be along as soon as he finds someone to take over for him.''

"I see," Octavia said.

Honey had the uncomfortable feeling that Seth's grandmother saw a lot more than she admitted. She could feel a telltale flush creeping up her neck, and glanced away. Thankfully, she spied her tea on the low table in front of her and quickly reached for the cup.

"This is a beautiful room," she said, praying that they'd all accept the abrupt change of subject.

"Why, thank you, my dear," Octavia said. Obviously prepared to let Honey tell her story in her own way and in her own time, the older woman glanced around the room, too, her expression proud and pleased. "It holds a lot of memories, as you can see."

Honey did see. In addition to the display case of Triple Crown memorabilia and pictures of famous racehorses on the walls, there was a trophy cabinet at one end of the room that held some of the racing awards won by Dunleavy horses over the years. The air itself seemed imbued with memories of some of the brightest moments in the history of racing. Honey knew it was a dangerous feeling, but in that instant, she felt as though she'd come home.

She'd always dreamed of putting down roots someday, of settling in one place and staying for longer than a race meet or a season. She longed for a place where she could raise a family and where she could sit on her own front porch with Seth and watch their children and grandchildren grow up.

Octavia must have seen something in Honey's face, for she leaned toward her and took Honey's hand. Quietly, she said, "You were right to come. Stubborn pride has always been the bane of this family. I'm glad to see that you have more sense."

The words were out before Honey could stop them. "Then you don't think I was wrong to leave Seth home alone?"

"Oh, I didn't say *that*," Octavia answered gently. "Like the women of the family, the Dunleavy men sometimes need a little time to adjust to things. Seth will come, my dear. Don't you doubt it."

She couldn't help herself. "Do you really think so?"

Honey didn't realize the note of desperation in her voice until Octavia squeezed her fingers. While Nan and Carla were silent, the old woman said, "Yes, I do. From what you've said, I can tell that my grandson loves you. He'll come if only to be with you."

Honey wanted with all her heart to believe it, but she knew Seth, and Octavia didn't. He'd always been closemouthed about his family, admitting only that his father had run out on them, and that he and his mother had come to a parting of the ways when he was about sixteen. Familiar with the big names in racing, she had once jokingly asked him—never suspecting that it might be true— if he was related to the Dunleavys of Dunleavy Farm. He'd angrily denied any relationship, and she hadn't pursued the issue.

Then they'd received the letter from Octavia, and Honey had seized on it like a lifeline. Desperate to revive her dying marriage, she'd believed that if she could introduce Seth to his family, everything would be all right. No matter what Seth said about her father, she and Davey had always had a close relationship that had sustained them both. She was sure that if Seth could develop the same ties with his kin, he wouldn't feel he had to shoulder everything alone.

Families *helped,* Honey thought. They closed ranks; they shored up those who were down. And heaven knew, she and Seth were about as *down* as they could get. That's why she had taken such a chance and come to the farm without him; she hoped that if she gave him time to think about it, he'd follow her.

And then?

"... what do you think, Honey?"

Guiltily, Honey realized that the conversation had moved on without her. Flushing, she said, "I beg your pardon?"

"Carla was saying that perhaps you should call Seth, just to let him know you arrived safely," Octavia said. "We wouldn't want him to be concerned."

Honey almost said that after the way they had parted, *worry* about her was probably the last thing on Seth's mind. But she'd already revealed enough and what she hadn't said aloud, she suspected Octavia might have already guessed. Reluctantly, she glanced around and saw a telephone on a table behind her. "I suppose you're right," she said. "If I could use the phone..."

"Oh, not in here," Carla said. "Nan and I can show you to your room—I mean, the room where you'll be staying, of course. It has a phone, so you'll have some privacy."

"Oh, I hadn't thought I'd be staying...here."

"But of course you'll stay here!" Octavia said in genuine surprise. "Why would you think otherwise?"

"That's very kind of you," Honey said, "but I can't just barge in. It would be different if Seth were here—"

"Nonsense," Octavia said firmly. "You're family. Dunleavy Farm is your home as long as you want it to be."

Dunleavy Farm. Even the name was magical, Honey thought. Before she knew it, she was confessing, "You know, when I was a little girl, I used to wonder what it was like to live on a beautiful farm like this. In fact, I even had pictures of all the big Kentucky farms taped to the wall of my bedroom. I'd look at them every night before I went to sleep, thinking that one day—"

She stopped, realizing anew that that *one day* had arrived. After all these years, she was finally here. *But what good is it if Seth isn't here to share it?* she wondered, and felt the sudden sting of tears.

"I'm sorry," she said, blinking rapidly. "I guess I'm more tired than I realized. It was a long trip."

"And we've kept you chatting away when you need to rest for a while," Nan said. "I'll show you to your room."

Gracefully, languidly, Carla rose from the couch. "I'll come, too. And after you've had a chance to relax, we'll show you around the farm."

Honey wanted that most of all. But she *was* tired, and she supposed she should call Seth. She turned to Octavia. "Thank you for making me feel so welcome. I appreciate it, especially in view of the recent troubles with the Dunleavy horses."

Octavia's eyes clouded. "You mean Done Driftin's accident, and the theft of Done Cryin'."

Honey was certain that everyone in the racing world knew about the tragedies surrounding two of the most promising three-year-old colts in the country. First, a freak stable accident had ended Done Driftin's racing career; then, Done Cryin' had disappeared right off the track. Despite a massive hunt, no trace of the horse had been found. Honey looked at Carla.

"How is your colt?" she asked.

"He's getting along. He'll never race again, but soon he'll take his old man's place in the stallion barn."

Honey turned to Nan. "Has there been any news of Done Cryin'?"

"No, but we haven't given up hope. Trent has posted a big reward, and we have all sorts of people looking for him."

"I'm sure you'll find him," Honey said. But they all knew that the odds shrank considerably every day that the horse was gone.

Honey took a deep breath. "And what about the filly?" she asked.

Nan and Carla glanced at each other, then they both looked at Octavia. It was Carla who spoke.

"Funny you should ask," Carla said, trying not to smile and ruin the surprise. "As we speak, the queen is at the barn, waiting to receive visitors."

Honey didn't trust her ears. "Never Done Dreamin' is...here? At the farm?"

Nan couldn't hide her grin. "It *is* her home, you know."

Octavia smiled, too. "Would you like to see her, my dear?"

Honey looked from one to the other. In that moment, she loved them all. "Could I?" she breathed.

So, not five minutes later, fatigue forgotten, Honey was standing in front of the stall containing the horse that was already being called the filly of the century. Trying to tell herself this was not a figment of her imagination, she gripped the stall bars. She had always dreamed of owning a horse like this—a filly so delicately built that one could see the blue-blooded veins lying just beneath the glossy skin, a filly with such blazing speed that she seemed to fly on her own wings.

Unable to take her eyes off the vision inside, she whispered, "She's...beautiful."

"Would you like to go in?" Octavia asked.

Honey managed to tear her gaze away from the horse long enough to ask, "Oh, could I?"

Nan pulled aside the stall door. "Be our guest."

As Honey slipped inside, the filly turned toward her, ears pricked. Then, the horse who sometimes needed two grooms just to hold her, stepped daintily to Honey's side and nuzzled her outstretched hand.

"She's yours, Honey—and Seth's," Octavia said mistily. "If you'll have her."

If they'd have her?

Honey realized she could never accept such a magnificent gift. *But Seth could,* she thought with a thrill, and knew that this horse could be exactly what he needed to get back on his feet. Just *looking* at her made people believe that anything was possible.

I believe in Never Done Dreamin', Honey declared silently. *And, if I have anything to say about it, Seth will, too. All I have to do is figure out a way to get him here.* She knew that, after one glimpse of this horse, Seth would realize that dreams could come true.

CHAPTER TWO

OUT IN ARIZONA, Seth Dunleavy was in the barn when he heard someone behind him. His heart jumping a little at the thought that Honey might have changed her mind, he looked quickly over his shoulder. To his annoyance, his father-in-law was standing in the doorway. Seth immediately frowned.

"What are *you* doing here?" he growled.

"Well, what do you think, boyo?" Davey LaRue asked nonchalantly, sauntering in on his bowed legs. "I came to see my daughter, that's what."

Seth reached for his crutches and levered himself to a standing position. He'd been treating a wound on one of the few horses remaining in his care, but the position had been awkward, and as he straightened, his face was red. The thought flashed through his mind how much he missed Honey's help—not to make it easier on him, but because no one could treat a sick horse the way she could. Under her touch, the most fractious horse became calm; the sound of her voice could make a nervous horse stand still. He'd never seen anything like it; it was as though she could conjure spells.

But he didn't want to think of his wife, who was hundreds of miles away at this minute, visiting a place he knew only from pictures, talking to people who should have remained strangers. The thought made him angry all over again, and when Davey saw his face, the older man retreated a step.

"If this isn't a good time," Davey said, squinting warily at his six-foot-two son-in-law, "I can come back later."

"It won't matter," Seth said. He came out of the stall and pulled the door shut behind him. "She won't be here then, either."

"Where'd she go—into town or something?"

Town—what a laugh that was. Here in Buckboard, Arizona, the nearest town was twenty miles away and consisted of a post office, a general store and a Laundromat. With a grimace, Seth put the crutches in place under his arms and glared at Davey.

"How did you find us?" he asked.

"It wasn't from anything you said or did, I guarantee that," the little man declared. "It's a fine state of affairs when a man has to ask complete strangers for the whereabouts of his only daughter. The least you could have done was leave me a note at the last stable office."

If Seth had been in a better humor, he might have cracked a smile at his father-in-law's resemblance to a banty cock. With Davey's unruly head of gray hair, some of it sticking up in points, and his darting little eyes—not to mention his diminutive stature—Davey LaRue could have been the scourge of the barnyard.

But Seth was hardly amused. He'd heard this line before and he wasn't sympathetic. Starting out of the barn, he said, "Well, you're here now, so what do you want?"

He knew Davey would tag along after him, but when he heard the footsteps behind him, he tensed anyway. It wasn't that he despised the man; it was only that he had little use for him. Davey might be his wife's father, but Davey was an opportunist who wasn't above taking advantage of someone else's bad luck. He and Honey had had more fights than he cared to count over her constant caving in to the old man. Seth always maintained that if Davey put half as much energy into honest work as he put into figuring out how to make an easy buck, they'd all be a lot better off.

Despite Seth's crutches, Davey had almost to trot to keep up with his son-in-law's long legs. Plaintively, he asked, "Do I always have to *want* something?"

"Yes. What is it this time—money?" Seth laughed shortly and answered his own question. "But of course it is, what else could it be?"

Davey looked pained. "Couldn't it be that I just wanted to see my—"

"No, it couldn't," Seth said. The cramped trailer that he and Honey shared—until she left for Kentucky, that is—was straight ahead. If he didn't invite the man in, Seth thought, maybe Davey would get the hint and leave.

Davey never did get hints. He was still right behind when they came up to the door.

"Here, let me help you with that," Davey said. He reached for the door handle, but dropped his hand when Seth glared at him again. "Hey, I was just trying to help," he said defensively.

"Well, don't," Seth said. He knew he was being rude, but he didn't care. If Honey were here, she'd be giving him that *look* that said he'd better straighten up if he knew what was good for him. But Honey wasn't here, and as he hauled himself awkwardly up the three metal steps into the trailer, he wanted to smash something. She'd only been gone two days, but already he missed her like hell. There was an ache in his heart—and in his groin—that wouldn't go away. How could he have let her go? He couldn't believe that things between them had deteriorated as badly as this.

Angrily, he told himself that it had been her decision to leave, not his. If she'd listened to him, he decided, none of this would be happening. Who cared if some crazy old woman in Kentucky took it into her head to write and say she was his grandmother? Why should he believe it? And why now, after all this time? He was almost thirty years old; if he'd had any other family but his mother, wouldn't he have known about it long before now?

In his agitation, Seth forgot to shut the door behind him. As though he'd been invited, Davey followed him inside.

"Seth, my boy," Davey said, "you look like you're in a bad humor today. If you have a couple of beers, I'll be glad to get them, and then you can tell me what's put the burr under your tail."

Seth's last two beers were in the side door of the little refrigerator. Before he could protest, Davey had them out and open. Keeping one, he handed the other to Seth.

"Down the hatch," he said, and took a long, thirsty draft.

Seth wasn't in the mood for a beer. He set the bottle aside and carefully lowered himself to the love seat at the "living room" end of the trailer. His leg hurt, and out of a habit he couldn't seem to break, no matter how long he'd been wearing this damned cast, he reached down to rub his knee before he remembered it was encased in unforgiving fiberglass.

Frowning fiercely, he leaned back against the couch and closed his eyes. He was tired, and tonight his bones ached like the devil. Usually when that happened, he tried not to think about it. After all these months of being encased from foot to midthigh, wondering when he was going to get out of the cast could drive a man wild.

But this evening, his thoughts seemed more difficult to control than usual, and he thought resentfully that things were worse because Honey wasn't here.

He'd been a fool, he told himself. He should have said or done anything to stop her from going.

"So, where is she, boyo?" Davey asked, taking another swig of brew. He was still standing in the kitchen area, and he glanced in the direction of what passed for the bedroom, at the opposite end of the trailer. "Is she sick or something?"

"No, she's not sick," Seth said sharply. "And stop calling me *boyo*. You're not my father, and I'm not your son, so put a lid on it."

"Okay, okay." Davey was silent a beat, then he asked, "You got anything to eat?"

Seth decided he wanted the beer, after all. Grabbing the bottle, he wrenched the top off and took a deep swallow. It tasted flat and he slammed it down on the table.

"No, and I don't recall inviting you for dinner, anyway," he snarled.

Davey looked wounded again. "Honey would, if she was here," he said.

"Well, Honey's not here! I told you that, so leave it alone!"

As though he hadn't heard, Davey asked curiously, "Did you two have a fight?"

"If we did, it's none of your damned business."

"My, my, you're touchy tonight, even for you. Come on, boy—come on, Seth, what's up? If you tell me, maybe I can help."

"You?" Seth laughed derisively. "What could you do?"

"Hey, now," Davey protested. "I know you don't think too highly of me, but Honey and I get along just fine. If something's wrong, she'd tell me."

"Oh, you think so?"

"I know it. Why, there was a time when the two of us were tight as ticks. It was just us, you know, me and Honey."

Seth was really in a foul mood now. "And I came along and ruined it, is that what you're saying?"

"I'm saying nothing of the kind. I'm merely pointing out—"

Seth was too out of sorts to argue about it. Wearily, he asked, "What do you want, Davey?"

"I told you. I just wanted to stop by and visit a spell. Can't a man come and visit his own daughter without his son-in-law suspecting the worst?"

"Maybe in another family—not this one," Seth retorted. But he knew that Davey wouldn't go until he'd gotten what he came for, so he said, "Come on, I know you too well. You've either got money troubles, or you've got something up your sleeve. Which is it?"

"Well, now that you mention it—"

"I knew it. Goodbye, Davey. Don't forget to close the door on your way out."

"No, no, you've got me all wrong! Will you just wait a minute and listen to what I have to tell you?"

Short of picking up the little man and throwing him out bodily—a temptation, to be sure, Seth thought—he didn't seem to have much choice.

"You've got two minutes, Davey," he said. "Make the most of them."

"Aw, now..." Davey must have seen the look in Seth's eyes, because he hastily asked, "Is it true that you're related to the Dunleavys of Dunleavy Farm?"

Seth sat up so abruptly that Davey jumped. "Where did you hear that?"

"Hey, don't get excited, I just asked. It's a rumor going around, that's all. I heard it up in Pleasanton the last time I was there."

Seth threw himself back against the couch once more. His leg itched like crazy, and he reached for the long piece of welding wire he'd fashioned into a scratcher. Shoving it down the inside of the cast, he moved the little hook up and down viciously as he said, "Yeah, well, that's just what it is—a rumor. You ought to know better than to pay attention to gossip, Davey—especially when it comes from the backside."

"It didn't come from the track," Davey said. Nervously, he finished his beer, then set the bottle down. He gestured to the one he'd given Seth. "Do you want that?"

Hoping Davey would leave when the beer was gone, Seth growled, "Help yourself. And what do you mean, you didn't hear it at the track?"

"You're in such a bad mood that maybe I'd better not tell you—oh, all right, I guess it doesn't matter," Davey said hastily when saw Seth's face darken. He took a quick swallow of the second beer. "Maybe you won't like it, but to tell the truth, it was Honey who mentioned it."

"Honey!"

Davey winced. "I knew you weren't going to like it."

"You're right about that. Honey had no business gossiping about family business."

"I'm family, ain't I?"

"You're a pain in the—" Just in time, Seth stopped himself. Instead, he said, "What do you mean, Honey mentioned it? Exactly what did she say?"

Seth's tone was so dangerous that Davey's eyes slid toward the door, as if calculating how long it would take him to skip out before Seth could catch him. Apparently, he decided it would take too long, for he sighed before saying, "I wish I hadn't mentioned it."

"So do I, but you did, so give. Tell me exactly what she said."

"How can I remember *exactly?* I ... Oh, all right. Look, it wasn't any big deal, she just mentioned that you'd gotten a letter a while ago from Octavia Dunleavy. You know, of Dunleavy Farm."

"Go on," Seth said ominously.

"There's not much to go on *with.* Honey said that this woman had written to say that she was your grandmother. Your grandmother!" Davey said, clearly still marveling at the idea. "Imagine! All this time, and no one knew you were related to the Dunleavys of racing fame!"

"Put your eyes back in your head, Davey," Seth said. "It's all a mistake. Honey got it wrong."

Davey looked disappointed. "You didn't get a letter?"

Oh, he'd gotten a letter, all right, Seth thought. Honey didn't know it, but he'd read it so many times, he'd memorized it by now. It read:

Dear Seth,

Permit me to introduce myself. I am your maternal grandmother, Octavia Whitworth Dunleavy.

When I think of the bitter circumstances under which your mother and I parted company, I
feel safe in guessing that you've probably never
heard of me. So I imagine this letter will come as
quite a shock, but please bear with me.

My dear grandson, I need to see you. I have a
proposition to discuss that I hope you will find
most interesting . . . .

There had been more, an invitation to visit the farm,
the promise of one of the Dunleavy horses if he stayed
a month. It was too unbelievable to be true, and
yet . . . and yet . . .

Honey had believed it. Seth had a mental picture of
how she'd looked when she'd read the letter. Those
beautiful lake blue eyes of hers had widened, her lips
had parted. He'd never forget the expression on her
face; it would stay with him forever.

"Oh, Seth!" she'd breathed, her eyes as bright as
stars. "Imagine, being related to the Dunleavys of
Dunleavy Farm! Why didn't you ever tell me?"

He hated like hell to disillusion her; he hated even
more to be the cause of that bright hope fading from
the face he'd grown to love more than life itself. But
he had to do it; he couldn't allow her to think that
what that crazy old woman had said was possible.

"Because it isn't true," he said flatly.

"What do you mean?" She looked down at the letter she was still holding. It was written on expensive parchment-like paper; even from his position halfway across the room, he could see the blazing Dunleavy logo in one corner. Just for an instant, he allowed himself to wonder...

But no. His mother had told him repeatedly that they had no family. "There's only the two of us," Jamie Dunleavy always said. "Just you and me. But we can make it, we can. All we need to do is keep trying."

Well, he'd tried, and so, he supposed, had Jamie. But they'd been at loggerheads over his friends at the nearby racetrack long before she sent him to a military school back East. He hadn't lasted long there; one night, he'd just walked out. And he hadn't gone home. Instead, he'd done exactly what they'd fought about: he'd headed straight for the nearest racetrack and hadn't looked back.

As for his father... Seth never knew who the man was, and he didn't care. Jamie wouldn't talk about him. She'd put "Dunleavy" on Seth's birth certificate and said she had no use for a man who would only tie her down. She was planning to be a great artist. And when she sent Seth away, he was sure it was because he was just something else standing in the way of her career. That's why, when he left the school, he didn't see any point in going back home.

Angrily, he shook his head. He didn't like to think about those times. Whenever he remembered his mother as she'd been when he last saw her, standing grimly at the airline gate, determined to stay until the plane left, to make sure that he was on it, he felt that same rage all over again. Despite the fact that they couldn't seem to see eye-to-eye about anything, he had loved her. To be cast aside while she blithely went on her way had cut him deeply. He'd never forgiven her.

But then he'd met Honey, and even though it had taken him two years to admit it, he'd fallen for her— hard. She was so lovely, he thought. She was all he could have asked for in a woman...a partner, a wife. Knowing her had dissolved some of the hard knot that had grown inside him. With Honey, he'd finally allowed himself to dream again.

Annoyed anew by the direction of his thoughts, Seth shifted on the couch. What good were dreams when what you had to deal with was reality?

It irritated him that Davey was still preoccupied with that damned Dunleavy Farm back East. "You know," Davey said, "I don't believe Honey would make up a story like that. It isn't like her."

"Believe what you like," Seth said. "But I'm telling you, it's got nothing to do with me."

"But think what it would mean if it did!"

Davey's face glowed at the thought, and Seth looked at him disgustedly. "It wouldn't mean anything," he said. "Even if I *was* related to those people—and notice I said *if,* what do you think I'm going to do— plunk myself on their doorstep and ask to join the family?"

"Well, why not?" Davey asked. "That old woman can't live forever, you know. The farm has to go to someone, and you could get a piece of a pretty big pie."

"I wouldn't want it."

Davey looked at him in disbelief. "You wouldn't *want* it? What kind of talk is that? Why, that farm's famous. Look at some of the horses it's produced. Done Roamin' was a Triple Crown winner! Lord above, Seth, I always knew you were a pigheaded, stubborn, proud man, but I never thought you were a fool!"

Seth didn't want to discuss it anymore. He slammed his fist down on the table. "Look, it's my life, not yours, so butt out!"

"You're right about most things, Seth, I won't deny it," Davey said. "But you're dead wrong about this. It may be your life, but my little girl's involved in it, too, and I don't want to see her hurt."

Seth was so enraged, he wanted to throttle the man. "You know I'd never do anything to hurt Honey!"

"Yeah?" Davey squinted at him again. "Then where is she, Seth? Has she left you? Is that why she isn't here tonight?"

"She didn't leave me!" Seth said furiously. But, try as he might, he couldn't meet Davey's bright little eyes. "She just went ... somewhere for a while. Now you know. I hope you're happy."

Davey was silent a moment. Then he said, "She went to Kentucky, didn't she?"

"You know so much, you tell me!"

Sorrowfully, Davey shook his head. "You shouldn't have let her go, not without you. You should have gone with her."

"Yeah, well, I didn't, so shut up about it, will you?" Seth shouted. "If you came because you need some money, there's twenty dollars in that drawer. Take it and leave."

"Aw, Seth, I didn't mean to make you mad. And I don't want your money—not right now, anyway," he amended hastily. "I was hoping we could have a little supper together, and then I could use your couch for the night. It's awful far back to town, and from what I recall, Buckboard doesn't have a hotel."

Seth's anger had vanished as fast as it had appeared. Too empty to argue about it, he said, "Oh, all right, do what you want. I'm going to bed."

The bedroom, such as it was, was closed off from the rest of the trailer by a curtain. Seth jerked it shut. Feeling it was too much effort to get out of his clothes in the cramped little space, he lay aside his crutches and threw himself down on the bed fully clothed. For a while, he listened to Davey trying not to make noise as he rustled up something for dinner, and then settled down to watch TV, but long after Davey had gone to bed and the trailer was quiet, Seth couldn't sleep. Finally, he got up, put his crutches in place and went outside.

The Arizona night was warm and still, the stars glimmering by the millions in the jet black sky. But tonight, its beauty was lost on Seth, who felt so out of sorts, all he wanted to do was climb on a horse and ride as far as it would take him. Of course, he couldn't do that, he thought bitterly. With his leg like this, he'd probably fall off and then where would he be?

Doomed to inactivity for even longer, that's where, he thought as he clumped over to the big paddock and leaned against the fence. Two of the horses, old pensioners he and Honey had picked up in Ferndale and had agreed to care for in return for a monthly stipend, ambled over to join him. Absently, he stroked the head of the nearest one and was rewarded by a soft nicker. The comforting sound should have helped, but it didn't. All it did was make him realize again just how much he missed his wife.

"Damn that old woman," he muttered, thinking of Octavia Dunleavy. If she hadn't written that letter, Honey would be here right now. But no: Honey was in Kentucky and he was alone, and it was all his fault. If he'd been able to jump out of the way when that damned Twisted Fate reared up and fell over in the cross-ties, things would be different. They'd still be on the fair circuit, making some money with those promising runners they'd had in the barn. If things had worked out the way they'd planned, this could have been a good year for them.

But then that horse had flipped over and everything changed. From one instant to the next, the future became even more uncertain than usual, and not long after that, Octavia Dunleavy had written. The final blow had been the call from Kentucky a while ago. Until his supposed cousins had phoned from Dunleavy Farm, he'd been hoping he could ignore the letter. He might have succeeded, if Honey hadn't answered the phone that day.

"Seth, we just had a call from Kentucky," she'd said.

He hadn't even changed expression. "We don't know anyone in Kentucky."

That wasn't quite true, but Honey didn't remark on it. Instead, she said, "Remember the letter we received from your grandmother? Well—"

"I don't want to talk about that," he said.

"Well, that's too bad, because we *have* to talk about it."

"There's nothing to discuss," he insisted. "I told you, I don't have a grandmother."

"I suppose you don't have any cousins, either."

He made the mistake of allowing the merest flicker of interest to show. "Cousins?"

"That Kentucky call was from Carla and Nan Dunleavy—Octavia Dunleavy's granddaughters." She added pointedly, "Your cousins."

Because he didn't know what else to do, he'd exploded. "Are you on again about this mythical connection I'm supposed to have to the Dunleavys of Kentucky?" he demanded. "I've told you a million times that we're not related. I should know, shouldn't I? Do you think my mother lied when she said the name was just a coincidence? I mean it, Honey, just let it go!"

Honey rarely lost her temper. She hated confrontations and angry words; normally, she did everything possible to avoid them. In fact, in almost any situation he could think of, Honey was the arbiter, the compromiser, the one who gave in. She did it with her father, and until that fateful afternoon, she'd done it with him.

But not that day, he thought bitterly. Just when he needed her to be the Honey he knew, she decided to become someone else.

"They've invited us to come to Dunleavy Farm," Honey had said. "I think we should go."

"And I don't. We've talked about this—"

Her eyes flashing, she declared, "I'm telling you, Seth Michael Dunleavy, we're going. This opportunity is too good to be missed."

"It's not an opportunity at all!" he'd shouted. "Don't you see? It's all a mistake. I'm not related to them. They've got the wrong guy, it's someone else!"

"Why are you so afraid of this, Seth?" she shouted back. "Just tell me why!"

But he couldn't explain, not to Honey, not to himself. It had to do with his mother and how she'd abandoned him—or near to it. It had to do with him never knowing who his father was, or why the man had deserted them. It had to do with the fact that if he was related to the Dunleavys of Dunleavy Farm, why in the *hell* hadn't anyone come forward before now?

All those years ago, barely sixteen and on his own, he'd needed *someone,* and no one had come.

Oh, yeah, he thought acridly. Where had Octavia Whitworth Dunleavy been back then?

"I mean it, Seth!" Honey cried. "You'd better tell me why you're resisting this! Because if you don't, I'm going to . . . I'm going to Dunleavy Farm by myself!"

He'd stared at her as if he didn't recognize her—and he hadn't, not then. Somehow, he'd managed to say, "You . . . what?"

Her head lifted. Emotion had turned her blue eyes nearly black. Then, to his shock, his compliant, sweet-tempered wife, the woman who would do anything to avoid an argument or even a harsh word, had looked him straight in the face and said, "You heard me, Seth. I'm going. Now, you can come with me—I hope you do. But if you decide not to, for whatever reason, don't expect me to change my mind. I know how you feel about taking a handout, but this isn't that. This is your *family*, Seth—do you understand? Your family! We need them right now. You can deny it all you like. But for once in your life, you have to accept help. If you won't think of yourself, think of—"

She stopped, her color high. She had never looked more beautiful—or more like a stranger. He was still standing there, stupefied, when she came out of the bedroom, carpetbag in hand. Color still burning in her cheeks, she'd stopped.

"Are you coming, or not?" she asked.

He couldn't answer; he was fighting too many emotions. He shook his head, and her lips tightened.

"Fine," she said. "Have it your way. You know where I'll be, in case you want to get in touch."

He finally found his voice. Reaching for her as she went to the door, he said, "Honey—"

She paused, and his heart leapt. She couldn't leave, he thought desperately. He needed her so much! But he couldn't tell her that, and after a tense moment when they just looked at each other, she shrugged off his hand. Opening the door, she went out and didn't look back.

Remembering how she'd looked as she walked down the road to catch the bus, he closed his eyes. As though sensing his misery, one of the horses nuzzled his shoulder. Without thinking, he twined his fingers in the animal's mane and held on tight. In that moment, he wished with all his heart that he could turn back the clock.

CHAPTER THREE

WHEN CARLA AND NAN showed Honey to the guest room, she stopped in sheer amazement at the door.

"Oh, no," she said immediately. "This is too much just for me. Don't you have something . . . smaller?"

She meant, *less grand*. From the rose-colored damask draperies on either side of the window, to the thick carpet of the same color on the floor, to the pictures on the walls and the cherry-wood furniture, everything bespoke elegance and wealth. A huge four-poster bed, covered in a puffed satin quilt in a delicate shade of blue, dominated the bedroom, and there was even, Honey realized, a *settee*—was that what it was called?—where someone might lie down and rest in the afternoons.

Then she caught a glimpse of the adjoining room, and knew that she must be dreaming. It was a bathroom, but none like she'd ever seen. It had the same rose, pale blue and cream color scheme of the bedroom, but in addition to the usual accoutrements, it boasted a built-in dressing table and fixtures with flowers painted right into the porcelain. Thick, fluffy towels in rose and blue hung perfectly from the towel rods, and on the cream-colored tile in front of the bathtub, was a rug that looked soft enough to wrap up in.

"Do you like it?" Nan asked.

Helplessly, Honey looked at Seth's two cousins. Too awed to disguise her lack of sophistication, she said, "I've never seen a room like this, not even in pictures."

Nan laughed. "I know what you mean," she said. "I felt the same way when I first came. At the ranch, everything was so rustic and sturdy. Here, it all seemed much too pretty to touch."

Whether what Nan had said was true or not, Honey was grateful for the woman's kindness. Carla was more brisk, but equally as considerate when she said, "You must enjoy it, Honey. Grandmother would be devastated to think you weren't comfortable here."

Amazed, Honey said, "How could anyone not be comfortable here? It's like a fairyland."

Nan's eyes twinkled. "And you haven't even seen the rest of the farm yet."

"There's plenty of time for that tomorrow," Carla said firmly. She tugged at Nan's arm. "We'll let you get some rest now." At the doorway, she said, "Dinner's in about an hour—if that's not too soon?"

"No, it's fine," Honey said faintly. She'd forgotten all about dinner. Now that she'd seen this room— and the living room downstairs—she could just imagine what the rest of the house looked like.

Nan shot an amused glance at her cousin before she said, "And don't worry about having to deal with company tonight, Honey. Grandmother and Carla invited Trent to dinner on *my* first night, but I thought it would be easier if it was just us women.''

"Thanks," Honey said gratefully. She hadn't thought about meeting anyone else today; she already felt a little dazed by everything she'd experienced since her arrival. And, as Nan had pointed out, she hadn't even seen much of the farm yet.

''Would you like Teresa to help you unpack?''

Honey had met Teresa downstairs. The capable housekeeper of Dunleavy Farm had taken one look at her and clucked. ''My, my,'' she'd said. ''You're just like these other girls—nothing but skin and bones. It seems to me that I'm going to have to fatten you up a little, Miss Honey.''

Nan and Carla had both laughed at that. ''And she's the one who can do it, too,'' Carla had said. ''With that hummingbird metabolism of hers, Nan doesn't have a problem, but I had to *beg* Teresa not to tempt me with all those wonderful pastries she turns out. I wasn't here two weeks before I was having trouble fitting into my clothes.''

The thought had flashed through Honey's mind that soon she might have that problem herself, but for a very different reason. But she didn't want to say anything yet—not until she was sure. So, in answer to Carla's earlier question, she glanced at the carpetbag she'd brought. It was so ancient that the tapestry upholstering was threadbare. Fighting the urge to giggle hysterically at the idea that she needed help with the few things she'd brought, she shook her head.

"No thank you. I can do it myself," she said, and paused. "I really should call Seth, but I can get time and charges—"

"Don't you dare!" Carla exclaimed. "You're grandmother's guest, *our* guest. Whatever we have is yours."

"Oh, but I couldn't—"

"Yes you can," Nan said gently. "Please, Honey, as Carla said, grandmother would be so disappointed if you didn't feel at home here."

Before Honey could reply, they were gone. Left alone in the elegant room, Honey stood there for a moment. As she looked around, she wondered again if she was really here. Maybe it *was* all a dream, and soon she'd wake up in her own little trailer.

Grimacing at the thought, she left the carpetbag where it was and crossed over to the shining cherry-wood table. She lifted the receiver of the elegant cream-colored telephone and then quickly put it down again. Her hand was shaking.

Why was she so nervous? Seth was her *husband*. She shouldn't feel anxious about calling him; she should *want* to hear his voice.

But she didn't, she thought miserably. The idea of getting into another argument with him made her feel queasy, and she sat down on an intricate needlepoint chair near the table, rubbing her cold hands.

You have to call him, she told herself. *He's probably worried sick.*

On that thought, she reached for the receiver again. Before she could change her mind, she dialed the number and listened to it ring four times, five, six. She was about to hang up when she counted ten rings, but just then she heard a click. Despite herself, she tensed as Seth's deep voice grunted a hello.

"Hi, it's me," she said in a small voice.

He was his sarcastic best. "Well, well, so you deigned to call, after all."

"You knew I would."

"Oh, really? After the way you stormed out of here, I wasn't sure I'd ever hear from you again."

"I didn't storm out," she said quietly. "I told you I was leaving."

"And I told *you* how I felt about it. Not that it mattered. Your mind was made up and no husband was going to change it, right?"

She took a deep breath. "Seth, I don't want to fight—"

"It's a little late for that, isn't it?"

"Seth, please!" she cried, and instantly looked toward the door. She hadn't meant to be so loud, and she lowered her voice. "I just wanted you to know that I arrived safely."

"Thanks for that much, at least."

She was determined not to get into another argument. "How are things with you?"

"How do you think they are? I want you here, Honey. Not gallivanting off on a fool's errand."

"It's not a fool's errand." She thought of all she'd seen since she'd arrived, the women she'd met, and knew she had to convince him to come. "If you would just consider coming for a few days. You won't believe how beautiful it is here. And the horses. Oh, Seth, I saw Never Done Dreamin'! She's everything you'd expect, and more. She's going to the Kentucky Derby. Imagine, the *Kentucky Derby!* You can't miss that. Please reconsider! You could take the bus and—"

"Forget it," he said harshly. "If I've told you once, I've told you a thousand times, I'm not going to step foot on that farm. I can't believe you're still on about it. You know how I feel."

She could no longer ignore his tone. Resentful and angry at his stubbornness, she said, "As a matter of fact, I *don't* know how you feel. In all those thousands of times when you refused even to consider coming here, you never once said why. Don't you think it's about time you explained?"

"I don't have to explain anything to you."

"I'm your wife!"

"A wife's place is beside her husband," he declared pompously. "And the way I see it, that's not where you are."

"I can't believe you even said that, Seth Dunleavy. You make it sound like I'm supposed to walk five paces behind you!"

"Right now, that doesn't sound half-bad."

"What?" she cried, outraged.

"Oh, forget it. When are you going to regain your senses and come home, where you belong?"

"If you feel that way, perhaps I don't belong there anymore, Seth. What do you think of that?"

"You've just been waiting for an excuse all this time, haven't you?"

"An excuse? What are you talking about?"

"What do you think, Honey? About leaving me, of course."

"*Leaving* you! I never said that!"

"Why not? You seem to like it at Dunleavy Farm a whole hell of a lot better than you do here with me."

"That's not fair!"

"That's the way it goes," he said cruelly. "Good-bye, Honey. Call me when you have something to say."

"Something you want to hear, you mean!" she cried.

He didn't answer. When all she heard was a click in her ear, she pulled the phone away and looked at it incredulously. For a few seconds, she was tempted to call him right back, but then she realized he wouldn't answer, and that would only make her angrier.

"Well, fine!" she said furiously, banging down the receiver.

Instantly, she was sorry. Anger was no excuse to mistreat the lovely things in this room, she thought. What if she had cracked the phone, or broken it?

Close to tears, she clasped her hands and pressed them against her lips. *You're not going to cry!* she told herself, blinking rapidly. *If you do, they'll see your swollen eyes at dinner and wonder why.*

Too agitated to sit, she sprang up. She'd known Seth would be angry with her for leaving him alone, but she hadn't expected that the conversation—such as it was, she thought miserably—would degenerate as badly as it had. How could it have gone so wrong? She'd known he would tell her to come back again, so why had she reacted like a harpy when he'd demanded it?

Because, she thought, *despite what he'd said, he had sounded as though he didn't really want her to come home. In fact, he'd sounded as if he ... hated her.*

Maybe she should call him back, she thought. She'd say...

What?

That she couldn't come home just yet because she wanted him to see Dunleavy Farm? That he had to see Never Done Dreamin' and watch the filly race, at least once, before he decided whether or not to accept the horse? Or that, most of all, she wanted him to meet his grandmother and his cousins, because once he did, he'd realize that they really *were* his family?

Oh, she wanted to say all that and more, she thought mournfully. But what would be the point? It was obvious that Seth wasn't listening to her these days, especially when she said anything concerning this farm.

Blinking back tears, she went to the open window. A light early-evening breeze wafted through, ruffling her hair as she stared out. Everything smelled so fresh; she closed her eyes and took a deep breath. Oh, she knew Seth would love it here as much as she did. Why was he being so stubborn about it?

Hoping to distract herself, she looked down. The guest room was on the second floor of the house, and from this vantage point, she could see the front pastures—*paddocks,* they were called here, she remembered—and the beautiful old trees lining the driveway. By craning out the window a little, she glimpsed barns to the left. A movement on the hill caught her eye and she leaned out a little farther. When she saw the horse there, she caught her breath.

The stallion—and it had to be a stallion, she thought, noting its muscular arched neck and proud stance—was silhouetted on the crest of the hill. Somehow she knew it was Done Roamin', the farm's famed Triple Crown winner.

Just the sight of him gave her a thrill; the horse was a legend. In the entire history of the Triple Crown races, there had been only eleven horses strong enough, and fleet enough, and determined enough, to attain the sport's highest glory. Done Roamin' was one of the eleven.

She couldn't wait to see him. She hurried downstairs, let herself out the front door and ran to the paddocks.

When she got to the fence, Done Roamin' was still on the hill. He was too far away to see clearly, but Honey, who had watched tape after tape of his famous races, had no need to glimpse him up close. Head up, ears pricked, he stared proudly over his domain like the monarch he was. Then, as Honey gazed at him in awe, he suddenly turned his magnificent head and looked straight at her. A chill ran down her spine. It was like being noticed by a king.

"He's beautiful, isn't he?" someone said behind her.

Recognizing Octavia's voice, Honey began to turn toward her. But just then, Done Roamin' let out a shrill whinny and started down the hill. The instant he moved, Honey was transfixed with horror. She'd read about the terrible, and still-unexplained, stable injury the horse had sustained several years before, but seeing the effect of it right before her eyes was devastating. For a few awful seconds, she wasn't sure she could stop herself from sobbing. In front of her eyes, the glorious, splendid horse who had inspired her just moments ago turned into a crippled animal pitifully and carefully lurching down the slope. The sight was so painful that for a moment, she couldn't speak.

Apparently sensing her distress, Octavia touched Honey's arm. "It's shocking when you see it the first time, I know," she said. "I should have warned you."

With an effort, Honey pulled herself together. "I read about the accident," she said, "but I had no idea it was so...so..." Words failed her, and she just shook her head.

"We're lucky he's alive," Octavia said sadly, watching her horse's slow progress. She paused a moment, then added, "If I didn't know better, I'd think there was a curse on this place. First it was Roamy, then Done Driftin'. Now Done Cryin' has disappeared." Her troubled glance turned in the direction of the mare barn, where Never Done Dreamin' was safely ensconced for the night. Her voice was even lower when she added, "I wonder who will be next."

At the thought that something might—could—happen to Done Roamin's fastest and most beautiful daughter, especially before Seth had a chance to see her, Honey felt a stab of fear. "No one's going to be next," she said. "The bad luck's all over. I'm sure of that."

Done Roamin' reached the fence and imperiously put his head over the top railing. Leaning on her cane, Octavia took a piece of carrot from her pocket and gave it to him.

"There, old son," she murmured. "Now, are you happy?"

When Done Roamin' seemed to be too busy chewing to answer, Honey smiled. "He seems to be, doesn't he?"

Octavia turned to her. "And what about you, my dear?"

"What do you mean?" Avoiding Octavia's sharp eyes, Honey patted Done Roamin's glossy neck.

"I think you know what I mean, Honey. Horses might be happy with carrots and a little show of affection, but we humans are a bit more complex. You haven't said much, but you'll forgive me if I get the feeling that you're not very happy yourself right now."

"Oh, that isn't true. I'm delighted to be here. The farm is wonderful. It's the most beautiful place I've ever..." She faltered to a stop. "That's not what you mean, either, is it?"

"If you don't want to talk about it, I understand," Octavia said. "I realize we don't know each other, and the last thing I want to do is have you think of me as a prying, meddling old woman."

"I'd never think that!"

"Thank you, my dear. But I have to be honest. I *am* a prying, meddling woman. I always have been. It's just that now I've reached the age where it's more acceptable. Or at least," Octavia added with a smile, "more tolerated."

Honey had to smile in response. "I don't mind. It's nice to know you care. After all, you don't have to. I'm just... Seth's wife."

"Oh, you're much more than that. You're part of the family."

"Thank you." To hide her sudden emotion, Honey turned to Done Roamin' again.

Octavia waited a moment, then she asked, "Are you sorry you came here?"

"Oh, no. As I said, it's beautiful. It's what I imagined heaven to be. It's just..." She stopped and bit her lip.

"Go on."

Octavia's kind tone was her undoing, and she blurted it out. "I shouldn't have come. I never should have deserted Seth."

"Desertion is a strong word," Octavia said mildly. "All you did was accept my invitation to visit."

"No, no, it was more than that." She couldn't seem to stop herself. "It sounds awful, but I was so *tired* of him feeling sorry for himself all the time. I know it's been a problem for him, his being in a cast and all. I know it's hard having a broken leg, and feeling confined. But he's not the only one in the world who's ever suffered! It hasn't been easy for me, either!"

To her horror, the tears that had been threatening ever since she'd boarded the bus—no, since she'd defiantly told Seth she was going to come without him—suddenly overwhelmed her. Before she knew it, she was sobbing into her hands.

"I shouldn't have said that," she said through her tears. "I don't mean to sound self-pitying, especially when Seth is the one who..."

"There, there," Octavia said, stroking Honey's pale blond hair. She tried to pull Honey's hands down so she could see her face, but Honey couldn't look Octavia in the eye. Crying even harder, she turned away.

"I'm so ashamed!"

"I think the first thing we need to do is find a place to sit down so we can discuss this rationally," Octavia said sensibly. She transferred her cane to the other hand and took Honey by the arm. "Come along, my dear. Let's go up to the house."

Honey didn't want to discuss anything rationally; she wasn't sure she could. Her voice muffled, she said, "There's nothing to discuss. I abandoned Seth when he needed me, and I'll never forgive myself!"

"Never is a long time," Octavia said calmly. She was stronger than she looked; as she spoke, she tugged Honey along. Unless Honey jerked away, she had to follow.

"Now," Octavia said when they were seated on the swing at one end of the front porch. "Why do you feel that you abandoned Seth?"

Honey wiped away her tears. "Why? Well, because...because...I *left* him there, to fend for himself!"

"Oh, I see. Then his injury is more serious than just a broken leg?"

"*Just* a broken leg? You don't understand. He's—"

"Completely helpless?"

"Well, no, not *completely* helpless. But—"

"Oh, I understand. Then you mean, he *can* get around...if he chooses."

"Yes, but it's awfully difficult. He has to use crutches, and he gets so impatient, and—"

"And when he gets...impatient, what do you do?"

Honey blinked. "What do you mean?"

"Well, for instance, do you tell him that he has to manage on his own? Or do you say he needn't bother—that whatever he wants, you'll get it for him yourself."

"Of course I help him! Wouldn't you? I mean, it's so hard for him to—"

"And he's *just* a strong young man, is that right?"

Honey looked at her suspiciously. "What are you implying?"

"I'm not implying anything," Octavia said. "I'm merely trying to understand the situation."

"There's no *situation* to understand! The fact of the matter is that Seth broke his leg, he's in a cast from foot to midthigh, and I just...deserted him!"

"Perhaps you should go back, then," Octavia said calmly.

Honey was silent. Octavia was right, she thought. She didn't belong here; Seth did. And if he wasn't going to come here, then she should leave the farm and go home to be with him.

Biting her lip, she looked around. Now that Done Roamin' had gotten his treat, he'd wandered away from the fence. Beyond his paddock were additional enclosures, where other horses grazed. In one of the barns to her right was the mighty Done Driftin', still being treated for his injury; she hadn't even seen him yet. And in the mare barn farther down was the filly who might make history by being the first distaff runner to win the Triple Crown.

Seth had to see this, she thought. He *had* to. But if she left now, he'd never come to Dunleavy Farm, and what would that accomplish?

"I don't know what to do," she said at last. "I've tried everything, but..." She looked down at her hands, clasped tightly in her lap. "I really wanted to unite Seth with his family. He's always denied it, but I know, deep down, he's envied my relationship with my father, and wished he had an extended family of his own. I thought that if I said I was coming here, he'd come, too. And then he'd meet you all and realize that he wasn't alone."

She stopped again, then went on painfully. "But he's not coming, and I... I'm at my wit's end. I don't know what else to try. Maybe I should just go home."

Octavia put a hand over hers. Quietly, she said, "I don't know Seth personally, but from what you've said, he's like all the Dunleavy men—proud and stubborn, even when it's to their own detriment. If you want my advice—"

"Oh, I do!"

"Then here's what I think. I think you should stay here for a while longer, my dear. Seth needs time to work things out in his own mind."

"But what if he doesn't?" Honey asked plaintively.

Octavia smiled. "Oh, I have a feeling he will. And when he realizes what he's missing, he'll join you. He just needs to be left alone to come to his senses."

"I don't know..."

Octavia patted Honey's arm again. "Trust me," she said. "You'll see. He'll come around."

With all her heart, Honey hoped that Octavia was right.

CHAPTER FOUR

HONEY MET CARLA's fiancé, Wade Petrie, the day after her arrival at Dunleavy Farm. Wade had been Octavia's farm manager but was now starting his own training stable. He was tall and rangy, with arresting blue eyes under a Stetson hat. Honey liked him immediately. And when she saw them together, she understood why he and Carla had fallen in love. For one thing, as Nan had teasingly confided to her, Wade was the only man who could keep the strong-willed Carla in her place. But for another, they were obviously made for each other.

Trent and Nan seemed to be the perfect couple, too, Honey decided. She met Trent that afternoon, when he came over to the farm to discuss some business relating to the loan he'd arranged for Octavia. Honey happened to be in the living room when Trent arrived, and when she saw Nan's anxious gaze go directly to him, she guessed why. Trent had put up a big reward for any information on the disappearance of Done Cryin'. Trent shook his head at his fiancée's unspoken question.

"There's been no word yet," he said, gathering Nan to him and giving her a kiss. "But don't worry, we'll find him, even if we have to turn the entire country upside down."

From what she'd heard about the abduction, Honey was just thinking that they might have to do just that, when Trent turned to her. Like Wade, he was tall and athletic-looking, but much less the cowboy type. Perhaps, she thought, it was the silver at his temples. It made him appear distinguished as well as downright handsome.

"You must be Honey," he said. "It's a pleasure to meet you."

"Where are my manners?" Nan murmured. "I'm sorry. I should have introduced you."

"No need," Trent said, still holding Nan close. "I'd know Honey anywhere." He smiled, his deep brown eyes twinkling. "You look just like your name."

"I'm not sure if that's a compliment or not," Honey said. She smiled, too, and held out her hand. "It's nice to meet you, Trent. I've heard so much about you."

He pretended dismay. "Already? Didn't you just get here?"

"Last night," she said with a laugh.

"And you women had a lot of catching up to do," he said, giving Nan another hug. "So, Honey, what do you think of the farm?"

"It's beautiful. What I've seen of it so far."

"Nan will have to take you on a tour."

"I plan to," Nan said, grinning. "After all, I have a new pickup truck now."

Honey had heard about the accident that had to-
taled Nan's previous vehicle, when she'd been run off
the road one night by a still-unidentified motorcy-
clist. Just the thought of it made Honey shiver, and
she said, "Maybe we'd better take some horses instead."

"One thing we *won't* do," Nan said firmly, "is ask
Derry if we can borrow his friend's motorcycle."

Honey knew about Derry's unauthorized esca-
pades with the motorcycle, as well as the fact that father and son had nearly come to blows over whether
the teenager could get his driver's license. Apparently, the Spencers had reached a compromise that
didn't suit the impatient Derry at all: Trent had agreed
to buy his son a car—*if* Derry brought all his grades up
to A's. Until then, Trent had decreed that it was a bicycle or Derry's own two feet.

"Don't mention that bike," Trent said. "It's caused
us enough trouble, don't you think?"

"I do indeed," Nan agreed. "But look at the re-
sult. Isn't Derry studying hard now? Hasn't he
changed?"

"Only because of you. You're a good influence on
both of us."

Pleased and obviously a little embarrassed, Nan
flushed becomingly and murmured, "I feel the same
way about you."

Trent turned to Honey again. "Nan told me about
your husband's accident. I hope he's better now."

Honey didn't want to talk about Seth. It was too
painful to remember that they'd once been as tender

and loving toward each other as Nan and Trent were, and as Carla and Wade seemed to be. But she couldn't be rude, so she said, "I'd like to say he is, but unfortunately, he's still on crutches."

"That must be difficult, for you both."

"It hasn't been easy," she said. "Especially since Seth is such an active man. If he'd had an office job when this happened, he could have gone right back to work. As it is—" She stopped, not wanting to get into it. "Let's just say, we'll both be glad when he's out of that cast."

"I can imagine," Trent said. "In the meantime, is there anything we can do?"

"You can send up a good thought or two that Seth's broken bone will start to heal soon. Otherwise, the doctor says they might have to operate, put a plate and screws in his leg."

"But it's been six months. They'd do that after all this time?" Nan asked, surprised.

"I know." Honey didn't want to sound as glum as she felt, but it was difficult not to. "You'd think that approach would have been considered months ago."

She obviously hadn't been as successful in hiding her feelings as she'd hoped, for after a brief pause, Trent said, "Honey, we really don't know each other—not as well as I hope we will—and I don't like to intrude on private affairs, but a friend of mine is one of the most highly respected orthopedic surgeons in the country. If you and Seth would consider seeing her, I'm sure I can get you an appointment."

Touched, Honey said to Nan, "I can see why you fell in love with this man. Thank you, Trent. That's very kind of you. I . . . I'll speak to Seth."

"Good," Trent said, and gave Nan a quick kiss. "Well, I'm off. I'll call you later, sweetheart. And Honey, it was a pleasure. By the way, Derry would like to meet you. I'll send him over to introduce himself."

"I'd like that," Honey said.

Honey met Derry, a younger, equally handsome version of his father later that afternoon. From all she'd heard about the teenager, she hadn't been sure what to expect, but he was a perfect gentleman. His affection for Nan, and hers for him, was obvious in their banter, and when he proudly told her about an A he'd gotten on an exam, Nan couldn't have looked more pleased.

"You don't look old enough to have a sixteen-year-old boy," Honey told Nan after Derry had said goodbye and left on his bike. "But I swear, if I didn't know the truth, I'd think he was your son."

"I don't think I could love him more if he was," Nan said. "But he was on his best behavior today, believe me. He can be a handful, and I know there are more stormy times ahead."

"You'll weather them," Honey said confidently.

"I hope Trent and I *survive* them."

They both laughed. But later that night, when she was getting ready for bed, Honey remembered that conversation and stopped to stare thoughtfully at her reflection in the full-length mirror opposite the dresser. She was in her nightgown, and as she slowly turned sideways, she pressed the gauzy material close to her body. Her stomach was still flat as a washboard. Disappointed, she bit her lip—and then felt impatient.

Well, what did you expect? she asked herself caustically. It hadn't been three months yet; even if she *was* pregnant, she couldn't possibly be showing.

But still...

She stood there, her hand on her belly. Did she really need a test, or a doctor, to tell her what she already knew? Like the miracle it was, she could feel the life force pulsing inside her. It was filling her up, taking her over, making her... whole.

Awed by the thought, she realized that she was part of a vast sisterhood now, comprising all the women who had come before her, and those who would follow. It was a process more sacred than anything men could name. She felt privileged, exultant.

Then Seth's face flashed into her mind, and she bit her lip again. As she had so many times, she wondered guiltily if she shouldn't have told Seth, at least about her suspicions, before she left. She'd wanted to, but then they'd had that fight about her coming here, and in the end, she hadn't said anything. It hadn't seemed the right time. It still didn't. Maybe now it never would.

Frightened by the thought, she turned away from the mirror. She was confused about so many things. But on one thing she was clear: no matter what happened between her and Seth, she was *not* going to use an innocent child either to hold him or to get him back. She knew what kind of man her husband was.

If she told him he was about to become a father, he'd feel obligated to stay, whether he wanted to or not. He'd say it was his responsibility.

Fiercely, she clutched her middle. She couldn't live that way, wondering if duty bound Seth to her, not love. She'd rather lose him entirely than live with him in an empty sham. That would be the worst thing of all.

HONEY TRIED to put her problems with Seth out of mind the next few days. Nan was a big help in that regard; with Carla away, Seth's petite cousin did everything she could to make Honey feel welcome.

Nan was even kind enough to pretend that Honey was a help. With Wade starting up his own training stable at Churchill Downs in Louisville, Nan not only had to fulfill her new duties as barn manager, but had taken over as the farm's manager. Each morning, she and Honey would meet in the barn office to discuss what needed to be done that day.

To Honey, Nan's job seemed an awesome responsibility, but Nan appeared more than equal to the task. As she pointed out herself with a laugh, she'd had good training in running the Saddleback, the dude ranch she and her father had owned for years.

"Do you miss it?" Honey asked her one day.

They were in the barn office, having a cup of coffee. Nan was behind the desk, and at Honey's question, she sat back thoughtfully.

"I do, and I don't," she finally said. "I miss Yolanda very much—"

"Yolanda?"

Nan smiled fondly. "Yolanda Bonney, my surrogate mother. She was with my father and me for years—all the while I was growing up. I don't know what I would have done without her."

"Is she still in Montana?"

"Yes. She absolutely refused to come with me. She said she was too old to move. But I still have hopes that I'll at least be able to persuade her to visit. And I'm sure that once she does, and sees how beautiful it is here, she might agree to stay on."

"That would be nice for you."

"The best," Nan agreed.

"But what about the ranch itself?" Honey asked. "Do you miss it?"

"Yes, I do. The Saddleback was the only home I'd ever known. When I was a child, it was wonderful. I loved the horses, and because it was a popular place, there were always people around—at least in the summer. But as I got older—" She stopped and shook her head. "I loved my father, but he had...problems. Then the economy took a downturn, and our reservations started falling off. We worked hard, but we kept getting further and further behind."

"I know what you mean. When Seth and I got married, we had such high hopes. We were going to train the next Triple Crown winner, and we'd have so many good horses in the barn that we'd have to turn dozens away." She paused. "But like most dreams, it didn't happen that way."

"Not yet, you mean," Nan said with a gleam in her eye. "Or have you forgotten Never Done Dreamin'?"

Honey thought of the spectacular filly who had been taken to Churchill Downs to train with the farm's horse trainer, Dwight Connor. Fervently, she said, "How could I forget her? If all goes well, it's going to be a thrill to see her actually run in the Kentucky Derby."

"It's going to be an even bigger thrill when you meet her as an owner in the winner's circle."

"Oh, I don't think so," Honey said. "Seth would never accept the filly. She's much too valuable."

"But Grandmother *wants* you to have her."

"Seth, you mean."

"I mean *both* of you."

"It's a wonderful gesture. But it doesn't change the facts. Never Done Dreamin' belongs to Dunleavy Farm."

Nan leaned forward. "That's what I said about Done Cryin'—and what Carla felt about Done Driftin'. But in the end, we accepted Grandmother's wishes because we realized just how important this was to her. Honey, she wants to do this. Don't deprive her of it."

With all her heart, Honey wished there was some way to convince Seth to accept Octavia's gift, but she knew that, no matter how much he might want the horse, he'd never agree. It would be charity to him, something he'd never taken and had sworn he never would.

Maybe she should persuade him, she thought. No, that would only make things worse. Even if she and

Seth could work out their own problems, she couldn't force something like this on him. He'd feel that he couldn't make it on his own, or that she didn't believe he could, and that would cause an even deeper rift between them.

Damn him! she thought in sudden anger. Why did he have to be so obstinate? Why did she have to love a man who would rather fail on his own than succeed by accepting a hand from his own grandmother?

"At least think about it," Nan said, interrupting Honey's thoughts. "Will you do that?"

Honey didn't want to tell her that she'd been doing nothing but thinking about it ever since Octavia had sent that letter. "I will. In the meantime, what do you have for me to do today?"

Nan looked at her in exasperation. "You know, this is supposed to be a vacation for you. You really don't have to work for your supper around here."

"I know. But *you* weren't happy just sitting around while everyone else was busy, were you?"

"How did you know that?" Nan demanded, and then grimaced. "Never mind. I imagine it was a little bird named Carla. Well, you're right. The truth is, when I first came here, I was so determined to prove I could be useful, I was prepared to muck out stalls."

Honey laughed. "I've done plenty of that in my time. Just point me to the rake, and I'll have at it."

"Not in your wildest dreams!"

"But I want—"

"I know what you want. You're determined to contribute something. That way, you can justify staying on."

Honey flushed. "I didn't realize I was that transparent. But yes, it's true. I do feel that I have to justify my presence here. After all, Seth is Octavia's grandchild, not me."

"But you're his wife, and that makes you family—in Grandmother's eyes, and in mine, and in everyone else's, too."

"You're all so kind—"

"Oh, pooh. It's true."

"So, getting back to the original subject," Honey said. "What can I do?"

Nan sighed. "Since you're so determined, let me think." She looked down at the paperwork covering the desk and wrinkled her nose. "I've already seen how good you are with horses, so, since I have to plow through all this, would you like to treat Done Driftin' again today? I checked on him this morning, and that poultice you put on his leg looks like it took a lot of the swelling right down."

"That's the Mississippi mud," Honey said. "It works every time."

"But it's not from Mississippi, and it's not really mud, right?" Nan said.

"It depends on who you ask," Honey said. "But you're right. This recipe is from a guy I know who worked on racehorses all his life. He knew his stuff."

"He certainly did," Nan agreed. "But I also know that medicines like that are guarded at racetracks more carefully than the crown jewels. How did you ever persuade him to part with such a secret?"

"Oh, he just liked me, I guess," Honey said, and didn't explain that Jesse Daystrom had been an old racetrack groom whose hands shook so badly, he could hardly bring the whiskey he craved up to his lips. But he'd loved horses, and the track had been his entire life. So, when no one else would, Honey had given the seventy-year-old man a job. She hadn't been able to pay much, and all she could provide was a cot in the tack room, but in the end, he'd told her that what she'd given him was worth more than money: because of her, he'd regained his self-respect.

In return, Jesse had taught her everything he'd learned in all those years of treating racehorses. She'd cried when he died, and she always felt that she'd gotten the most out of their relationship.

But Jesse was in the past, she reminded herself, and she had work to do today. Eager to get going, she stood and started toward the door, only to stop with a sudden thought. Looking back at Nan, she asked, "Do you think your grandmother would mind if I took a look at Done Roamin'? I know he's had all that expensive care, and people who are smarter than I'll ever hope to be treating him, but I'd like to see if I could ease his pain a little bit."

"If you could help Done Roamin' in any way," Nan said fervently, "I'm sure Grandmother would deed you the farm and anything else she owns. But I don't have to tell you to be careful. You know how stallions are, and even now, Done Roamin' can be a handful."

She shook her head ruefully. "Sometimes I think he gives the grooms a bad time just to prove he still can."

"And from what I've seen, they let him get away with it."

"Well, wouldn't you? After all, he *is* the king around here, and you know how Grandmother feels about him."

Honey grinned. "Truth to tell, I feel the same way."

Nan laughed again. "Truth to tell, so do I."

"YOU KNOW," Octavia said that night, "Roamy was moving a lot better tonight when I went out to give him his carrot."

"Oh, really?" Honey murmured, sharing a covert glance with Nan. "That's nice to hear."

Octavia sat back. "Yes, it is. You wouldn't have anything to do with that, would you, Honey?"

"I did look at him this morning," Honey said anxiously. "I hope you don't mind."

"Mind?" Octavia's eyes misted. "I haven't seen him walk that well since...well, never mind. What did you do, Honey? Whatever it was, it's a miracle."

"It's no miracle," Honey said. In fact, she wished she could have done more. But the damage to the stallion's hock was so extensive that there was only so much anyone could have done, even Jesse. "It's a form of massage and acupressure that a racetrack groom taught me."

"Have you seen how much better Done Driftin' looks?" Nan put in. "Honey worked her magic on him, too. Carla's not going to believe his leg when she sees it."

"I saw it," Octavia said, "and I agree. You're a wonder, Honey Dunleavy. What you've done for those two horses puts most veterinarians I've known to shame."

"I just use some of the old, simple remedies. It's no big deal."

"No big deal?" Octavia echoed. "My dear, when you can take a horse like Done Roamin', who's suffered for years with that bad hock, and make him walk even a little easier, it's the biggest deal in the world—especially to me."

"I wish you could see Seth in action," Honey said proudly. "He can *look* at an animal and know if something's wrong with it. And the things that he's come up with to help horses! He's always fooling around with one invention or another. He's even sent a few ideas off to big companies for backing—" Honey's bright look faded. "So far, no one's responded. But when they do—"

"All it takes is one great idea," Octavia agreed. "By the way, have you made any progress in convincing him to visit?"

Suddenly wishing she hadn't mentioned Seth, Honey glanced down at her plate. "No, I'm sorry to say I haven't."

"I do hope he decides to come," Octavia said fretfully. "Soon it will be Derby week—or to be more accurate, Derby's *two* weeks. It's an event not to be missed, if I say so myself. And following that, the running of the Kentucky Derby itself. With Never Done Dreamin' entered, it would be a shame for Seth to miss it.''

Honey couldn't have agreed more. She almost promised Octavia that she'd call Seth again that night, but she decided she wasn't up to another quarrel with him. At least not yet.

Fortunately, the conversation moved on to the exciting events of the upcoming Derby week, and she was diverted by all the interesting stories Octavia told of famous visitors to the farm, of horses who had won in the past and the celebrations that went on from dawn to dusk and culminated in the race itself.

Later that night, alone in her room, Honey looked longingly at the telephone. It would be nice to hear Seth's voice, she thought wistfully. What was he doing right now? Was he all right? He never bothered with proper meals when he had to fend for himself; she could just imagine an empty refrigerator and him managing on a diet of doughnuts and pretzels.

What if he was sick? she thought suddenly. How would she know? The place they were renting was so far away from town, no one ever came there. He could have hurt himself again. If he had, who would care?

Stop it! she commanded herself. She was getting worked up for nothing. Seth could take care of himself. In fact, knowing him, he was enjoying the solitude. For months now, their tiny trailer had been a battleground. He was probably reveling in being alone.

SETH WASN'T ALONE. In fact, at that very moment, he was in more trouble than he'd been in a long, long time. He didn't know how she'd found out—he sure hadn't said a word—but the woman who ran the post office in town had suddenly appeared at his trailer this evening, wearing an off-the-shoulder blouse and long skirt that clung to her hips and thighs. She was bearing a homemade apple pie.

"Hello, Seth," she purred, while he barricaded himself on the opposite side of the flimsy screen door. "You remember me, don't you? My name is Dorinda Comstock, but you can call me…DeeDee. May I come in?"

The last thing he wanted to do was let her into the trailer. With her looking at him like that, heaven knew what might happen. But he couldn't let her stand outside, either. Wishing Honey were here—and suddenly feeling angry that she wasn't—he managed a nod.

"Yeah, sure," he said, opening the screen door. "Come on in."

Lifting her skirt with the hand that wasn't holding the pie, she sashayed—there was no other word for it, he thought, swallowing hard—up the three metal steps. Her perfume wafted into his nostrils, and even though he normally didn't care for such strong scents, he breathed in deeply.

Or maybe he was breathing heavily because when she passed him, she made sure that her breast brushed his arm. Resisting an urge to run a hand through his hair, he gripped the hand guards on his crutches and turned warily toward her.

She smiled provocatively. "I made you a pie, Seth," she said. "Where would you like me to put it?"

In the car on your way out, he thought. But he said, "On that counter is fine."

She turned toward the kitchen area, her skirt revealing a long slit that exposed bare tanned legs more than halfway up her thighs. Momentarily distracted by the sight—she did have nice legs, Seth mused—he managed to jerk his eyes away just as she turned his way again.

"Would you like a piece?" she asked.

For a second or two, all sorts of wild things caromed through his head. Then he realized she was asking about the pie.

"Uh . . . I just had dinner," he lied. "Maybe later."

"It's apple," she said persuasively. "I don't know a man in the world who isn't partial to apple pie."

He swallowed again. "I appreciate it. But you shouldn't have gone to all this trouble."

"Oh, it was no trouble," she breathed. She gazed at him for a long moment, then she lowered her lashes. "When I heard that your wife left you, I had to come. I mean, no man should be alone at a time like this."

Good Lord, was that what people believed? Quickly, he said, "Honey didn't *leave* me. She's coming back."

DeeDee lifted her eyes to his. "That's too bad," she said slowly.

She started toward him; he backed awkwardly away until he felt the couch behind his legs. He suspected that if he sat down, she'd be all over him, and he was trying to decide how to handle this, when she put her hands against his chest.

"What are you doing?" he asked hoarsely.

She gazed up at him. He could feel her breasts pressing against him; he thought he could also feel the heat of her thighs. Her voice husky, she said, "What do you think?"

She began to unbutton his shirt. Hastily, he grabbed her hands. He had to let go of the crutches to do it, and when they clattered to the floor, he knew he was in trouble.

"Stop it," he said. "I'm a married man."

She gave him that lazy-lidded look again. "And I'm a married woman. So what?"

This was a bad sign. Feeling foolish and a little desperate at the same time, he said, "What about your husband? Does he know you're here?"

"Harvey?" She laughed contemptuously. "He's snoring in front of the TV by now. He wouldn't care, anyway."

If Honey knew about this, *she'd* care, Seth thought. He tried to get control of the situation by saying, "Look, I really appreciate the pie, but—"

"Oh, the pie's nothing," she murmured seductively. "The real dessert is right here."

Before he realized what she was doing, she withdrew her hands from his grasp and pulled down her peasant blouse. She wasn't wearing a bra, and when he saw the round globes of her breasts, he quickly glanced away. But not quickly enough. It took him a second or two to realize that even though she was tanned, she had no tan line. Without even trying, he pictured her sunbathing in the nude. He felt a stirring in his groin and was appalled at himself.

"I think you'd better—"

"I think so, too," she said throatily, and took his hands. Before he realized what she was doing, she'd placed them over her breasts.

Her warm flesh felt so good that, for the merest instant, Seth was tempted. He and Honey hadn't been getting along; that was for sure. They hadn't made love in almost longer than he could remember. In fact, he couldn't recall the last time he'd even touched his wife. But now here was a woman who was not only offering it to him, she seemed eager to give him anything he asked.

What would it hurt? he wondered. Who would know?

He would, he thought, and was ashamed of himself. He realized he was still touching her, and jerked his hands away so fast that he lost his balance. He tried to catch himself, but without the crutches, he fell heavily to the couch. Before he knew it, DeeDee had thrown herself down with him.

"I knew you wanted it as much as I did," she murmured, her breath hot against his face. She reached underneath for his belt.

That did it. Galvanized into action, he sat up, taking the surprised woman with him. She was even more astonished when he shoved her away.

"That's enough," he said. "I think you'd better leave."

Leaning toward him, she said, "You don't mean that—"

He pushed her away a second time. He reached for his crutches, could find only one and used it to lever himself to a standing position. Balancing on one leg, he said, "Yes, I do mean it. I'd appreciate it if you'd go."

She looked up at him. When she saw his expression, her own darkened. She got to her feet, her big breasts bouncing. Ominously, she said, "You'll be sorry."

He already was—but not for the reason she'd intimated. He should have thrown her out when she'd first made a move on him. Hell, he thought, he shouldn't have let her in, to begin with.

"I'm sure I will be," he said, trying to afford her a little dignity. It was difficult; she either seemed not to realize, or care, that her blouse was still down around her waist. "I appreciate the pie, but—"

"The pie?" she repeated. "That's all you can think about, is the damned *pie?*"

"Well, I—"

Her face contorted. He only had time to think that now she looked more like a harpy than a seductress, before she whirled, grabbed the plate off the counter and threw it straight at him.

"There's your *pie!*" she cried. "I hope you choke on it!"

It took Seth more than an hour to clean up the mess. But after DeeDee had burned rubber getting out of the yard, he still felt that it was worth it. He was just finishing when he had a sudden thought: what if she came back?

The notion stopped him in his tracks. For the first time since he'd gotten that damned letter from Octavia Dunleavy, he wondered if it might not be a good idea to visit Kentucky. Maybe the next time Honey called—*if* she called, he thought grimly—and asked him to change his mind, he could casually agree to come for a few days. Just to check the place out.

And if Honey didn't ask him to come?

She'll ask, he told himself. But if she didn't, he'd find some excuse. Because one thing was for sure: he didn't want to stay around here, not with DeeDee Comstock on the loose.

CHAPTER FIVE

HONEY HAD NEVER experienced anything like the Derby fever that gripped Louisville two weeks before the running of the Kentucky Derby. It was estimated that over a hundred thousand people would pour into Churchill Downs on the day of the big race, but for the fourteen days preceding, the Kentucky Derby Festival offered more than seventy events—everything from lab-rat races to costume balls. Caught up in the excitement, Octavia announced at dinner one night that she might even revive Dunleavy Farm's annual Southern Masquerade Ball.

"*Southern* Masquerade Ball?" Carla asked.

"Oh, I know what you're thinking," Octavia said slyly. "I realize there are some people who believe that Kentucky isn't part of the South. But I've always maintained that this is where southern hospitality begins."

"I don't believe I've ever heard you mention an annual ball," Nan said.

"Oh, I haven't bothered with it for a long while." Octavia beamed at them. "But the idea is irresistible, isn't it? Never Done Dreamin' is going to race, and I'd like to show off my beautiful granddaughters."

"Isn't it a little late to plan an event like that?"

"We could hold it after the big race," Octavia said, her eyes sparkling. "What do you think?"

"I don't know what to think," Nan murmured.

Honey had never been much of a party-goer, and she asked hesitantly, "Did you say it was a costume ball?"

"Oh, yes. Such fun!" Octavia said, laughing like a girl. "I have all sorts of things in the attic—long gowns, all the petticoats you could ask for, even hoops for skirts. Alvah did so love the ball. He started it, you know, the year his beloved Donnagal was running in the Derby. Then, of course, when Donnagal won, the celebration became even more meaningful."

"It does sound wonderful," Carla said enthusiastically. Then she made a face. "My problem is going to be convincing Wade to come. As you know, Grandmother, he's not much for parties."

"Appeal to his vanity," Nan teased, "and tell him he'll make a wonderful Rhett Butler."

Carla looked thoughtful. "You know, that just might work. I'll try it. What are you going to do about Trent? And Derry?"

"Oh, Trent loves parties," Nan said. She shook her head fondly. "Probably because he knows how handsome he looks when he's all dressed up. As for Derry..." She turned to Octavia. "Would he be invited, too, Grandmother?"

"Your future stepson? Of course. We'll invite other young people his age, as well. They can have their own party out by the gazebo."

"Under supervision, naturally," Nan said.

Carla teased, "You sound like a parent already."

Octavia turned to Honey. "Do you think Seth would come for that? It would be a special occasion, you know."

Honey thought they'd have a better chance convincing Seth to run for president. But she didn't want to dampen Octavia's enthusiasm, so she said carefully, "I don't know. Like Wade, Seth isn't much on parties."

"But Never Done Dreamin' is going to be running in the Derby!" Nan exclaimed. "Surely he won't want to miss *that*."

"You wouldn't think so. But as I told you before, he can be obstinate."

"I'm sure you can convince him to make the trip," Octavia said confidently.

The message was clear and Honey swallowed. "I'll try. I'll call him after dinner tonight."

"Excellent," Octavia said with satisfaction. As though it were all settled, she changed the subject, and for the rest of the meal, entertained them with stories of past balls and some of the people who attended the parties at Dunleavy Farm. The governor was a regular, she said, and sometimes both members of the state legislature. Racing people came, of course, and at times, they'd been privileged with the presence of a secretary of state and a general or two. As if that illustrious guest list wasn't enough, some members of the Hollywood elite had been known to drop in.

"My goodness," Carla said, "we're going to be awash with VIPs. Don't tell Wade, or he'll manufacture a stable crisis or two to keep him away that night."

"Speaking of stables," Nan said, "how is Wade's training barn coming along?"

Carla actually glowed. "He's already got eighteen horses coming in—and the promise of almost half a dozen more."

"That's wonderful!" Honey exclaimed, hoping she didn't sound jealous. She was genuinely happy for Wade and Carla, but when she thought of what she and Seth could have done with twenty-four horses in training, it was difficult not to feel just the tiniest twinge of envy.

"It certainly is," Nan confirmed. "And there's quite a distinguished list of pedigrees among them. I know, because I saw the list."

"You know," Carla said, laughing, "because you helped to compile it."

"Oh, I didn't do that much, I just confirmed what Wade had already decided."

Carla turned to Honey. "Nan's a whiz at racing pedigrees," she said. "Ask her anything about any racehorse who's ever lived, and she knows all about it."

"I had a lot of time to study," Nan said. "Those Montana winters are long and cold, you know. There's not much else to do if you don't have a satellite dish."

Honey knew Nan was being modest. She'd experienced just how much Nan knew about pedigrees the other day when she'd asked Nan a question about one of the horses scheduled to run in the Derby. Without having to look it up, Nan had recited the bloodline all the way back to the great Sir Barton himself.

"You can say what you like, Nan," she said. "But if I knew half of what you know about pedigrees, and what Carla knows about finances, Seth and I would be a lot better off."

"Don't be so hard on yourself, dear," Octavia said. "You have talents of your own. I declare, Done Roamin' is feeling so good since you've been working your magic on him that he's almost as frisky as a colt."

"And Done Driftin' looks so much better, too," Carla said. "Even the vet is amazed at what you've been able to do."

"You're all very kind, but I can't take any credit. It's not something I plan, it's just something...I do."

"Oh, *just* something she does!" Carla exclaimed in gentle mockery. "Well, let me tell you, cousin, if we could bottle your ability and sell it, we'd all be rich and famous."

"Not to mention what it would do to help all the suffering horses," Nan murmured.

Everyone fell briefly silent. Carla and Honey exchanged quick looks. They knew Nan was thinking of Done Cryin'. Honey could imagine how Nan felt, and she wanted to say something to comfort her—but what? Every effort was being made to find the horse, but there had been no word. As Nan had said, it was as though he'd just vanished from the earth.

"My, my," Octavia said after a moment. "Look at the time. I think I'll leave you, my dears, and go watch my television program. Oh, by the way, do any of you have plans for the end of the week?"

"Nothing I can't put off," Carla said at once.

"My time is yours," Nan told her cheerfully.

"Likewise," Honey said.

"Good," Octavia said with a smile. "Because I'd like to invite all of you to be my guests at lunch. I thought we'd kick off Derby Week at the Galt House in Louisville, and then maybe take in the new art exhibit at the Kentucky Center for the Arts."

"Who's the artist?" Carla asked. "Anyone we should know?"

"Her name is Jane Dunne, according to the paper. There wasn't a picture—apparently, she dislikes having her photograph taken. But the article said she's spent a lot of her time in San Francisco, even though her work has been exhibited in most of the world's major cities."

"Why is she giving an exhibit here?" Nan asked.

"It's in conjunction with the Derby. Supposedly, she's a marvel at capturing the essence of life in bluegrass country. All of Kentucky, in fact."

"That's intriguing," Honey said. "Especially if she's never lived here."

"Yes, it is," Octavia agreed. "That's why I thought it might be interesting to go."

Carla spoke for all of them. "You've got a date, Grandmother. What time shall we be ready?"

Clearly delighted at the prospect of an outing with her granddaughters, Octavia said, "Your carriage will be waiting by the front door at eleven-thirty."

"Oh, this *is* an occasion," Carla teased. "Grandmother's getting out the Rolls."

Octavia drew herself up. "If you think I'd trust these old bones to that fast little sports car of yours—or to Nan's new pickup, you've all got another think coming. Besides, Honey hasn't ridden in the old car yet, and I think she needs a treat."

Honey smiled at Octavia's obvious pride. "I can't wait," she said. She glanced mischievously at Seth's two cousins. "The only problem is—who's going to drive?"

"I am, of course," Octavia said at once.

Dinner over, Carla stood and placed her napkin by her plate. Without missing a beat, she said, "We'll talk about that later."

HONEY KNEW she couldn't put off contacting Seth any longer. After excusing herself, she went up to her room and closed the door. She'd been delaying calling him since their last horrible conversation because she didn't want to get into another quarrel. Now she had no choice. She couldn't confess to Octavia that she was afraid of her own husband, so, before she lost courage, she headed toward the phone and dialed.

Seth answered on the second ring.

"Hi," she said, trying to ignore the little jump her heart made at hearing his voice. "It's me. I hope I'm not calling too late."

Now that he knew who it was, his voice changed. He sounded...strange. "We're two hours behind you here in Arizona, remember? It's not even eight o'clock yet."

Wondering what was wrong *now,* she asked cautiously, "Is everything all right?"

"No," he said flatly. "That Inverness mare cast herself in her stall last night and now her fetlock is as big as a football."

"Did you call the vet?"

"What do you think?" he asked sarcastically. "I might be a cripple, but I still have a brain in my head."

"You're not a cripple," Honey said quietly. "And . . . I just asked."

"Well, you wouldn't have to ask, if you were here, would you? I could have used you today, Honey. I've had to ice that horse's leg on and off all afternoon."

Honey knew she couldn't possibly be to blame for the mare's injury, but she felt guilty all the same. Seth had a point, she thought. If she'd been there, she could have taken care of the problem. With Seth's leg immobilized, it was so difficult for him to maneuver.

"I'm sorry," she said. "Do you want me to come home?"

He seemed determined to be nasty. "Oh, no. I *like* having my wife thousands of miles away when I need her here to help out."

Honey was tired of Seth's self-pitying tone, and annoyed that he seemed to hold her responsible for everything that had gone wrong—not only lately, but throughout their marriage. It wasn't *her* fault, she thought resentfully, that that horse had fallen on him. If they were going to start throwing around blame, she could just as easily demand to know why in the hell he hadn't gotten out of the way faster.

Instead, she said, "You could always hire someone to help. There are plenty of people around who would like to earn a little extra money by cleaning out stalls and grooming horses."

"And that's just what they'd get from me—a *little* extra money. Since you're out there living the high life, you've obviously forgotten that we don't have enough cash on hand to start throwing it around on stall cleaners and grooms. What we have, I use to pay the feed bills and the rent."

"No one knows better than I do what a tight squeeze we're in. I do the books, remember?"

"When you're here, that is."

She counted to ten. "Well, I'm not there, am I? So until I am—*if* I decide to come back—you'll have to manage by yourself."

"What do you mean 'if'?" he said sharply. His voice rose. "Are you trying to tell me you're going to stay there?"

She didn't mean to say it; the words were out before she could stop them. "If you're going to continue to act like this, maybe I will."

"Well, that's just great!"

"What do you expect? You've been moping around for months now, doing nothing but feeling sorry for yourself."

"I have a right to feel sorry for myself. You don't know how it feels, having to watch your wife run herself ragged, doing things you're supposed to do, seeing everything you've worked so hard for—as little as that is—going right down the drain!"

Honey started to answer, then fell silent. Closing her eyes, she wondered how she could bear the pain she heard in his voice. Finally, she asked, "Has it been that difficult for you?"

"Difficult?" As though he realized how much of his feelings he'd exposed, he laughed harshly. "Let me put it this way. If it hadn't been that I couldn't leave you with this mess, I would have disappeared long ago."

She gasped. "You wouldn't have!"

"I thought about it. The way I figure it, you'd be a lot better off without me."

"I wouldn't," she insisted, trying not to panic. She dared to add, "I love you. I want to work this out. Don't you?"

"You'd be a lot better off with someone else—someone who's a success."

"You *are* a success!"

"Oh, yeah, right," he said bitterly. "I'm so successful that I'm stuck out in the godforsaken desert, living in a hot box of a trailer, my business shot to hell, while my wife has moved to Kentucky."

"I haven't *moved* here! You know why I came."

"Without me."

"You wouldn't come! One of us had to acknowledge your grandmother's letter!"

"Why? Octavia Dunleavy is no kin of mine."

"You're wrong. Octavia Dunleavy is a wonderful woman who is anxious to meet you. If you would think with your head instead of this misplaced pride of yours, you'd realize that she has nothing to gain by what she's offered. In fact, the truth is, she has a lot to lose."

"You can't lose what you never had."

"I'm talking about the filly, Seth. Never Done Dreamin' is entered in the Derby. And the way she's been racing—and training—she has the potential to go all the way. To the Preakness and the Belmont Stakes. Seth, she could win the Triple Crown! I'm not saying you should consider Octavia's gift of the filly—I know you'd never do that. But don't you think that the least you can do is come and watch Never Done Dreamin' race?"

"Why? You make her sound like a sure thing. But she's got some tough competition, and we both know how hard it is for a filly to win against colts, especially in derby races."

"Winning Colors did it, and so did Genuine Risk and Regret."

"That was then," he said flatly. "This is now."

"Will you at least think about it?" she asked desperately.

"Maybe," he said.

Honey refused to give up hope, even after she'd hung up. *He'll come,* she told herself shakily.

But would he? Octavia was positive that, given enough time to work it out himself, Seth would see the light. But as Honey got ready for bed that night, she wasn't so sure. Octavia didn't know him, she thought. She did. And the signs weren't good.

SETH COULDN'T sleep that night. His leg itched like crazy, and as he tossed and turned, trying to get comfortable, all he could think about was how much he missed Honey. Finally, he sat up. It was time, he decided, to stop messing around and go to Kentucky to get his wife.

"And that's all," he growled to himself. He wasn't going to stay at that damned farm, and he wasn't going to accept anything that family had to offer. He might not have been much of a man these past months, but if nothing else, he could start acting like a husband. He wanted Honey *here,* with him, and he wanted her *now.*

Whatever happened after that was still to be determined. For the moment, it was enough to know that, come first light, he'd be on his way to Kentucky to bring back his wife.

SETH ARRIVED at Dunleavy Farm late the next afternoon. Right up until he boarded the plane, he wasn't convinced he would actually go so he hadn't called Honey until he landed in Lexington. He left a message with someone named Teresa, and then took a cab out to the farm. Honey must have been haunting the windows, for the instant the taxi pulled up, the front door opened, and she was flying down the porch steps and right into his arms.

"Seth!" she cried, hugging him fiercely. "Oh, I'm so glad you're here. I've missed you so much. And I have so much to tell you!"

"Hey," he said, embarrassed by her display. He glanced uneasily toward the big house as he disengaged her arms from around his neck. "It hasn't been *that* long."

"It's been a—" She stopped midsentence. Her eyes widened as he took a cane from the back seat. "What happened to your crutches?"

Despite his growing feeling that he'd made a big mistake coming here, he felt like a kid with a new toy. "The doctor changed my cast a couple of days ago," he said. "Now it's just from my knee to my ankle. He took away the crutches at the same time. I still have to use the cane, but—" he demonstrated "—at least I can bend my leg now."

She looked thrilled. "Why didn't you tell me?"

He took his duffel bag from the cab. "I wanted to surprise you."

"Well, you certainly did!" She grabbed his arm. "Come on, let's go inside."

He looked up at the house again. He'd seen pictures of it, but standing in front of it was an entirely different matter. He hadn't realized it would be so big—or that the farm itself would exert an immediate tug.

It was a dangerous feeling, he thought. "I don't know," he said. "I'm not sure I should."

She looked at him in dismay. "What? But you came all this way. You're here! Of course you have to come in. What will I say?"

She was right. He knew he couldn't just turn around and walk away. Reluctantly, he said, "I guess you're right."

"Of course I'm right," she said, beginning to tug him up the porch steps before he could change his mind. "There's so much to see!"

The first person he saw when he went inside was Octavia Dunleavy herself. The grande dame of Dunleavy Farm was sitting in the living room, and when she saw him with Honey, her hand went to her throat.

"My goodness," she said. "I'd know you anywhere, Seth. You look so much like—"

He stiffened. "If you say I look like my mother—"

"Seth!" Honey hissed.

"It's all right, my dear," Octavia said to Honey. She turned to him again. "I wasn't going to say that at all, Seth. I was about to remark that you're the image of your grandfather, Alvah. He also had the same handsome features, the same air of confidence. It's obviously a family trait—on the male side, of course."

"I don't know why you insist that we're related," he said angrily.

Octavia was wearing a locket around her neck, and she gestured him closer. Opening it, she pointed to the tiny picture inside. It was as if he were staring into his own face. The man in the photograph was wearing clothing that hadn't been in fashion for fifty years or more, but there was no mistaking the resemblance. Seth could have been looking at his twin.

"Is that—"

"Yes, it is," Octavia answered. "Your grandfather, Alvah Dunleavy."

Put in his place, Seth had no choice but to take the imperious hand she offered him to shake. "I didn't mean—"

"Of course you did," she said calmly. "But no matter. The important thing is that you're here, and I'm absolutely delighted to see you."

"I'm not staying," he warned.

"A pity," she remarked. "Does that mean you'll miss the Derby?"

He flushed. No matter what he said, he thought, he couldn't seem to rattle her. In fact, he decided uneasily, he was the one who was rattled. He hadn't expected that picture; it changed things in a way he didn't want to admit yet.

Stubbornly, he said, "I just came to take Honey home. That's all."

"Well, that's a shame," Octavia said mildly. "Could you at least stay for dinner? If you're really in a hurry, I can ask Teresa to move the meal up an hour or two."

Now he really felt like a fool. "That won't be necessary," he muttered.

"Good," Octavia said solemnly, but with a trace of a twinkle. "In the meantime, perhaps Honey could show you the farm. I know how you feel about it, but it really would be a shame to have come all this way and not even take a tour. What do you think, Honey?"

Seth knew what Honey thought: her shock at his boorish behavior was evident on her face. But even if he hadn't seen that *look* in her eyes, he knew he had to apologize, and he turned to the woman he could no longer deny was his grandmother.

"I'm sorry, Mrs. Dunleavy," he said. "I shouldn't have been so rude."

"Apology accepted," Octavia said, but with that twinkle again. "To make up for it, you can call me Grandmother."

She really was irrepressible, Seth thought, smiling despite himself. "All right . . . Grandmother."

Octavia let out a long breath. "Well! I'm glad *that's* settled. Now, I'm sure you two have a lot to discuss, so why don't you run along. We'll talk again at dinner about this Derby business."

When she waved them out, they had no choice but to go. But as soon as they were alone in the hall, Honey whirled around to him and said, "How could you? I was so embarrassed, I could have died!"

Avoiding her eyes, he said, "You're right. Maybe I shouldn't have come."

"Oh no you don't!" she exclaimed. She grabbed his arm. "Come on. We're going upstairs and discuss this!"

But by the time she showed him to the guest room, he couldn't wait any longer. The door had barely closed behind them when he took a chance and pulled her into his arms.

"What? Oh...Seth," she said, looking a little overwhelmed by his gesture. To his alarm, she began to cry. "I've missed you so much!"

He had always hated to see her cry. Awkwardly patting her shoulder, he said, "Come on, Honey, stop it. I missed you, too."

She looked at him. "You did?"

She was so beautiful that she almost broke his heart. "You know I did," he said gruffly.

She was still gazing at him when he bent his head and kissed her. Almost before his lips touched hers, desire raced through him like a flash flood. It had been so long. They hadn't been together in months, not sexually...or any other way. He felt her body tremble. Holding on to her, he pushed her onto the bed.

"Hey," she murmured, looking at him with surprise. "What's gotten into you?"

He wasn't going to let her go. "You," he whispered back. "Oh, Honey, I've missed you so much!"

She pulled him down on top of her, kissing him with such passion that he responded without thought. His arms went around her, and as his lips left her mouth and moved to her throat, he wished he could vaporize their clothes. He wanted to feel her, all of her, and to his amazement and delight, she seemed to feel the same way. When she began to unbutton his shirt, he helped her by pulling it free of his jeans. Sighing with pleasure, she put her hands under the material. At her touch, he gave himself up to the sensation of having her in his arms once more.

Seth might have endured months of inactivity, but he hadn't been idle. He'd always been lean and muscular, but all this time of balancing on crutches while he bucked hay, or cleaned out stalls, or labored in other ways, had built up his shoulders and arms. As Honey ran her hands over him, he began to tremble.

"I can do more than the last time we made love," he said hoarsely.

"What do you mean?" she whispered.

He grinned wickedly. "Don't you remember? I was pretty useless in that other cast. You had to do all the work."

She pulled back a little to look at him. "I remember." Smiling, she pulled his head down again. "This time you can help me take off your jeans...."

He would have gotten those jeans off if he'd had to rip them apart with his teeth. As it was, the denim slipped off without much trouble, and then he reached for her. She was wearing a cotton shirtdress that had a million buttons down the front. Finally, he unbuttoned enough of them to push the dress off her shoulders. He looked down at her and closed his eyes.

"You're still the most beautiful woman I've ever seen," he said softly. Gently, he put his hand on her shoulder and caressed her. "Your skin's so soft...."

He dropped his hand lower, to her breast. Even through the material of her slip and bra, the feel of her warm flesh was enough to electrify him, and he drew in a sharp breath. Slowly, he moved his thumb over her nipple and groaned with pleasure.

HONEY HADN'T consciously planned a seduction scene, but with Seth's hands on her, the thought flashed through her mind that even if she had, she never would have been able to keep to a script. His touch after so many long, empty days and nights was like spontaneous combustion; every nerve in her body felt on fire, and she couldn't delay any longer. Ripping off her panties and slip, she reached for her bra, but he said, "Let me..."

In the "old" days, before things had turned so cold between them, they had joked that Seth wasn't like the heroes of novels, who were always able to undo buttons and clasps and hooks with a mere snap of the finger. But this afternoon, no man could have done it better. Naked, she stood up and reached for the comforter covering the bed, intending to pull it back with the sheets so they could climb in. But Seth stood up with her and pulled her to him. His touch light as a feather, he ran his hands down her back, making her shiver with anticipation and press closer to him.

"Oh, Honey," he murmured, his lips in her hair. "How I've missed you...."

Honey wouldn't have cared if their lovemaking had been interrupted right there. She had waited months to hear those words, and when she finally heard them, she sent up a prayer of thanks. Until now, she'd thought that he'd never want her again. But every tremor of his body, every tightening of a muscle, every shaky breath he took, told her that, no matter what he said, he still loved her.

Lifting her head, she looked into his eyes and whispered, "Make love to me...."

He couldn't wait any longer, either. Gently pressing her down onto the bed, he climbed in beside her, careful to position the leg with the cast so it wouldn't chafe against her.

"I'm not sure how we're going to do this," he said, panting a little.

She smiled, pressing her lips against his. "Don't worry. We'll find a way."

And somehow they did. Caught up in passion and desire, they forgot about awkwardness and broken legs and casts and canes and crutches as they explored each other, once again, after so long. After all these years of marriage, Honey knew her husband's body as well as she knew her own—better, perhaps. But for some reason she couldn't explain, it was as though this were the first time for both of them. To be with someone she knew so intimately, and yet feel as though she were with a stranger, was an erotic sensation. She knew him, but the way he touched her and stroked her, and parted her thighs so he could caress her with finger and tongue, was so seductive that long before he finally entered her, she was mad with desire.

The magic worked on Seth, too. Swept up in the sensations he was evoking in her, Honey became someone else for that afternoon. She was not only the wife who loved her husband, but a wild creature who was capable of inciting a tumultuous response from her lover. By the time she was ready to take him inside, he could no more have refused her than he could have voluntarily stopped breathing.

"My God," he said at one point, gasping and blinking sweat out of his eyes. "Where have you been all my life?"

She smiled and murmured, "Right here, by your side."

Words failed them both. Thrusting hard, Seth seemed to fill her up, but she wanted—needed—more. She opened wide, taking him in deeper, until he groaned and threw his head back.

"I can't wait much longer...."

She had no breath to speak. Urging him on with every movement of her hips, every touch of her hands, every kiss from her lips, she followed his lead until something swept her up and hurled her forward.

"Seth!" she cried, hoping he was right there with her. She couldn't stop to make sure; her body was no longer her own, but a separate entity that seemed about to explode with pleasure.

Seth uttered a sound between his teeth that was half moan, half groan. His body shuddered, and he grabbed her to him with all his strength. He didn't let go until the last tremor.

"Lord," he muttered, and collapsed beside her.

CHAPTER SIX

THE NEXT DAY, with Seth driving, they all rode in style to the Galt House in Louisville in Octavia's old but well-kept Rolls. Seth hadn't wanted to come, but Honey had been persuasive. But as much as his new-found cousins wheedled, adding their pleas to his wife's he drew the line at having lunch with everyone and agreed to meet them at the nearby Kentucky Center for the Arts to view the exhibition by the artist Jane Dunne.

When Honey walked into the huge exhibition hall, she felt as though she'd stepped into a picture post-card in oils. Octavia had said that the artist was famous for her scenes of life in bluegrass country; from the painting of a horse emerging from the mist, to the poignant depiction of an old tobacco sharecropper leaning exhaustedly against a fence, the skill and talent of the artist shone. Horses seemed to breathe; people appeared as though they would turn toward the viewer and blink at any second. Lost in such visual delights, Honey wandered away from the others. She turned a corner, and gasped.

For a moment or two, she thought she was dreaming. She blinked, but it was no mistake. On the wall right in front of her was a painting of Octavia that seemed so real, she almost expected Seth's grandmother to speak to her.

Sure it was a trick of the light, or at the least, some kind of mystical coincidence, Honey moved closer. But from only a few feet away, the resemblance to Octavia was even more astounding. The portrait—if that's what it was, Honey thought dazedly—was of a younger Octavia. In the picture, she was wearing an evening gown of rich green velvet that featured perfect white shoulders and emphasized a Scarlett O'Hara-size waist. Her hands gracefully resting in her lap, she was posed in a wing chair, her head tipped slightly, a faint provocative smile playing at her lips. Heavy-lidded eyes the color of emeralds held Honey's gaze, and it took her a moment to realize that the subject's shoulder-length chestnut hair—the same color as Carla's—was pulled back and up on the sides and held with jeweled clips.

If she'd needed anything more to convince her that the woman in the portrait was Octavia Dunleavy, the sight of those hair clips clinched it. Not two days ago, Octavia had shown her that exact pair.

"My father gave these to me on my eighteenth birthday," Octavia had told Honey. The clips were carefully wrapped in a soft cloth, and when Octavia had gestured for her to take them, Honey had done so reverently. Surprised at their weight, she'd looked up.

"They're so heavy!" she'd exclaimed.

"That's because the pearls and the diamonds are real," Octavia said, and then laughed. "Of course, in those days, my hair was much thicker and longer and could hold them. Now, they'd just fall right out.''

"They're beautiful," Honey said, handing them back.

"Yes, they are, aren't they?" Octavia agreed softly. She rewrapped them carefully in the cloth. "I had planned on allowing my daughters to wear them when they got married, but things... didn't work out that way."

"It's a shame," Honey murmured. She didn't know the whole story—she doubted anyone did—but she was aware of the years' long estrangement between Octavia and her two daughters: Carla's mother, Meredith, and Octavia's youngest child, Jamie, who was Seth's mother.

"Yes, it is," Octavia said. Her glance turned inward. "I made so many mistakes..."

She sounded so forlorn that Honey gave her a hug. "We all make mistakes, Grandmother," she said. "Lord knows, I have."

"But you're young. You still have time to rectify them."

Boldly, Honey said, "But isn't that what you're trying to do now? Not only have you contacted all your grandchildren, but you've made all these lovely gestures. First, it was giving Done Driftin' to Carla—"

"That didn't work out so well, did it?"

"His injury wasn't your fault. And no one could have predicted that Done Cryin' would be stolen."

"That's true. You know, I'd never say this to Nan, but sometimes I doubt we'll ever get him back."

Honey doubted it, too, but she remained silent.

Octavia put a hand on Honey's arm. "You're very comforting, my dear, but the fact remains that my plans have gone awry. First it was the two colts, and now Seth won't even come to the farm for a visit."

"I haven't given up yet," Honey had said with more confidence than she felt. For Octavia's sake, she'd added, "He'll come if I have to drag him out myself."

But it had turned out to be a little easier than that, Honey thought that afternoon as she gazed at Jane Dunne's painting of Octavia. Sure that they were going to work things out now that he was here, she decided to find the others and bring them here to show them the startling portrait. She was just turning around, when she realized someone was behind her.

"Oh, you startled me!" she exclaimed when she saw a woman standing there.

"I'm sorry," the woman said. "You seemed so deep in thought that I didn't want to disturb you."

"I was looking at that portrait," Honey said. "It looks so much like my husband's grandmother that I can't quite believe it."

"Did you say, your *husband's* grandmother?"

"Yes, I—" Honey stopped. There was something familiar about this woman, she thought, but what? She was sure they'd never met; she definitely would have remembered such an exotic-looking creature. From the scarf around her head to the ballet-length skirt, the woman was dressed in layers of chiffon that seemed to float in some invisible breeze. The golds and violets and purples of the gauzy fabric shimmered like a romantic tropical sunset, and when the woman moved her arm, there was the musical sound of dozens of thin silver bracelets tinkling together. Earrings to match reached the woman's shoulders, and her heavily made-up eyes were the color of emeralds.

It was the eyes that made Honey draw in a breath. She knew those eyes; she had looked into a similar pair every morning across the breakfast table for six years. She had seen replicas at Dunleavy Farm, in Carla, and Nan, in Octavia herself. The Dunleavy green, Octavia had laughingly called it: everyone in the family had those green eyes... including Octavia's youngest daughter, Jamie.

Seth had rarely talked about his mother. The only thing he'd ever said was that he and Jamie had parted company when he was sixteen because he wanted to work with horses, and she had forbidden him to do it. She hadn't wanted him to "waste" his life at a racetrack.

Before she realized what she was saying, she stammered, "Are you... are you... Jamie?"

A variety of expressions flashed across the woman's striking face. Finally, she asked, "How did you know?"

Honey blinked. *It was true,* she thought. *Oh, Lord, now what was she going to do? Where was Octavia? Did she know?* A sudden notion struck her and she froze. *Seth was going to meet them here.* How would he react to this?

Before Honey could gather her whirling thoughts, they both heard footsteps. As though on a rusty spring, she turned jerkily just as Nan, Carla and Octavia appeared.

"We've been looking all over for you—" Nan stopped midsentence when she saw Honey and the woman standing there.

"What is it?" she asked as Honey's eyes went over her cousin's shoulder and widened.

Honey couldn't answer. At that instant, Seth came into view, and she realized time had run out.

She'd been intending to—to what? To try to warn him? It was too late. Seth took one look at them and came to an abrupt stop himself. His glance went to Jamie, and his face reddened.

Carla was staring at Honey in consternation. When she saw Honey turn pale, she, too, asked, "Honey?"

Honey hardly heard her. Staring at Seth, she said, "Seth, did you . . ."

Her voice trailed away as his eyes narrowed, first at her, then at his mother. In a voice as cold as ice, he said, "Well, well. If it isn't . . . Jamie."

No one said anything for a long, tense moment. Transfixed, Honey didn't know who to watch: Seth, his grandmother, who couldn't have looked more shocked, or her own mother-in-law, who was standing tautly beside her.

Then Jamie broke the ringing silence. "Hello, Seth," she said neutrally. "I didn't expect to see you."

Seth's features could have been carved from stone. "No, I imagine not," he said. He transferred his gaze to Honey and said, "Come on. We're getting out of here."

Honey couldn't believe he was serious. "What are you saying?" she asked. "I know you're surprised, but—"

His voice was like etched glass. "You don't know anything. Now, I mean it. We're leaving."

Honey didn't care for his tone or his manner. His estrangement from his mother was no excuse for his rudeness. Lifting her chin, she said, "I'm not ready to leave."

"Don't fool around, Honey. I want to go, and I want to go *now*. Are you coming or not?"

She dug in her heels. "No."

He stared at her for a few seconds; she forced herself to stare back. Then, his words clipped, he said, "All right, fine. Stay if you like. But I'm going."

She thought he meant . . . back to the farm. Barely restraining her anger at his behavior, she said, "Go ahead."

And, to her outraged disbelief, that's exactly what he did.

"It'll be all right," Nan said quickly.

Carla glanced over her shoulder at her departing cousin, then looked back at Honey. "Yes, I'm sure it will be. In the meantime—"

"In the meantime," Jamie said, "we have a . . . situation."

"Indeed," Octavia said. "I'm as surprised as Seth apparently was. I had no idea you'd be here, Jamie."

"It wasn't my idea, Mother," Jamie said. "My agent insisted I do a showing here this year. I've resisted in the past, you know. Nothing anyone could offer would have induced me to visit the place that holds such a wealth of bad memories. But this time they made me an offer I couldn't refuse. Don't worry, though," she added coolly, "Louisville is a small town compared to some, but even so, it shouldn't be hard for us to stay out of each other's way."

There was another electrified silence. Struggling with all sorts of emotions—chief of which was whether or not to go after Seth—Honey wouldn't have said anything to her mother-in-law if she hadn't seen how Jamie's hateful words had wounded Octavia.

The despair that she saw in Octavia's eyes galvanized Honey. Seth's grandmother had been so kind to her, welcoming her with a warm heart and wide open arms, generously offering her everything Dunleavy Farm had to give. In that moment, Honey's loyalty was to Octavia, not to the mother-in-law she'd only just met—the woman who had so disapproved of her only son's career choice that she had cut him out of her life without a thought.

Her voice shaking—with anger as much as temerity—Honey said, "Please don't speak to Octavia like that. If you really despise this place, why have you painted all these wonderful pictures? Why—"

"That's enough, Honey."

Mercifully, Octavia's quiet voice brought her to a halt before she said even more to regret. Appalled at herself, she looked at the startled little group. Carla gazed at her with an approving smile playing around her lips; Nan was wide-eyed. But it was Octavia, pale and clearly shaken, who most concerned her, and she was about to blurt out an ashamed apology, when Jamie spoke.

"No, don't correct her, Mother," Jamie said. Her beautifully made-up eyes sought Honey's. "You're right. And I applaud you for having the courage to say it. Now that I've seen Seth and met you, Honey, I'd like to call a truce. What do you say, Mother?"

Octavia said quietly, "I'd like that. What happened took place long ago, and I've regretted it for a long time. You proved me wrong, Jamie. You did become a great artist."

"Why *did* you do everything you could to discourage my painting?"

"I thought you'd get hurt. I was afraid that failure would destroy you. It meant so much to you. But I... I was mistaken. I should have encouraged you to explore your talent, to pursue your dream, and I... didn't."

Octavia seemed to notice her portrait for the first time. Her eyes misted. She gazed at the painting for a long moment before she brought her glance back to her youngest daughter's face. "And now," she added, "you have more than fulfilled all that promise. I'm proud of you, Jamie, more than I can ever say."

As if suddenly aware that she and Octavia weren't alone, Jamie laughed self-consciously and said, "Well, if I'd known *that*, Mother, I wouldn't have been painting under an assumed name all these years. Now it seems as if I'll have to start building a following all over again. But in the meantime—"

"In the meantime," Octavia said, "I'd like for us to start over again, too. Would you—" She paused, obviously hesitant to ask the question. "Would you consider coming out to the farm? If not to stay for a while, just for a visit."

"Please come," Honey said. "After Seth has a chance to think about it, I'm sure he'll realize that you and he have a lot to talk about."

Jamie smiled sadly. "That's true. I just wonder—" She stopped and shook her head. "Maybe you're right. As Mother said, it's time to put the past to rest—or at least try to explain it."

Carla stepped forward and held out her hand. "I'm Carla Dunleavy, Aunt Jamie. Your sister, Meredith, is my mother."

Nan came forward, too. "And I'm Nan—your brother Gary's daughter. It's a pleasure to meet you after all this time."

Solemnly, Jamie started to shake hands, then gave both her nieces a hug instead. "I knew who you were right away," she said. "Carla, you're the image of your mother. And Nan...you look so much like Gary."

Finally, she turned to Honey. Almost shyly, she said, "I've been wanting to meet you for years. It was all I could do to stay away when I heard that you and Seth were getting married.''

Honey was startled. ''How did you know that?''

''I wanted to come to the wedding, but Seth made it clear that he didn't want me there. He—''

''Wait a minute,'' Honey said. ''What do you mean, Seth didn't want you to come? When did you talk to Seth? He's always told me that you and he haven't had any contact since he ran away at sixteen.''

''He told you that?'' Jamie looked down. ''I guess I can't blame him for that. He never has forgiven me for disapproving of his work with horses.'' She lifted her head to glance at Octavia. ''Supposed parental disapproval seems to be a trait in this family.''

Honey was still trying to digest the news that Seth and his mother had been in contact at least once over the years and he hadn't told her. Thinking that when she got back to the farm, he was going to have a lot of explaining to do, she said, ''*Supposed* disapproval? Seth told me—''

''I can imagine what he told you,'' Jamie said. ''The truth is . . . well, it's a long story.''

She might have explained, but they all suddenly realized they'd drawn a curious little crowd. One man, seeing that he had Jamie's attention, gestured to her. When Jamie saw that, she sighed.

''There's my agent,'' she said. ''Apparently, I've been remiss in my duties, so this will have to wait until later when I come out to the farm.''

Honey forced down her impatience. "All right," she said reluctantly. Then she thought of something. "I'm not sure what I should call you."

"Well, I haven't been much of a mother, so I haven't really earned that title, have I?" Jamie said. "I'll tell you what. Until we can talk things over, why don't you call me Jamie?"

HONEY COULD HARDLY wait to get back to the farm and find Seth. They had, she thought grimly, a lot to talk about. But when they all arrived and she went looking for him, he was nowhere to be found.

"Teresa, have you seen Seth?" she finally asked the housekeeper.

"Oh, my," Teresa said, wringing her hands. "Didn't he leave you a note or anything?"

"A note? What do you mean?"

Teresa looked even more distressed. "Oh, Miss Honey, I do hate to tell you this, but the truth is, your Mr. Seth, well, he . . . left."

"Left? You mean, he went somewhere?" Honey still didn't understand. "Where did he go?"

"I think he went back home."

"Home?" Honey realized she was repeating everything the housekeeper said and made an effort to focus. "He couldn't have gone *home*," she said. "You must be mistaken, Teresa."

"Oh, I don't think so, Miss Honey," Teresa said. "He took that duffel bag and everything. Just called up a cab and went. He seemed in a powerful hurry, too, like he was angry or something."

Honey knew he'd been angry—but angry enough to leave the farm? Shaken, she tried to remember exactly what he'd said at the gallery. *We're getting out of here... I mean it, we're leaving. Are you coming or not?*

She'd never dreamed he intended to go back home! Almost angrily, she looked at Teresa again. "Didn't you ask where he was going? How could you have let him go like that?"

"It wasn't my place to question him, Miss Honey," Teresa said, offended. "If he was determined to go, how was I supposed to stop him?"

Belatedly, Honey realized how she'd sounded and was ashamed of herself. "You're right. I'm so sorry, Teresa. It's just that I...I never thought he'd just...leave!" Hopefully, she looked at the housekeeper. "Didn't he say *anything?*"

"Yes, he did," Teresa said reluctantly. "He said that if you wanted him, you'd know where to find him."

CHAPTER SEVEN

HONEY CRIED herself to sleep that night. The next morning, she dragged herself from the bed she and Seth had so recently shared, hoping this had all been a bad dream. But that hope was dashed when she looked at the place where his duffel bag had been, and at the empty drawer where he'd put his clothes. She had to accept it: Seth's things were gone, and so was he.

Telling herself that she'd already cried much too much, she pulled on jeans and a T-shirt. The dress she'd worn to the gallery was still draped over the chair; she knew she should hang it up in the closet, but she didn't have the energy. What was the point? she asked herself wearily. Seth had left in a fury yesterday; right now, that's all that mattered.

Wondering mournfully how things could have gone so wrong, she went into the bathroom. When she looked at herself in the mirror, she winced. Her face was blotchy; her eyes were red and swollen. On top of everything else, she thought, she looked a mess.

She didn't know why she was bothering, but she took a washcloth from the rack and ran it under cold water. She pressed it to her eyes, but when she took it

away, she looked just the same—awful. She couldn't
go downstairs, she decided. Everyone would know—

What? That she was upset? But everyone already
knew that. After that scene yesterday, she wouldn't be
surprised if someone came for her today with a net.
Every time she pictured Seth turning on his heel and
leaving the gallery, she wanted to die. Why hadn't she
gone after him? Why had stubborn pride—the same
kind of obstinacy that she complained about in him—
stopped her? What must this family think of her, to
have let her husband just walk out like that?

She couldn't cower up here and wonder. She had to
go downstairs and face them sometime. Halfheart-
edly, she rummaged around for some lipstick and eye
shadow, but after she'd finished applying both, she
decided she looked worse than ever. Angrily, she
grabbed the washcloth again and scrubbed them off.
Without looking at herself again, she left the bedroom and went downstairs.

Breakfast was always served on the sideboard in the
dining room. The last thing Honey wanted was something to eat, but she did grab a cup of coffee before she
went to huddle in one of the dining room chairs. She
was just thinking that she was going to have to leave
the farm, too, when Nan and Carla appeared at the
door. When they saw her, they stopped. On their faces
were almost identical expressions of concern and
worry.

"We were going to come by your room on the way
down," Nan said, "but we didn't think we should

disturb you. Are you all right? Do you need anything?''

She needed her husband, Honey thought miserably, but she shook her head. "No, I'll be okay."

Nan and Carla exchanged a quick look that implied they both wondered if that was true. Carla asked, "Do you mind if we join you?"

Honey shook her head and took a sip from her cup.

Nan went to the sideboard and poured some coffee for herself. As she brought it to the table and sat opposite, she said quietly, "It wasn't your fault."

Again, Honey felt the sting of tears. "Yes, it was. I should have gone after him. I never should have let him go like that. I'll have to leave—"

"Leave?" Carla and Nan looked at each other in dismay. "Before the race? Oh, Honey, you can't leave now!"

"Yes, I can. I must." Honey began to get up.

"I think we should talk about this," Carla said.

"There's nothing to talk about," she said. But she sat down again. "As kind as you all have been to me, I'm not really part of your family—"

"That's ridiculous," Carla said. "Of course you are. Even if you weren't my cousin-in-law—is there such a thing?—I almost feel like we're sisters. Of course you belong here!"

"I agree," Nan said firmly. "I never just thought of you as my cousin's wife, either. You're family, Honey. You can't leave now!"

But Honey was adamant. "I should be with my husband. We all know that. It's not right that I'm here, and he's...wherever he is. We'll *never* work things out this way."

Carla was silent a moment. Then she said, "But if you leave, you'll never accomplish what you'd planned. You told us you wanted Seth to get to know his family. That's why you came."

"And a lot of good it did!" Honey said. "I should have just left everything alone!"

"You don't mean that!" Carla exclaimed.

"Yes, I do. I do! Don't you understand? It didn't work! Now, I'm here, and Seth is gone, and he'll never get together with his family."

"I'm sure if we put our heads together, we can figure out a plan to get things back on track again," Nan said encouragingly.

Honey turned to her. "It won't work, I tell you. If I want to save my marriage, I have to go back. There's no other choice!"

"Are you sure?" asked a new voice from the doorway.

Startled, they all turned toward the dining room threshold. As soon as Honey saw her mother-in-law standing there, her mouth tightened. There was a short silence, during which Carla fixed herself a cup of tea, then sat down next to Honey.

Jamie must have seen the way they all seemed arrayed against her, and she smiled ruefully. Still, she came into the room and stopped by Honey's chair.

"I know you're not going to like hearing this, Honey," she said, "but despite the way he acted, Seth is not a child. If he couldn't deal with his mother's sudden appearance—and I'm not saying that I shouldn't have handled it better myself—he shouldn't have taken it out on you."

Because she was so upset, Honey reacted angrily. She sensed she wasn't being fair, but she didn't care. "You don't know what you're talking about. Until you showed up, I had such high hopes that Seth and I would work everything out. He seemed so...so happy here. Then he saw you."

"I see." Jamie went over to the sideboard and lifted the coffee carafe and poured herself some coffee.

This morning, she was dressed conservatively—for her, Honey supposed—in a simple multicolored caftan that floated around her when she moved.

Cup in hand, Jamie turned and faced them. Leaning against the sideboard, she stirred her coffee for a moment, then she said to Honey, "So, you blame me for all your problems with your marriage?"

Honey flushed. She made herself look Jamie in the eye. "No, I don't blame you for that," she said. But she added evenly, "But I do hold you responsible for some of the problems Seth has."

If Jamie had erupted with anger, Honey wouldn't have blamed her. After all, who was she to judge? She waited for the explosion, but instead, her mother-in-law looked at her for a few seconds, then nodded.

"Well said," Jamie commented. "And you're right. I know Seth blames me for a lot of things—just as I blamed my mother. But all these years, you've heard only his side. Would you like to hear mine?"

Carla stirred in her seat and looked at Nan. "Um...I think we should excuse ourselves, don't you?"

Nan nodded and got up. "Yes, I do. We'll be in the—"

"You don't have to leave," Jamie said. "If you like, you can hear this, too."

Nan and Carla glanced uncertainly at each other, and Jamie prompted, "You're my nieces...we're family. Don't you think it's about time all the Dunleavys started acting like one?"

Honey was still so agitated that she almost burst into hysterical laughter. How could they suddenly start acting like a family, she wondered, when until recently none of them had been speaking to one another? It was all very well for Jamie to stand here this morning after her triumphant return to Louisville and give advice, but the truth was that it had been years—if ever—since the Dunleavys had been close. Hadn't she learned that so bitterly, and painfully, herself?

Carla and Nan exchanged another glance. Then Carla, who had never been known to mince words, said, "That would be nice, Aunt Jamie. But even though you and Grandmother seem to be on the verge of working things out, there's still *my* mother to convince."

"Ah, yes, Meredith," Jamie said wryly. "We haven't had a chance to talk about your mother, have we, Carla?"

"No, but you will," Carla said darkly. "Like the will-o'-the-wisp she is, she came in late last night."

"Is that so," Jamie said. "Well, well, it's getting to be like old home week. All we need now is—" She stopped and turned her exotic glance on Nan, tears suddenly glittering on her long lashes. "I was about to mention Gary, but... Mother told me that he died not long ago. I'm so sorry, Nan. There was a time when Gary and I were very close." Her expression turned far away. "We *all* were, before—" She stopped and shook her head. "Well, it doesn't matter. Water under the bridge and all that. Where were we?"

"I believe," said another voice, "that you were about to explain the complex workings of this family."

Reflexively, Honey turned to look at the newcomer. So unhappy about Seth's desertion yesterday, she'd gone to bed last night and hadn't been aware of Meredith's late arrival. Now, for a confused moment, she thought she was seeing Carla instead of Seth's aunt. *She and Carla look so much alike,* she thought blankly. If it hadn't been for the obvious age difference, the two women could have been sisters.

"Good morning, Aunt Meredith," Nan said.

Carla looked at Meredith in astonishment. "For heaven's sake, Mother, it's barely eight o'clock. What in the world are you doing up?"

"Good morning, Nan, dear," Meredith said. She looked in reproach at her daughter. "Must you always make me sound like a lazy slug, Carla? And here I made such an effort to join everyone at breakfast."

Carla got up to give her mother a kiss on her perfectly made-up cheek. "I'm just surprised," she said, and added pointedly, "After all, you came in so late last night."

"But how could I miss the first-ever Dunleavy family conference?" Meredith asked. She glanced around at them, her eyes lingering on her sister. "Hello, Jamie, darling. It's been a long time, hasn't it?"

Jamie set aside her coffee cup. A smile playing on the edges of her mouth, she looked at her older sister, whom she hadn't seen or talked to in years. "Indeed, it has, Merry. But I should have known. In all this time, you haven't changed. You're still the same—"

"Now, now," Meredith said. "Let's not give away *all* the secrets at once." She stepped back. "You look marvelous, my dear. But then, you always did have a flair. For the dramatic, of course."

"You should talk," Jamie said calmly. "Does Mother know you're here, or was it your intention to surprise her, as well?"

"Things have changed," Meredith said airily. "Mother and I are actually on speaking terms. But enough about our silly little selves for now. As irresistible as we are, I want to meet the newest member of the family."

She turned to look at Honey, who had to make an effort not to stare openmouthed. With a smile and a gracefully extended hand, Meredith said, "Hello. You must be Honey. It's a delight to meet you at last."

Scrambling to remember her manners—it was disorienting to be in the same room with such strong

personalities as those of Meredith and Jamie—Honey
got to her feet.

"It's nice to meet you, too," she said. "I've heard
so much about you."

"Obviously a topic we'll have to discuss," Meredith said with a smile. She glanced around. "But
where's Seth? Don't tell me my only nephew is still
abed. It's not every day that his aunt and his mother
actually stand on Dunleavy soil at the same time."

Honey saw Nan and Carla look at each other. She
knew Carla well enough by now to know that Carla
would try to smooth out the awkward pause, but she
couldn't have that. She might not be good at fighting
her own battles, she thought, but at least she could
make the attempt.

"He isn't here," she said. "We had...er...there was
a problem yesterday, and he...left."

"I see. Well, that's too bad. Tell me, is he gone for
good, or does he intend to come back?"

"I don't know," Honey said, trying not to sound as
miserable and uncertain as she felt. "We didn't...
discuss it."

"Oh. Well, we all understand that the farm has that
effect on people at times. Don't we, Jamie?"

"Merry," Jamie said, "I think we should go...
elsewhere...and talk."

"But I haven't had my coffee yet."

"You'll live," Jamie said. She linked her arm with
her sister's, leaving Meredith with no choice but to go
along.

Honey felt as though two whirlwinds had collided right over her head and then stormed away to begin the process somewhere else. It had been fascinating, and exhausting, she thought as she reached for her coffee. She wished Seth could have been here to—

But Seth *wasn't* here; that was the problem. The answer was to figure out what to do herself.

"You're not really going back to Arizona, are you?" Nan asked worriedly. "I mean, not before the Derby. You know you want to see Never Done Dreamin' run. It would be a pity to miss it."

Honey didn't know what to do. She couldn't deny that watching the filly run the Derby would be one of the biggest thrills of her life, but still . . .

"It's this coming week," Carla said persuasively. "I know it's none of my business, but if it were me, I'd stay here and give Seth time alone to think things through."

"That's right," Nan said eagerly. "And once he does think about it, he'll come around."

Honey thought that was about as likely as him joining the crew of a space shuttle for a trip into orbit. But she knew Carla and Nan were trying hard to cheer her up, so she said, "Maybe you're right." She forced a smile. "At this point, what have I got to lose?"

Despite her show of bravado, her lip trembled when she said the last, and she quickly reached for her coffee again. She was about to take a sip, when the phone rang. The sound jangled her already taut nerves; she jumped so badly, she nearly dropped the cup.

"Who on earth could that be at this hour?" Nan asked.

Honey was closest, so she reached for the phone. "Hello?" she said.

It was Dwight Connor. As she listened to what he had to say, she knew something awful must have shown in her face, for Nan and Carla both tensed. They stared at her, obviously wondering what was wrong, but when Carla plucked questioningly at her sleeve, Honey shook her head.

She listened intently for another few minutes, then she swallowed convulsively and said, "Yes, yes, I understand, Dwight. We'll be there right away." She listened again. "No, no, it's all right. We'll...decide what to do when we get there."

Dazed, she hung up the phone. Nan and Carla spoke at the same time.

"What is it?"

"What's wrong?"

Honey looked up at them with strained eyes. She tried to speak, and failed.

"For heaven's sake, Honey!" Nan cried. "Has something happened? Why did Dwight call? What did he want?"

Honey pulled herself together. She managed to say, "It's Never Done Dreamin'. Dwight says she's really sick."

"Sick?" Carla looked blank. "But we visited her yesterday, and she was fine."

Honey didn't realize she was wringing her hands until Nan reached out and stopped her. "What did Dwight say?" Nan asked.

Trying to concentrate on details instead of the pictures whirling in her mind, Honey said, "They were prepping her for the big race, and Dwight told the jockey to breeze her this morning during her workout. She did just fine until..."

"Until?" Carla prompted.

"Until they took her back to the barn," Honey said. She felt disoriented, as though the room had suddenly turned upside down. How could this be happening? she wondered. With so much at stake, everyone had been on pins and needles around that horse. How could the filly have gotten sick?

"At the barn, she started exhibiting signs of colic. Before they knew it, she went down." She looked at the cousins with wide, frightened eyes. "The vet is there right now. They're not sure they can...save her."

"No!" Carla whispered. She put a hand to her mouth. "No, I don't believe it."

Nan looked ready to cry. Her voice shaking, she said, "It can't be happening—not again. Not three in a row! It isn't fair!"

Honey couldn't think about fairness; all she could think about was that horse. "Let's go," she said unsteadily. "We've wasted enough time."

NEVER DONE DREAMIN' was still lying in her stall when they pulled up in a spray of gravel in the backside parking lot and hit the ground running even before the car rocked to a halt. The drive from the farm to the track had been quiet and intense; the only words spoken had been bleak assurances from Carla and Nan that the filly was going to be all right.

Honey couldn't answer; she could hardly think straight. Every time she thought of something happening to that beautiful horse, she felt sick. At least, she tried to console herself, it wasn't as if this was deliberate—as it had been with the filly's two half brothers, Done Driftin' and Done Cryin'. With a horse as closely guarded as Never Done Dreamin', there was no way anyone could have gotten near her long enough to make her sick. It had to be just one of those things, a swing of fate.

But her hands were ice-cold and her teeth were chattering by the time they ran up the shedrow to where a crowd had gathered outside the filly's stall. Dwight hurried to meet them.

"How is she?" Honey called tensely, when they were still yards away. "Is she going to be all right?"

The expression on Dwight's face spoke volumes. *She's dead!* Honey thought, and froze in her tracks. Nan and Carla stopped with her.

Dwight rushed up. Sounding like he was holding on to his own sense of control by a thread, he said, "We're doing everything we can. But I have to warn you, it doesn't look good."

"How can this have happened?" Honey asked, her voice choked. "She was just fine yesterday—"

Dwight's face turned even more grim. "That was yesterday," he said, "before she had her workout this morning on a bellyful of cold water."

Carla drew in a breath. "What fool allowed that to happen?"

Dwight clenched big, meaty hands. "That's what we're trying to find out. And believe me, when we do—"

Honey didn't want to debate the fate of a person cruel enough and insidious enough—and clever enough—to have given a horse heading toward a hard workout any water, much less a bucketful of something cold. She wanted to see the filly, and she wanted to see her *now*.

With Nan and Carla still trying to get the story from Dwight, Honey left them and went to the horse's stall. She was so intent on the sick animal that she barely nodded to the worried grooms and concerned stable hands who were crowded outside. The stall had Dutch doors; the top part was closed, and she bent down so she could see inside the stall.

The veterinarian, a young woman Honey had met named Krista Vallon, was inside. She was kneeling beside the prostrate filly while two men stood over them, one holding a light, the other holding up a plastic intravenous bag.

Honey didn't want to disturb either the horse or those attending her, but she couldn't just stand here. "Dr. Vallon," she called softly, "is it all right if I come inside?"

Dr. Vallon's expression was even grimmer than Dwight's had been. Making a sign to be quiet, she gestured that it was okay to join them. Holding her breath, Honey slipped into the stall.

She had seen horses in full-blown colic before; anyone who worked around equines had. But never had she seen a horse who was in such bad condition as the filly. Never Done Dreamin' was lying in the straw, and the intravenous line in her neck actually quivered with the shuddering breaths that shook the animal's entire body. Her neck and sides were soaked with perspiration, but most alarming were the damp patches above the filly's eyes. The only time Honey had ever seen a horse sweat there was when the animal had been in mortal pain.

I can't bear it, she thought, and gently placed a hand on the horse's sweaty side. The only reaction was an involuntary rippling of skin. The filly didn't even look up.

Honey dashed tears from her eyes. "How could this have happened?"

"We know how," the vet muttered. "We just don't know who—yet."

She had to ask the dreaded question. "Is she going to be all right?"

"The next twenty-four hours will tell," Dr. Vallon said. "I've got her loaded up on painkillers and everything else I can think of, and we're pumping fluids into her as fast as we can. But if we get reflux when we pass the tube into her stomach again—"

Dr. Vallon didn't finish the thought, but Honey knew what the vet had been about to say. Horses were incapable of vomiting, so if the intestinal system was blocked—the condition known as colic—the only way for that blockage to pass was for the symptoms to resolve themselves. If that didn't happen, and if, when the vet passed a tube into the stomach and the tube returned the contents, options suddenly became extremely limited.

"Will you operate?" Honey asked, mentioning one option.

"That's up to you and your husband," the vet told her.

Honey recoiled at the thought of having to make such a decision. "What do you mean? It's not up to us."

"Yes, it is. Dwight told me that you and Seth Dunleavy are the registered owners of the filly now."

"That's impossible!"

"No, it isn't. Apparently, Mrs. Dunleavy had the papers changed a while ago. I've seen a copy of the registration documents. So, whatever we decide to do... it has to come from you."

Honey could feel the color draining from her face. "No," she whispered. "I can't make a decision like that."

The vet looked grim again. "I'm afraid you're going to have to," she said. "Because at this point, I think surgery is going to become an option."

Honey looked down at Never Done Dreamin'. *Surgery!* She quailed at the idea. She knew that some horses came out of colic surgery just fine. But others never made it, and even those who managed to pull through might never race again.

I can't do it, she thought in a panic. No matter what the registration papers read, she couldn't make such a monumental decision by herself. What if she chose wrong? What if surgery seemed the only choice, but the filly died? What if it turned out that the horse could have made it without an operation?

Dr. Vallon apparently saw how frightened she was, for she put a comforting hand on Honey's arm and said quietly, "Let's not worry about that yet. Let's see what develops."

The following hours were agony for everyone concerned, the filly not least of all. The morning dragged on; lunchtime came and went. By late afternoon, Honey had left the horse's side only once, to call Octavia—and Arizona, to leave a message for Seth, in case he was there.

She didn't know where Seth was, but she needed him. At that point, when the filly's life might hang in the balance, she wasn't going to let their disagreements stand in the way. She needed him to help her make a decision about the operation, if it came to that.

Carla and Nan both stood by, at various times insisting that she take a break to eat something. But she couldn't bear the thought, and when they suggested that she at least have a cup of tea, she couldn't drink.

She appreciated their efforts, but all she could do was sit there with her hand on the filly's neck and croon meaningless nothings when the horse got restless.

One of the grooms sat with Honey at all times; if the filly started to thrash from the pain, they were both needed to hold her down. The colic was bad enough; they didn't want to risk a twisted gut.

Dr. Vallon came and went, trying to attend to her racetrack practice and keep an eye on Never Done Dreamin' at the same time. There were many moments during that nightmare day when Honey would look up with shadowed eyes to see the vet just standing there, ready to help.

Finally, when the last shot of pain medication—the strongest the vet could administer—failed to last even a half hour, Honey had to accept that decision time had come. She knew it was risky, but she sent the groom out of the stall for a few minutes so she could be alone with this horse of her dreams, the oh-so-fleet daughter of Done Roamin', who might never race again.

Wishing desperately that Seth was with her, she stroked the filly's neck, looking down at her all the while. Never Done Dreamin's breathing was labored; she seemed exhausted. Was she asking Honey to get it over with, to help her out of the pain?

"I don't know what to do, girl," Honey whispered. She didn't realize she was crying until a tear fell on her hand. Another slid down her cheek, and she brushed it away, willing herself not to burst into sobs.

She knew that if she told Dr. Vallon to go ahead with the operation, and it was a success, there was still the possibility that the filly might never race again. Would Never Done Dreamin' want that, she who had been born to run? Was saving a life the right thing to do when the decision to do so took away the animal's reason for living?

Just then, someone came into the stall. Lost in the filly's pain and her own dire thoughts, Honey didn't look up. She thought it was the vet, needing her decision.

"Honey?"

For a second or two, she was sure she was dreaming. *It couldn't be,* she thought, and was so afraid to move, she couldn't even look over her shoulder.

"Honey," the voice said again.

Jerkily, she turned around. Seth was standing in the doorway. She didn't question it, or wonder how he had come here, or known that she needed him so desperately. When she saw him, her face crumpled, and she was lurching to her feet when he came quickly to her side. His strong hands pulled her up, and he held her tightly to him. His embrace was the most comforting feeling she'd ever known.

"Oh, Seth," she said, her voice strangled with tears and relief that he was here. "Did Dr. Vallon tell you...?"

"She did," he said, stroking her hair. "And we'll make the decision when it's time."

She was just looking up at him when Never Done Dreamin' lifted her head. With eyes dazed from all the drugs she'd been given, the horse looked around for a few seconds. Then, with a snort, the swiftest distaff runner in the country got to her feet and shook herself. For the first time since the filly went down, Honey dared to believe Never Done Dreamin' was going to make it.

CHAPTER EIGHT

IN THE FLURRY of activity that followed Never Done Dreamin's recovery, Seth and Honey had little time for themselves.

Which was as it should be, Seth thought, relieved that the inevitable confrontation could be postponed for a while. Honey was so thrilled that the horse seemed to be all right, he didn't have the heart to tell her that they were still going back home.

In fact, as he stood outside the filly's stall with his arm around his wife, while the vet examined the horse from head to tail, the last thing he wanted to do was start an argument. He knew she didn't want to leave, and when the contact of her slender body next to his brought back memories of the lovemaking they'd shared, he felt a tightening in response. Without even trying, he could picture the way she'd looked and felt yesterday, how slim and pliant she'd been in his arms, her lips eager for his kisses, her breasts full and warm and soft. He'd never stopped loving her, but yesterday, he'd never loved her more.

They never should have come here, he thought. But now that they had, they should leave. Nothing had changed—in his mind, at least. He wasn't going to accept charity from anyone—either in the form of staying on as a guest at Dunleavy Farm, or especially in accepting a valuable racehorse like Never Done Dreamin'.

When Honey had said she wasn't coming with him yesterday, he'd gone to the airport intending to take the first plane back to Arizona. So why had he spent the night wandering around the airport, feeling so sorry for himself that finally he'd had to come to the track? He'd intended only to look in on Never Done Dreamin'—just to see her up close. Then he planned to leave again, with no one the wiser that he'd been there.

But things hadn't worked out as he'd anticipated. By the time he'd talked his way into the backside by showing his trainer's license, the filly had been down for hours. He couldn't leave then, not until he knew the outcome.

Or was he trying to rationalize the real reason that he was still here? He had to admit it. The truth was, he hated to hurt Honey. Every time he made her cry, he despised himself even more. After the way he behaved yesterday at the gallery, he wondered if they could go on. He'd acted like a fool.

Something was wrong with him. How could he be willing to jeopardize his marriage to the only woman he loved—the only woman he would ever love—because of his pride? Was it worth the high price?

Grimacing at the thought, he looked down at Honey. Her face was so luminous with joy, it almost hurt to watch. What made him think that she'd *want* to come back to Arizona with him? It was obvious that she belonged here.

As though she knew he was thinking about her, Honey looked up at him. "Isn't it wonderful?" she said. "Never Done Dreamin' is going to be all right, and it's all due to you."

"Me?" He was feeling too rotten to be recognized for anything, much less something he hadn't done. "I didn't do—"

"Yes, you did. You came back. Your mother is going to be so pleased."

His eyes darkened. "I'd rather not talk about my mother."

"But, Seth . . ."

"Please, Honey. I need some time to think about it."

Before Honey could pursue it, Dr. Vallon came out of the stall, and Dwight quickly came over from the aisleway. The veterinarian was carrying a stethoscope, and as she hung it around her neck, she grinned at all of them.

"Whatever you did, worked," she said to Honey and Seth. "That filly's got gut noises, she's hungry and things are looking and sounding normal again."

"Thank God," Honey breathed.

"Do you think she'll be able to run?" Dwight asked.

"Well, it's a little too early to say, but we'll keep monitoring her. If she continues like this, and there's no recurrence, I think there's a good possibility."

The trainer looked inside the stall at Never Done Dreamin', who was beginning to show interest in some hay. Shaking his head in amazement and obvious relief, he said, "I'll tell you right now, I've never seen anything like it."

Seth addressed the veterinarian. "Honey told me that you traced the possible cause of the colic to the filly's drinking cold water before she went out to work. I know that can sometimes cause bellyache in a horse, but full-blown colic...?"

"I know, it troubles me, too," the vet said with a frown. "It's unusual, I admit, but we have to realize that this filly is extremely nervous and high-strung. Things affect her that wouldn't bother other horses."

"I talked to the exercise rider," Dwight said, "and he told me that she acted a little sluggish when he first took her out to the track. But once she got warmed up, she was ready to go, so he let her breeze like I had instructed him to do. I know Jorge. He has good instincts, and if he'd thought there was something wrong, he wouldn't have run her." He frowned, too. "It goes without saying that if *I'd* thought anything was the matter, she wouldn't have left her stall."

"We all know that, Dwight," Honey assured him. "No one is blaming you for anything."

Except for allowing whoever had that bucket of cold water to get near the filly in the first place, Seth thought, and was instantly ashamed. He knew how he would have felt if he'd been in Dwight's place. He might not train horses of the same caliber, but he knew that, no matter how dedicated and careful one tried to be, mistakes could happen.

"Thanks, Honey," Dwight said, "but the fact is, it's my barn, and I take full responsibility. If you want to pull the filly out and give her to someone else, I'll understand. I know Wade isn't up and running quite yet, but I can recommend—"

Honey looked shocked. "Oh, I'm sure Mrs. Dunleavy wouldn't think of it! You've been her trainer for years!"

"With all due respect," Dwight said, "it's not her decision. I spoke to Mrs. Dunleavy this morning, and she made it clear that, whatever the filly's fate, it's in yours, and Seth's, hands."

"In that case, we'll just leave things as they are, Dwight," she said. "We'll talk to Seth's grandmother tonight."

The emergency over, everyone went their separate ways. Seth knew that this was the moment to tell Honey that they weren't going back to the farm, but before he could say it, she looked up at him.

"We'll leave in a minute, okay?" she said. "I want to make sure the filly's really all right."

Tell her! Seth commanded himself, and said, "Yeah, sure, go ahead. I'll look around."

A movement caught his eye as Honey disappeared inside the stall, and when Seth saw a flicker of someone slipping around the corner of the shedrow, he followed. There was something familiar about that figure, he thought, and he started after it, leaning heavily on his cane. He'd been walking around too much, he thought with a grimace. This damned broken bone was giving him fits.

It turned out that the leg was the least of his problems. The man who had tried to sneak away had stopped in the next shedrow, apparently to make sure he wasn't being followed. Well, he'd been mistaken. When Seth recognized who it was, his jaw tightened. No wonder the guy had looked familiar, he thought. "Davey!" he shouted. "Wait up!"

At Seth's shout, Honey's father, Davey LaRue, looked around, a guilty expression on his pale face.

Seth caught up to him a few moments later. Resisting the urge to grab the man by the collar and give him a shake, Seth demanded, "What are you doing here, Davey?"

Davey tried to look belligerent. "I've got just as much right to be here as you do."

"Oh, really? Tell me, how did you get onto the backside? Did you sneak in?"

"For your information," Davey said indignantly, "I've got a job here."

Seth squinted in disbelief. "A job? Doing what? For whom?"

"It's none of your business."

"I'm making it my business," Seth said, grabbing Davey's arm.

Davey tried to squirm away. "Hey! You've got no right—"

"Pop!" Honey cried just then. "Seth! What are you doing?"

Reluctantly, Seth let go of his father-in-law as Honey came hurrying up.

"What in the world are you thinking of, Seth Dunleavy, to... to *manhandle* my father like that?" she demanded. She turned to Davey. "Are you all right?"

Davey grimaced and began to rub his shoulder, obviously intending to pretend that Seth had hurt him. Apparently, Seth's glare made him change his mind, and he muttered, "Aw, I'm okay. It was just a misunderstanding."

Honey frowned at Seth before she turned back to her father. "What are you doing here, Pop?"

Davey brightened. "Well, now, I could hardly stay away, could I? Not when my daughter's horse is runnin' in the Derby."

Honey glanced quickly at Seth before she said, "Never Done Dreamin' isn't my horse, Pop."

"Oh, no? That's not what I hear."

"Well, you heard wrong."

Davey shrugged. "That's not going to stop me from watching the race. And don't worry," he added, "I've got a job that'll keep me in change while I'm here. I wasn't thinking of sponging off you."

Honey flushed guiltily. "I wasn't worried about that, Pop."

"Yeah, well, you should have been," Seth muttered. "He knows you're staying at Dunleavy Farm. Don't be surprised if he tries to wangle an invitation to stay there himself."

"Would I do that?" Davey said in outrage.

"In a minute," Seth retorted. "Now, do you mind, Davey? Honey and I have something to talk about."

Davey complied, but as he vanished around the end of the shedrow, Honey turned to Seth. Her voice a little unsteady, she said, "I don't know why you came back, but I'm glad you did. Please tell me you won't leave until after the race."

"Honey—"

"Please," she said, clutching his arm. "If something happens to that filly and you're not here to help, I don't know what I'll do!"

Made uncomfortable by the trusting look on her face, Seth was tempted. But only momentarily. "You're being ridiculous," he said. "That horse has more security, especially now, after this incident, than any other horse on the planet. I'm not needed—"

"Yes, you are, Seth. I, for one, need you more than you'll ever know."

When she threw herself against him, his arms instinctively went around her. He felt how delicate she was, how fragile, how...soft, and closed his eyes. *It wasn't fair, that she could do this to him,* he thought. How could one woman make him feel like the lowest of the low and the hero of her dreams, all at the same time? When he held her like this, there wasn't anything he wouldn't do for her. Without hesitation, he would have offered her his life.

The problem was, he just couldn't grant her what she was asking now. "Honey—"

"Please, Seth," she said softly.

Her arms encircled him, and when she pressed against him, he could feel her trembling. And when she put her head against his chest, he knew he was lost.

TOGETHER, Seth and Honey went back to Dunleavy Farm. *But only until after the race,* he'd told her. She hadn't answered, but he knew her well enough to know that the battle wasn't over yet. Whether Never Done Dreamin' won or lost, whether the filly even raced, he knew that Honey would try to talk him into staying on. He wasn't going to do it. He'd give in this much, but no more.

To his relief, Jamie wasn't at the farm when they arrived. She still had obligations at the art center in Louisville, and wouldn't be back until later. *Much later,* Seth hoped. He knew a confrontation was inevitable, but he didn't mind postponing it for as long as possible.

Octavia was resting after all the excitement, and to his surprise, Honey excused herself and went up to bed, too. It wasn't like her to turn in so early, but when he asked her if she was feeling well, she replied that she was just tired. It had been a long wait for the filly to get better.

He couldn't argue that; he hadn't had any sleep himself. But he felt too keyed up to join Honey, so after she'd disappeared upstairs, he went into the living room. He was standing by the glass case that held the memorabilia of Done Roamin's Triple Crown win, when he heard a discreet cough. He looked around.

A woman who looked so much like Carla that they could have been sisters was gazing at him from the opposite end of the room. He hadn't noticed her when he'd come in because she was half-hidden by the wings of the chair in which she was sitting. She saw that she had his attention and smiled, reaching for the cigarette case on the table by her elbow.

"You must be Seth," she said. She lit the cigarette with a gold lighter. As she snapped it shut, she added, "I'm your aunt Meredith, Carla's mother."

Nodding, he said, "I would have guessed that. I'm pleased to meet you."

"And you," Meredith said with a nod. She took a drag on the cigarette. "It seems you caused quite a stir yesterday."

He winced. "So you know about that."

"I hear about most things concerning this place." She stared thoughtfully at the tip of the cigarette for a moment before she tapped the ash into a crystal ashtray nearby. "But I must admit, my radar was badly askew concerning your mother. I had no idea Jamie was in town."

"Join the club," he said. He sat down on the couch opposite her. "Neither did I."

"You don't sound very pleased about it."

"Should I be?"

"Why, I don't know, Seth. You tell me."

"I'd really rather not talk about it."

She took another drag on her cigarette. Calmly, she replied, "I don't blame you at all. That's something this family doesn't do."

"What's that?"

"Talk about things. For example, I never told Carla that we were related to the Dunleavys of Dunleavy Farm. In fact, when the subject came up, I vehemently denied it." She paused. "I imagine Jamie did the same."

"Why do you say that?"

"We grew up here together, your mother and I. Remember?"

"Did you? I wouldn't know. My mother denied we had any connection to this place, too." He scowled. "There's something wrong with this family."

"You think so?"

"Don't you?"

She laughed merrily. "I know so. But perhaps I'm the wrong person to ask. Until a few months ago, it had been years since I'd set foot on Dunleavy property. Now, I'm a regular guest. It's ironic, really, but what can one do?"

"You don't have to answer, but why did you come back?"

"That's a good question," she said in an amused tone. "I've asked myself that many a time. I suppose that initially I came because my mother invited Carla. She even tempted her by offering her a horse if she accepted. Now, I admit that Octavia Dunleavy is an original, but this approach was novel, even for her. I wanted to see what Mother was up to."

"Did you find out?"

"Yes, I did," Meredith said, sounding surprised. "It appears that what Mother said in the letter was exactly what she intended to do. She gave Carla that colt, Done Driftin', and later, when Nan came, she gave Done Cryin' to her.''

"The colt who was stolen from the track."

"Yes," Meredith said, and for a moment looked almost frightened. Seth was wondering why when she added, "That was a terrible thing, awful. Nan was devastated, of course. We all were." She shuddered. "And now there's been this business with Never Done Dreamin'."

"Why include the filly in this? What happened was probably an accident. A stupid one, I admit. But an accident nevertheless."

"Do *you* think so?"

"I don't know what to think."

Meredith shuddered. "*I* think that this farm and everyone connected to it is cursed."

"That's a pretty strong statement."

"Is it?"

"From what Honey has told me, I guess it's true that things around here have been strange these past few months."

"Things have always been strange around here," she said, and before he could figure out how to reply to that, she stubbed out her cigarette and stood. He stood with her.

"It was so nice to meet you at last, Seth," she said. "I admit that Jamie and I have had our differences in the past, but I hope that won't affect our relationship." She smiled. "Now that we've started one, that is."

"What's between Mother and me is...between Mother and me," he said.

"Good. That's the way it should be. Now, if you will excuse me...?"

He watched her walk from the room, thinking how much he'd liked her. Still...there was something about her—an uneasiness that didn't seem characteristic.

Or maybe it was his own uneasiness that was affecting him, he thought, and decided to head out to the paddocks. He needed some air. But even more important, he needed some time alone to sort things out.

The splendid old stallion, Done Roamin', was standing outside when Seth emerged from the house and started down the porch steps. When he saw the horse, he paused for a moment, feeling a sense of awe, despite himself. As far away as the horse was, Done Roamin' still had such an air about him that Seth couldn't look away. He'd seen the tapes of all the Triple Crown races, of course, but the performance and the blazing speed of this particular horse had stayed with him. What he wouldn't have given to have been there!

An image of Never Done Dreamin' flashed into his mind just then, and he squeezed his eyes shut. Now there was a chance that one of the stallion's daughters might take the elusive prize, and what did he want to do? Head back to Arizona, where nothing awaited him.

Why don't you just give in? a little voice asked.

Hunching his shoulders, he kept walking. He'd always wanted to give Honey everything she desired; it was stupid to be so stubborn now, when things might finally be going right. Octavia had not only opened the door for success, she had thrown it wide. All he had to do was accept her gift and he and Honey would be on easy street the rest of their lives.

"Damn it all," he said through clenched teeth. So what if it was charity. Maybe he should just give in and get it over with. What did it matter if his grandmother's offer made him feel even more of a failure than he already did? Honey would be happy, and that's what counted, wasn't it?

He was still wrestling with the problem when Done Roamin' started toward the fence where he was standing. As he watched the horse's awkward, shambling progress, Seth forgot his own problems. It was a crying shame, he thought, that such a great horse had been brought to this. Because of his injury, Done Roamin' couldn't even service mares anymore. The two colts, Done Driftin' and Done Cryin', and the filly were the last of his get.

It wasn't fair, Seth thought, and was embarrassed by the childish thought. Who had ever promised fair? he asked himself.

Suddenly, he realized he wasn't alone. When he turned, he saw Octavia coming slowly toward him. Despite his ambivalent feelings about the woman, he immediately went to assist her.

"It's so nice to know that chivalry isn't dead," Octavia said, gratefully taking his arm for the last few steps to the fence. "Although, if you think about it, with these canes, we make quite a pair."

"As long as I'm rid of the crutches, I can't complain," he said.

She took a piece of carrot from her pocket and gave it to Done Roamin', who had put his head over the fence. Stroking the stallion's head, she murmured, "How're you doing tonight, Roamy?"

"He's still a beautiful animal," Seth said.

"He is, isn't he?" She gave Done Roamin' another piece of carrot, then turned to him. "I'm glad the filly recovered so quickly. She gave us all quite a scare."

Until she'd mentioned Never Done Dreamin', Seth didn't know what he was going to say. But suddenly it came to him—so clear that he didn't know why he hadn't thought of it sooner.

"I'd like to talk to you about her," he said.

"About what? The filly getting sick? But Dwight—"

"This has nothing to do with Dwight. It has to do with your offer of Never Done Dreamin'."

"Now, Seth, please don't say that you can't accept her. I've made up my mind. I want you to have her."

"Aside from everything else, she's too valuable—"

"She *is* valuable, but not in the way you mean. I know she's worth a tidy sum, but that's not what's important to me."

"Well, it is to me."

"That's because you're young. When you reach my age, things look different."

"That may be. But—"

She put a hand on his arm. "No buts about it, Seth," she said. "I want to do this. Please let me."

He'd thought it out. "Maybe," he said. "On one condition."

She looked surprised at his quick turnaround. "What is it?"

"You have to give her to Honey, not to me."

"But *you're* my grandson."

"And Honey's my wife. She deserves this gift far more than I do."

Octavia was silent a moment, studying him. Her scrutiny made him anxious, and he glanced from her toward Done Roamin', who had wandered away. As Seth stared at the horse, he thought of the idea he'd sent a while ago to that equine products company. Honey indulged him in his fooling around with his "inventions," as she fondly called them. But maybe that one would—

"That's a lovely gesture on your part, Seth," Octavia said, interrupting his thoughts. "But the fact is, Never Done Dreamin' is registered to both of you now."

"You shouldn't have done that."

"Why not?" she said serenely.

"Well, for one thing, you don't even know us. And until Honey came here, you'd never even met either of us before."

"It didn't matter. You were family."

"But—"

She put a hand on his arm again. "I've made mistakes, too, Seth. With all my children, it seems. Meredith had good reason to hate me, and Gary believed I never approved of his marriage. I even drove Jamie away. Then, after all these years, I finally found a way to make up for the past."

"That's why you wrote the letters?"

"Yes. I wanted to meet my grandchildren. But even more, I wanted to give you all a sense of your family history. No, no, you don't have to say it. I know how you feel about family right now. But whatever problems you have with your mother, you'll have to work out with her. Just as I have to."

"Do you think you'll be able to put aside your past differences?"

"I hope so, yes. We've already made a good start. But one can only conciliate to a point, you know. I can't undo what happened, I can only try to explain my side of it. If Jamie will listen, I'll be glad to tell her."

"And what is your side?" Seth asked.

"That's between Jamie and me. She'll tell you when she's ready." She paused. "Or when you are."

Seth glanced away. He didn't want to talk about a possible reconciliation with Jamie Dunleavy. The pain was still too near the surface. "Well," he said, "she came out here to see you. Maybe that's a step."

"That's true. But in this case, I think it's a situation of two steps forward and three back. After all these years, you and your mother finally came to visit. But the instant she set foot inside, you left."

"I admit it was a shock seeing her there, but I didn't mean to cause a scene."

She patted his arm. "The men in our family have always been hotheads. Your uncle Gary was, and so was your grandfather, Alvah." She looked at him sternly. "But that doesn't excuse you, young man. Now, I hope you will at least stay on until the Derby."

"I promised Honey I would. If I'm still welcome, that is."

"You'll always be welcome, Seth," she said. "But then, you always were."

When she seemed ready to go back inside, he offered to assist her, but she waved away his help. "You stay out here for a while and keep Roamy company," she said as she started off. She looked back. "Maybe he can convince you to accept his daughter."

Seth frowned. "I told you—"

"Don't give me an answer now. Think about it. Will you do that much for me?"

She was impossible, this old woman, he thought, and said, "I'll think about it. But I can't promise anything."

"That's good enough."

When Octavia had gone, Seth leaned against the fence, preoccupied with his problems once more. For a while, he idly watched the old stallion ambling around his paddock, and he was about to go inside himself, when he saw that his mother had come out of the house and was heading toward him. As he watched, he felt himself tense.

Jamie stopped about ten feet from him. Quietly, she asked, "Are you going to run away again?"

"I didn't run away," he growled. "I just felt the gallery was too small for both of us."

"The way you've acted all these years, the *country* is too small for both of us."

"You should talk," he scoffed.

"I'd like to. Do you have a minute?"

"It depends," he said. "What do you want to talk about?"

"Oh, I don't know. You . . . me . . . us."

"Oh, you mean, there's an 'us' now?"

"You don't have to be sarcastic. We used to be a family."

"We were never a family . . . *Jamie,*" he said, and added bitterly when he saw her face, "What's the matter? Don't you remember that you didn't want me to call you Mom because it made you feel too old?"

She flushed. She was wearing wide pants, a long tunic and a longer vest, all in different shades of green. As he stared at her, even he had to admit that she didn't look like his mother—or like anyone's mother, in fact. Her skin was too fine, her eyes too vivid, her tousled hair styled too young. What she looked like, he thought unwillingly, was the renowned artist she'd become.

That thought prompted him to say, "Oh, sorry. Maybe I should have called you Jane. That *is* the name you sign to your paintings, isn't it?"

"Oh, you took the time to look at some of my paintings?"

He didn't answer.

She bit her lip, then said, "I like Honey. She's lovely."

"How would you know? Until the other day, you'd never met her."

"That wasn't my fault, was it? I wanted to come to the wedding, but you didn't want me there, remember? We did talk about it. And *you* were the one who called me."

"It was a mistake."

She started to reply, then stopped. Her glance went beyond him to the stallion, still nibbling desultorily at the grass in his paddock. Something changed in her face, and she shook her head. Her eyes came back to him.

"I was wrong," she said. "I never should have sent you away to that school. I know that now—"

"Oh, great. *Now* you know. You mean, you couldn't tell when I wrote letter after letter, and made call after call, begging you to get me out of that hellhole? You didn't realize *then* that something was wrong?"

"Something *was* wrong," she said. "You were out of control, Seth. You were running wild—"

"Just because I wanted to work with horses?"

"Horses were the least of it and you know it. You got involved with those . . . those *people* at the track. You know who I mean—that Joe Digby, and Larry Fenton, and that jockey Louis Ferro."

That took him aback. "You remember them?"

"I'll never forget them! Together, the three of them were responsible for taking away my son!"

Forcing himself to ignore the naked pain in her face, he said, "The only one responsible for taking away your son was you. You sent me away, don't forget."

"I did it because I loved you," she said. She reached out as though to touch his arm, but at his involuntary flinch, she dropped her hand. "I did it because I loved you," she repeated. "I know you don't believe it, but those men were a bad influence on you. They taught you to drink, and to gamble, and . . . God knows what else. Until you met up with them, you went to school, you studied, you were a—"

"What? A good boy? Don't bother saying it."

"All right, I won't. But you were, you know. We never had any trouble, you and I—until you met Joe and his boys."

He scoffed, but inside, he suddenly wasn't so sure she was entirely mistaken. "You make them sound like a gang."

"They *were* a gang. A gang of hoodlums and thugs and lowlifes who took advantage of anyone they could. You know it's true, Seth. Or at least, you should by now. You were young, then, I admit. And you'd never had a father to emulate. But—"

Now he was on safer ground. "Since we're baring our souls here, why don't we talk about that? You never have told me much about my elusive sire. I presume I had one. You may be a great talent, Jamie, but not even you can arrange an immaculate conception."

Her reply to that was so swift, it caught him completely by surprise. Before he knew what was happening, she had lifted her hand and delivered a stinging slap right across his face. As he stared at her, more astonished than anything else, she looked down at her hand as though it didn't belong to her. Then she raised her eyes to his.

"I'm not going to apologize for that," she said, her voice steely. "You had it coming. I might not have been the best mother in the world, but I *am* your mother, and I won't have you speaking to me like that."

He knew she was right. His sarcasm had been out of line. "Maybe if you'd done a little more of that when I was a kid," he said, "things wouldn't have turned out the way they did."

"I don't believe in hitting. I don't know what made me do such a thing," she said, "but it's typical for us, isn't it? We worked at cross-purposes before you . . . disappeared. And it seems that's still the pattern. I'm sorry, Seth. I thought we could try and work things out, but once again, I was mistaken."

She turned and began walking away. Part of him wanted to stop her, or at least follow her, but another part made him stand still and watch her go. *Too many years,* he thought.

None of them could be erased in a single instant.

CHAPTER NINE

NOT LONG AFTER she recovered from her bout of colic, Never Done Dreamin' stunned the racing world at the Kentucky Derby. In a field of ten horses—including nine of the best colts in the country—the filly defied all the odds-makers and confounded the experts by taking the lead right out of the gate.

Stride by stride, she increased the distance between herself and the other horses, while the huge crowd filling Churchill Downs went wild. It was obvious, even to a novice, that Never Done Dreamin' was racing easily, almost with disdain. The only time she was ever challenged was when a big chestnut named Striking Distance tried to move to the inside rail on the final turn. With the flicker of an ear, the lightning-fast filly simply put on a burst of speed and left the horse behind.

With the throng screaming her on, Never Done Dreamin' was all by herself at the wire. The filly's jockey, Ian McKenzie, was so jubilant when he stood in the stirrups and waved his whip to signal no contention that he almost fell off.

In the stands, the elation was equally as great. The Dunleavy family, filling their box for the first time in more years than anyone could count, celebrated the filly's decisive victory in full view of television cameras and hovering reporters and well-wishers who couldn't get near, but who screamed up their congratulations, as well.

Oblivious to the hubbub, Honey had eyes for only one horse and rider while the official results were announced. Ian and Never Done Dreamin' were cantering around to the backstretch, when an outrider dressed for the occasion in a red coat, white breeches and tall black boots caught up to them. When the rider clipped a lead to the filly's bridle to turn her and bring her back to the winner's circle, the red-and-white pompoms tied to his horse's mane bounced like cheerleaders, adding to the festive air spreading in the outfield.

Honey felt transported as she watched Never Done Dreamin'. Only one thought kept running through her head: *She won. She won!*

If she never saw another race, this one would stay with her forever. The filly had more than fulfilled the promise of generations of her ancestors; she had proved herself worthy to take the crown.

"Honey? Honey!"

Still feeling dazed, she looked up at Seth, who was shaking her arm. "What is it?" she asked blankly.

"They want you to go down to the winner's circle."

In her euphoria over the win, she had forgotten all about that. Seth started to turn away, but she grabbed his arm. "Where are you going? Aren't you coming, too?"

He hesitated, then said, "No, you go ahead."

"What? But why?"

"Let's not argue about it, okay?" he said in a tone that brooked no discussion. "I just don't want to be down there, pretending I own the horse. You understand that?"

"But what about your grandmother?" she asked.

He deliberately misunderstood her. "She's over there."

Wondering how she was going to explain this to Octavia, Honey followed his glance. Octavia Whitworth Dunleavy was holding court just outside the box. Dressed in a royal blue suit and matching hat with touches of gold—the racing colors of Dunleavy Farm—she had defied her doctor's orders to stay home and had arrived in style with her family at Churchill Downs. Honey knew that Octavia was considered one of the doyennes of racing, but she had been amazed at the attention paid to Octavia on this exciting day. Everyone seemed to know who she was, from the valets in the VIP parking lot, to the president of the track itself. From the moment she'd stepped onto the grounds, she'd been surrounded by an admiring crowd.

All the attention had been good for her, Honey thought, when she realized that Octavia was giving yet another impromptu interview to a national sportscaster. Under the wide brim of her gold and blue hat, Octavia's green eyes sparkled, and today the color in her cheeks was natural. She'd never looked better—or happier.

Honey was about to say so to Seth, when she glimpsed him disappearing down the stairs. *Damn it!* she thought, and started to follow him, when a thrilled-looking Nan elbowed her way through the growing throng to appear at her side. Trent was following close behind, and with them was his son, Derry, who had abandoned his bored-teenager pose to look as excited as everyone else.

"Congratulations!" Nan cried, giving Honey a hug.

"Ditto," Derry said shyly.

"That was quite a race," Trent added, bending down to kiss Honey's cheek. "The way that filly left those colts in the dust, I'm almost glad my Majnoon wasn't entered."

"So am I," Nan said fervently. "It would have been terrible for me to have had divided loyalties. This way, with Trent's colt sidelined with that sole bruise, I could scream for the filly all I liked."

"And scream she did," Trent said, laughing. "She was so excited, she almost fell out of the box."

"I wasn't worried," Nan said. "I knew you and Derry were there to catch me. Oh, Honey, wasn't it the most glorious race you've ever seen? Aren't you so proud of her, you could burst?"

Before Honey had a chance to answer, Carla joined the group. Wade wasn't with her; Dwight had been so nervous that Wade had stayed down at the rail to watch the race with him. Honey was hoping that Seth had gone to join them, when Carla gave her a hug.

"Where's Seth?" she asked.

"I think he went down to the track."

"Where you should be," Carla said, and sighed with pleasure. "This almost makes all the turmoil this past week or so worth it, doesn't it? But hang on to your hats, dearies. From now to the Preakness, the pressure's only going to get worse."

Honey turned to look at Carla, who as always, was impeccably dressed in an apricot-colored silk suit with a matching broad-brimmed hat. It was a tradition that women who came to the track for Derby Day wore hats, and the Dunleavy women were all turned out. Nan had chosen a smart fedora slanted over one eye, and looked as chic as could be in hues of green. Honey had never owned a hat—at least not a stylish one. But today, in addition to a new blue silk dress, she was wearing a boater in the same shade that made her eyes appear almost royal blue.

This week especially had been hectic at Dunleavy Farm. The news of the filly's illness had spread with the speed of light, and anyone even remotely connected with Never Done Dreamin' had been besieged for quotes, comments, or failing those, conjecture. And the phone at the farm hadn't stopped ringing; so many reporters and television crews had driven up to the door that, for the first time since word had gotten out about Done Roamin's accident, Octavia had ordered the front gates closed.

Now the race was over, and Never Done Dreamin' had won. Honey had tried not to fantasize about this moment, but again and again in her dreams, she had seen the filly first under the wire; again and again, in nightmares, she had watched in terror as something terrible happened during the race.

But the dream had come true, and because the horse was registered in hers and Seth's names, Honey was supposed to go down to the winner's circle and brave all the hot lights and television cameras and reporters anxious to record every word and reaction—apparently without her husband. It wasn't right.

She and Octavia had discussed it earlier this week, and she had insisted that if Never Done Dreamin' won, Octavia had to be the one to accept the trophy. She'd said, "After all, you bred her, you raised her, and your trainer trains her—"

"That's true," Octavia had said. "But you own her."

Octavia wouldn't listen to any more of Honey's protests, and now the moment was here. Honey looked around, but Seth was still nowhere in sight. Making up her mind, she grabbed Nan and Carla.

"Come on," she said. "You two are going with me."

They both immediately protested.

"Oh, no—"

"It's not—"

"I'm not taking no for an answer," Honey said firmly. "And furthermore, we're taking your grandmother with us. She's really the one who deserves to be there. Now, let's go, or they'll start without us."

With three granddaughters flanking her, Octavia had no choice but to give in gracefully. As soon as the matriarch of the Dunleavy clan appeared in the flower-strewn winner's circle, another roar went up from the crowd. Ian and the filly were there, covered by the traditional blanket of roses, and as flashbulbs popped and the band played "My Old Kentucky Home," and camera crews and photographers crowded one another for the best shot, they all smiled and smiled and smiled.

LATER, after the ritual trophy presentation and the awards ceremony were over, and all the other hoopla involving the winners of the Derby had taken place, Dunleavy Farm gave a victory party. Despite Seth's defection that afternoon at the track, Honey was still so excited that she couldn't be angry at him.

But as she was changing clothes for the affair, which Carla had cannily designed to be either a victory celebration or a consolation party, Honey glanced at the clock and wondered what had happened to him now. She hadn't seen Seth since they'd all arrived back at the farm, barely managing to close the gates on the horde of reporters who were following close on their heels.

Now it was hours later, and he should be here, getting ready for the party. Frowning, she went to the open window and looked out. Early evening had always been her favorite time, especially here at the farm. The dying light made everything appear in soft focus, and even the slight breeze coming in the window was like a caress. She stood there for a moment, eyes closed, breathing in the sweet-scented air. When she opened her eyes, she spotted a lone figure down by the paddocks and knew instantly it was Seth.

What was he doing down there? she wondered, and was about to call out to him, when she realized he was too far away to hear her. Squinting in the growing darkness, she watched him for a moment, and then let out a breath of relief. She even smiled. He's checking the horses, she thought, that's all. It was a ritual with him at this hour of night—patrolling one last time to make sure that all was well. Still smiling, she turned away from the window to finish getting dressed.

As she reached for her slip, she paused. One hand went to her belly, and she straightened. She still hadn't told Seth about the baby; she'd been waiting for the right time. But what time could be better than the day Never Done Dreamin' had won the Kentucky Derby?

She'd tell him tonight, she thought excitedly. She'd wait until they were ready to go down to the party, and then she'd say they had something more to celebrate than the filly's victory. Oh, she could see his face when she told him! They'd always talked about having a family, but with money so tight, the time had never been right.

Now it was. With all their dreams coming true, a baby would make things perfect. She couldn't wait to give him the news, and after she finished dressing, she sat down to wait.

IN THE PADDOCK AREA, Seth was wrestling with the problem of how to deliver some news of his own. Horses always had a calming effect on him, so he'd come here to think things through. Unfortunately, even the presence of Done Roamin' didn't help. Seeing Seth there, the stallion had come to the fence in search of a treat, but had wandered away again when he realized Seth had nothing for him.

Being empty-handed was the story of his life, Seth thought, and then felt disgusted with himself. Self-pity wasn't going to help him sort this out. He had to think about what he was going to say to Honey, and with guests arriving at any minute, he didn't have much time.

But that was the problem, wasn't it? He'd run out of time. At the realization, he tightened his jaw. He had to tell her tonight. If he didn't, he might not be able to make the break. Already he was more involved with this place and the people here than he wanted to be—to an extent he wouldn't have believed possible only a short while ago. His stubborn stand about not accepting charity of any sort was wearing a little thin, even with him.

It would be hard to leave this place, but he didn't belong at Dunleavy Farm. Not the way Honey did....

Honey.

Tears filled his eyes and he dashed them away. He didn't want to leave her, but what choice did he have? He had to do what was best, for her, not for him. A part of him would die without her, but it was a small price to pay for seeing her happy at last.

He clenched his jaw. He'd had such big dreams when he was young, he remembered derisively. He was going to be one of the greats. He'd be rich and famous, so good at running horses that he would be in the position to choose only the best of the best.

But it hadn't turned out that way. Once, he'd dreamed of giving Honey everything in the world she could possibly want: a big house and a fancy car and more clothes and jewels than she could ever wear. The reality was that all he'd done for her was drag her down. Honey deserved more than he'd given her, more than he could ever give now. He was almost thirty years old; he couldn't just go on hoping he'd make it. It wasn't fair to Honey. He'd been trying to find a way to work things out, and he'd finally come to a decision.

He had to leave her: there was no other way. He knew how loyal she was. She would never agree to leave him. She'd feel it was her duty to stay to the bitter end.

Well, it was the end, and it was bitter, and since she wouldn't leave him, he'd leave her. It was the perfect time for him to say their marriage was over, that he just couldn't—didn't want to—go on. He couldn't have done it before because she wouldn't have had anyone to turn to. Now she did.

He knew that Octavia loved Honey as much as she loved her own granddaughters; she'd told him so. That was good enough for him. He'd be leaving Honey in good hands.

He had worried about that a lot in the past: leaving her alone, with no one to turn to. Her father was no help. Davey LaRue loved his daughter, Seth knew. But the man couldn't take care of himself, much less anyone else.

So it had all worked out perfectly. All Seth had to do now was convince her that he meant what he said. Steeling himself, he realized it would be the acting job of his life—the last thing he could do for her before he set her free. Trying to ignore the gnawing pain inside him, he went into the house to tell his wife he wanted a divorce.

HONEY LOOKED UP when she heard the door open. She'd been sitting on the bed, but as soon as she saw Seth's face, she jumped up. She knew instantly that something was wrong. Terribly wrong. Her heart already pounding hard, she made herself ask, "What is it?"

He hesitated a moment, then he closed the door. "Honey, we have to talk."

Without knowing why, she was suddenly so frightened that she thought she might faint. The only thing that held her up was the thought of the baby. She didn't know what had happened to put that grim look on his face, but telling him about the baby would make things right. She said, "I know. But first I've got something to tell you."

"Can it wait? I need to get this out."

She had to stop him. Somehow, she knew that if she didn't, whatever he had to say would change things forever. "But this is really important—"

"So's this," he said.

He started to say something more, but he paused again, as if he'd changed his mind—*or couldn't say it?* Honey wondered fearfully. What could be so bad that he couldn't get it out?

Her lips numb, she said, "All right. What is it?"

He took a deep breath. "I want a divorce."

She looked at him blankly. "Wh-what?"

"You heard me. I want a divorce."

"What are you saying? A *divorce?* Now, when we're finally seeing all our dreams come true?"

"What dreams?" he said, sneering.

She looked at him as though he was crazy. "What *dreams?* For the first time in years, you have a family!"

"I *had* a family," he said harshly.

"I mean someone other than me! Everybody at Dunleavy Farm is—"

"I don't care about Dunleavy Farm. It's nothing to me."

"But your grandmother—"

"I don't know her."

"But you could! And now your mother—"

"I don't want to talk about my mother."

"Then think about that wonderful horse!" Honey said desperately. "Never Done Dreamin' just won the Derby. If all goes well, she'll run in the Preakness in a few weeks, and maybe the Belmont after that—"

He was angry; she could see it in the sudden flash of his eyes. Well, she didn't care, she thought shakily. He couldn't mean it. No one just decided they wanted a divorce! A decision like that didn't come out of the blue.

"Look," he said, "I did as I promised. I stayed for the first race. I know you've forgotten, but I've got responsibilities at home. I've got to get back, but since it's obvious that you've no intention of coming with me, I think the simplest thing to do is just to end it here."

He means it! Honey realized, appalled. So shocked she didn't care what she said, she shrilled, "What responsibilities are you talking about? That broken-down old trailer? A few pensioned-off horses? What responsibilities do you have that could possibly compare to what you have here?"

"Oh, you mean this fancy place and everything connected with it?"

"No, I mean your family!" she cried. "You've always wanted a family, well, now you have one! How can you abandon them because of your stupid, misplaced pride?"

She hadn't meant to say that—or at least she hadn't meant to say it *like* that. Before she could try to make it right, his eyes narrowed furiously, and he said, "Somehow, I don't think you're talking about the people here as much as you're talking about the *place.*"

"I'm not talking about the farm! I told you—"

"I know what you told me. But I told *you* before that I wouldn't accept charity—in any form."

"It's not charity! Why can't you get that through your head?"

"Maybe because I can see things a lot more clearly than you can, Honey. You always were dazzled by rich people and material things. It's one of your least attractive characteristics."

He couldn't have hurt her more if he'd slapped her face. "You...you can't mean that," she gasped.

Implacably, he said, "Yes, I do. So, what do you say? Can we make this easy, or are you going to be difficult?"

She looked at him as though he'd turned into a monster right before her eyes. "I'm going to be as difficult as possible, Seth!" she cried. "If you think you can just walk in here and say you want a divorce, you've got another think coming! We've been married six years. I'm not going to give that up without a fight!"

"There's nothing to fight over," he said. "We want different things, that's all. It's never been more clear to me than since we came here. You *like* this life—"

"And why shouldn't I? You'd like it, too, if you gave yourself half a chance. You might even like the people here—the people who, no matter how much you try to deny it or ignore it, are your family. All they want—"

"All they want is to make me beholden to them," he countered angrily. "Well, I won't do it! I might not have much, but what I do have, I've earned. I'm not like you."

Again, it was as though he'd struck a blow. She was so stunned that she stepped back. "How can you say that? I've worked hard, right alongside you. I never complained, I never criticized.''

"Oh, no? What about all that talk of 'one day'? What about that?''

"I had dreams! What's wrong with that?''

"Dreams are for kids,'' he said harshly. "It's time for you to grow up and face reality.''

"And reality is a trailer in Arizona?''

"If that's what I have to offer.''

"Well, it's not good enough!'' she cried. Too late, she realized what she'd said. "I didn't mean that. You've got me so upset, I don't know what I'm saying.''

"Oh, you meant it, all right,'' he said coldly. "But you know what? I'm glad it's finally out in the open. I always suspected you felt that way, and now I know. It's a relief.''

How had everything gone so wrong? Frantic to make him understand, to try to repair this terrible rift that widened with every word, she started across the room toward him. The expression she saw on his face stopped her in her tracks.

"Okay, Honey,'' he said. "I think we know where we both stand now.''

"No, you're wrong!''

"Am I? For years, we've been trying to pretend that everything was all right when it wasn't. It's been like trying to fix a leaky rowboat with a plastic bandage. The bandage just keeps falling off.''

She couldn't believe the words coming out of his mouth. Fright and fury rose side by side inside her, and all she could think was: *Not now! Oh, not now!*

She tried again. "When we got married, we promised—"

"Things don't always work out like you want them to. No one should know that better than us, right?"

She felt desperate; he looked so cold. She had never seen him look like that, not even in the past when they'd had some terrible fights. Frantically, she said, "But things are working out now—"

"For you, maybe. But not for me."

She had to make him change his mind. "You can't mean this. We can work it out, I know we can. We'll go to a counselor—"

"I'm not about to spill my guts to some stranger. Forget it, Honey. We've tried. I have, and you have, and it's not working. I don't blame you for wanting to stay here. In fact, I think you should. But not me, I'm going."

"Going?" She put a hand to her head, wondering why she couldn't seem to think straight—why she couldn't seem to think at all. "And you want me to...to stay here. Without you?"

"Aren't you listening? Do I have to spell it out word for word?"

She knew he was serious; she could tell by the look in his eyes, by the set expression on his face, by the way that muscle bunched in his jaw. She felt panic rising in her like a wild tide, but she held it back. She couldn't fall apart now, not when everything she held dear was at stake. Her lips shaking with the effort, she said, "You can't mean this. You can't intend just to...walk out."

"Don't you mean, *limp* out?"

When he cracked the cane against his cast for emphasis, her nerves were so taut, the sound made her jump. "We can fix that!" she said. "Your leg won't be in a cast forever. Oh, Seth, if this is about—"

He cut across her protest. "This isn't about the damned leg, Honey! This is about us. Why can't you understand? It's simple enough!"

"It's not simple at all!" she shouted. "We've argued and fought about a lot of things, but never—*never!*—can I recall either of us mentioning the word *divorce.*"

"So I'm bringing it up now."

"Why now? Why not last week, or last month, or last year, whenever you decided you didn't want to be married to me anymore?"

"I didn't want to hurt you."

"Oh, so, *now* it's all right? What made you change your mind?"

"Look, I don't want to fight about this any more than we have to. I'll wait, if you want. I know how important the next two races are for you."

"Who cares about the damned races?" she cried.

"You do," he said simply.

Honey stared back at him for a long moment, unsure whether she felt rage or fear or just an overwhelming sense of hopelessness. She couldn't believe it had come to this.

Tell him about the baby! a voice inside her commanded, but she shoved the thought aside. If Seth didn't want *her,* a baby wouldn't help the situation. It would only make him feel obligated to stay. He'd resent her and they'd end up hating each other, which would be infinitely worse than if they just went their separate ways.

But her heart was breaking when she looked at her husband again. He might make her angry; he could infuriate her at times. But in the end, he was so... so *dear* to her that she didn't know how she was going to live without him. Willing her voice not to tremble and give her away, she said, "All right, Seth. If that's the way you feel, I won't stand in your way. If you want a divorce, I'll give it to you."

He didn't say anything for a few seconds; he just looked at her with such an expression of sadness and regret that she nearly flung herself across the room and told him she hadn't meant it. How could she live, knowing that she'd never feel his arms around her again, or that he wouldn't be there to comfort and protect her as he once had? Who would laugh with her and tease her, and look at her in that way that made her melt? What kind of life would it be if they never made love again... if he didn't see his son or daughter grow up?

"All right, then," he said finally. "We can settle things later."

She didn't want to settle anything. Once he left, she knew she wouldn't be able to bear seeing him again. It would be too hard, knowing he was lost to her, wondering what had gone so wrong between them that it couldn't be fixed.

But she'd always wonder that, wouldn't she? Trying not to think of all the days and nights fanning out into a bleak future without him, she said, "Whatever you say, Seth."

He seemed about to say something more, but then obviously changed his mind. When he went to the door, she stayed where she was, not sure her legs would support her. But then, when he paused to look back at her, her heart gave a leap. Foolishly, she thought, *He's going to say he changed his mind.*

What he said was, "I'm sorry, Honey. I wish it could have been different."

Her lips so stiff she could hardly speak, she replied, "So do I."

He went out, the door closed. Her life over, Honey sank onto the bed, so numb she couldn't even cry.

CHAPTER TEN

THE HARDEST THING Seth had ever done was to leave Honey standing there alone, that stricken look on her face. He shut the door, but once he was outside in the hallway, he leaned against the door, his hand on the doorknob. He was shaking.

It's not too late, he thought. He could still go back in there and say he was sorry, that he'd made a mistake, that he hadn't meant what he said, that he wanted to... start over.

He wrenched his hand away. He couldn't do it. He'd made the break; now he had to live with it. The only thing that propelled him down the stairs and out the front door was the thought that even though he'd never be the same, Honey would eventually get over him and be happy. He might not have been able to give her much these past few years, but he could give her this last gift.

But every time he thought of the look on her face, he almost lost his resolve. The last thing in the world he'd ever wanted to do was to hurt Honey—in any way. He loved her. He loved the smell of her hair, the softness of her skin, the way her eyes changed color according to her moods.

Hell, he loved everything about Honey LaRue Dunleavy, and that's why he was leaving her. He loved her too much to hold on to their marriage and insist that she suffer because of his pride. Here, she'd finally have the life she deserved to have, the one he would have given everything to have provided for her.

He felt the sting of tears again and clenched his jaw in an effort to control himself. *For heaven's sake, stop feeling sorry for yourself!* he commanded. *Just get in the damned truck and go. Don't make this any harder than it is already.*

Octavia had insisted he use one of the farm trucks whenever he needed transportation, and he had taken her up on her offer only because it was too expensive to keep taking cabs whenever he had to go somewhere. Tonight, as he headed toward the place where he'd parked, he debated briefly about whether or not to drive out. If he took it, someone from here would have to come and drive it back from wherever he left it, and he didn't want to put anyone out. On the other hand, the sooner he got away from here, the better.

He made his decision just as the headlights of a fast-approaching car swept across him. The driver had the high beams on; the lights were so bright they nearly blinded him. He threw up a hand to shield his eyes, and then had to leap back as the car came to a screeching halt not ten feet away from him.

"What the...!" he muttered. For a confused moment, he wondered why one of the party guests had arrived so early—and in such a hurry. He watched as the driver got out, slammed the car door and nearly ran into him again. Startled, he realized it was his aunt Meredith.

"Hey, watch out," he said, trying to warn her.

She uttered a cry and jumped back. Clearly, she hadn't seen him. "Seth!" she exclaimed angrily. "You frightened me to death! What are you doing out here in the dark, anyway?"

Thinking he might ask her the same thing, he gestured toward the nearby truck. "I had to... get something."

Obviously embarrassed as well as angry, she said, "Well, get it then, and stop skulking around!"

Now that she was close to him, he could see that she'd been crying. The realization shocked him. *Meredith Dunleavy cry?* Even from what little he'd seen of his aunt, he thought she was the most contained, controlled person he'd ever met. He couldn't imagine her breaking a sweat, much less shedding tears.

"Aunt Meredith," he said hesitantly, "are you all right?"

She drew back. "Why do you ask?"

"You seem a little... agitated."

"Is that a surprise? You scared me out of my wits!"

He decided to let it go. It wasn't his concern, anyway. All he wanted to do was get out of here before someone asked him why he was leaving.

"I didn't mean to scare you," he said. "I'll just get the truck and—" He stopped, suddenly realizing that her car was blocking his way out. "That is, if you'll move your car."

"Move the car? Why?"

"I can't get out."

She dug in her purse for her keys. "You move it. I'm too upset even to think straight."

He couldn't believe that he'd frightened her that badly, but he wasn't going to argue. She held out the keys, but as he reached for them, he felt her hand shaking. He looked at her in renewed consternation.

"Are you *sure* you're okay?"

"Will you stop asking me that?" she snapped. "I'm perfectly fine. I just had a . . . a little surprise a while ago. It's nothing more than that."

It seemed to be a lot more to Seth. Now that his eyes were adjusting to the dark, he could see that she was trembling from head to foot. Deciding he couldn't leave her like this, he said, "I'm sorry, Aunt Meredith, but you don't look well. I think you'd better sit down."

"I don't want to sit down! I just want to go inside and have a drink!"

He sympathized with that; at this point, he could have used a drink himself. "If you're sure—"

"I've never been more positive of anything in my entire life. Now, are you going to move my car or not? Oh, never mind, I don't care. Do what you want. Just leave the keys on the dashboard. I'm going in."

He didn't know if she'd forgotten about the party tonight or not, but he felt he had to say something to remind her. "Aunt Meredith—"

She'd started off. At the sound of his voice, she stiffened and turned back. Between her teeth, she said, "What *is* it, Seth?"

"I just wanted to remind you about the party tonight."

"Party?" Her voice rose. "What party?"

"You know, to celebrate the filly's win today."

"The filly?"

"Yes, you know—Never Done Dreamin'," he said, wondering if she'd spent the afternoon on the moon. All the news media had been full of the horse's win. Where had she been? He added, "She won the Kentucky Derby this afternoon, you know."

For a horrified instant, he thought she was going to break into tears. "I know. I'd . . . forgotten."

In the dim light that was spilling from the front windows of the house, he could see that she'd turned white as a sheet. Really beginning to worry about her, he put a hand on her arm to steady her. She was still trembling violently.

That did it. He was going to take her into the house whether she wanted help or not. It didn't matter if anyone saw him; he couldn't just leave and hope that she made it inside by herself.

"Aunt Meredith," he said, "let me—"

It was as if she didn't even hear him. Closing her eyes, she murmured, "He wouldn't . . . Not even he would be so—"

He didn't know what the hell she was talking about. At this point, it didn't matter. Wondering if she was sick, he took a firmer grip on her elbow. If he had to, he thought, he'd carry her.

"Aunt Meredith, please—"

Her eyes snapped open, and she grabbed him. Intensely, she said, "Seth, you have to do something for me."

He wasn't going to argue with her, not when she looked like that. Her eyes seemed to burn holes right through him, and he said, "Anything. What?"

Her grip on his arms tightened; he could feel her long fingernails digging into him. The pain was inconsequential compared to the look on her face. He couldn't describe it: she looked frantic and desperate and angry all at once.

"You have to go to the track, *now*, and make sure that the filly is all right."

He felt a stab of fear. It couldn't be happening, not again, he thought. He knew how Honey would feel if anything went wrong with that horse, so he tried to think. Dwight would have called if something was amiss. And what could possibly occur? Ever since Done Cryin's disappearance, Dwight had men watching the filly night and day.

But even so, someone had managed to put a bucket of cold water in the stall.

At the thought, he looked at his aunt. "Why do you want me to check on her? Do you know something I don't?"

"Never mind, will you do it?"

She hadn't answered him, but she didn't need to. He'd seen another flicker of fear in her eyes; it had been as plain as day. Why was she afraid? he wondered. What did she know?

Her nails dug into him again, this time making him wince. *"Please!"* she begged. "You have to do this, Seth. You must!"

By now he was more than a little anxious to look in on Never Done Dreamin' himself. "All right," he said. "I'll go."

Some of the tautness left her body. "Thank you," she said, exhaling a sigh of relief. She realized he was staring at her, so she tried to laugh it off by saying, "Sometimes I get...feelings about things. Usually, it's nothing, but it never hurts to check, does it?"

He wasn't convinced by the act. "Yeah, sure."

"Well, go, go," she said, making a shooing motion with her hands when he just stood there. "And Seth—"

He turned. "What?"

"I'd appreciate it if you kept this between us."

Wondering what the hell was going on, he nodded. Two minutes later, he was heading out the gates, trying to ignore the sinking feeling in the pit of his stomach. It was obvious that Meredith knew more than she was telling. He floored the gas pedal, more anxious than ever to get to the track and make sure that the filly was all right.

WHEN SETH ARRIVED at Churchill Downs, the backside was shut down for the night. This had always been one of his favorite times at the track; only a few lights were on, casting spools of gold down the shedrows, blurring lines, making everything look fuzzy and soft. The mingled fragrances of hay and horse filled the air, but as Seth hurried toward Dwight's barn as fast as his cane would let him, he didn't even notice.

The drive had seemed endless, but now that he was finally here, he couldn't wait to see the filly for himself. He knew his fear was irrational; after everything that had happened—to Done Driftin' and to Done Cryin'—Dwight was going to guard Never Done Dreamin' with his life. But Seth couldn't forget the look in Meredith's eyes, and as he hobbled quickly along, he wondered. Was she just being melodramatic? Had it only been a joke?

He knew it hadn't been a joke. He didn't know her well, but one thing he was sure of, and that was that his aunt Meredith wasn't the kind to play jokes, practical or otherwise. And no one could have faked the fear he'd seen in her face, not the best actress in the world. But exactly what was she afraid of—and why?

He didn't know, and that made him hurry even faster. He was panting by the time he reached Dwight's barn, and real fear shot straight through him when he turned the corner and saw that the lights were on in the filly's stall.

"Oh, my God!" he whispered. Meredith's feelings had been on the money. Something *was* wrong with Never Done Dreamin'.

He looked around, but he couldn't see anyone. Suppressing the urge to yell and charge, he crept up to the stall, his body hunched. When he heard voices inside, he tensed even more. But since no one was around to help, he hefted his cane like a club, stood up and stepped into the doorway, shouting, "Stop what you're doing!"

The three people inside jumped as though they'd been shot. As one, they turned to face him, and in the split second before he started swinging, Seth recognized Dwight and two of his grooms.

"Lord above, Seth," Dwight said, clutching his chest. "You scared the bejesus out of me."

"Dwight," Seth said, lowering the club. Feeling slightly embarrassed, he nodded an acknowledgment at the grooms. "I thought you were doing something to the filly."

"We are," Dwight said. "We're checking her legs to make sure she came out of the race okay."

"And did she? Is she fit?"

Dwight gave him a strange look as he stood. "She's just fine, Seth. I would have called if she wasn't."

"I know you would have, Dwight," Seth said. "I guess I just wanted to see for myself."

Dwight came with him out of the stall. Clapping a hand over Seth's shoulders, the trainer grinned and said, "I don't blame you one bit. But next time you make an entrance like that, will you give a fellow a little warning first? I nearly had a heart attack."

"I'm sorry. I'll be more careful the next time," Seth said. He laughed, until he realized that there wouldn't be a next time. Dejected by the thought, he asked, "What are you doing here, anyway? It's pretty late."

"Not for me. I'm bedding down in one of the tack rooms until the Preakness and the Belmont are over.

After what happened to the other two Dunleavy horses, I'm not letting this filly out of my sight.''

"You can't guard her all by yourself. What about some of the grooms helping out?"

"Oh, they'll help, all right. But the truth is, the only one I trust is myself. I found out how Never Done Dreamin' got hold of that cold water the other day. That kid named Jack who was supposed to be watching her fell asleep. I suspected it all along, but he wouldn't admit it until his . . . er . . . conscience got the best of him.''

From the way Dwight hesitated over that last, Seth had his own ideas as to how the hapless Jack had come to confess. But it wasn't any of his business; that was between the trainer and the people who worked for him. Or didn't, since Dwight told him he'd fired Jack as soon as he'd learned of the lapse.

"But he swears he didn't put the bucket in the stall," Dwight went on, "and I believe him. So whoever did it—"

He stopped, but Seth finished it for him. "Whoever did, did so on purpose. And is probably still around.''

"Exactly."

"Any ideas?"

Dwight shook his head. "But I swear, if I find the bastard, I'll drown him in that selfsame bucket.''

An idea had been coming to Seth as they talked. The more he tried to dismiss it, the more insistent it became. He knew how Honey would feel if harm came to the filly. If he couldn't do anything else for his wife, he thought, he could at least guard her precious horse.

He was aware that he was rationalizing. The truth was, he didn't want to leave, not yet.

He knew Dwight could hire an entire security force to protect Never Done Dreamin'; Seth Dunleavy wasn't needed. But before he could change his mind, he said, "I'd like to help, Dwight. Why don't you let me keep an eye on her at night? You can't be training all day and staying here at night, too. Besides, I'm not doing anything right now, and at least this way, I'd be useful."

Dwight squinted at him. "You sure you want to?"

Guarding the filly would give him an excuse to stay on—here, not at Dunleavy Farm. This way, he could keep an eye on both Honey and her horse.

"I'm sure," he said.

Dwight still looked doubtful. "All I've got is a cot and a sleeping bag in the tack room. Oh, and a hot plate in case you want coffee at night."

Seth grinned. "Sounds like my idea of heaven."

Dwight grimaced. "Better you young fellows than me, then. All right, if you want to, the job's yours. Although, I'm not sure I should let an owner do my work for me."

"I'm not an owner," Seth said. "Honey is. And Dwight—" he held out his hand "—no one can do your job for you. You're the best there is."

"Thanks," Dwight said gruffly, shaking hands. Then, obviously embarrassed by the compliment, he slapped Seth on the shoulder so hard that Seth nearly lost his balance. "Well, good night. My number is on the board. Call me, even if it's only a mouse getting into the grain."

"Sure thing," Seth said.

Once he was alone in the barn, Seth decided to make a tour of the stalls, just to make certain everything and everyone was tucked in. He'd just reached the end of the row when he heard men's voices. He stopped to listen, every muscle tense.

He couldn't hear what the men outside were saying, but it sounded as if they were arguing about something. He might have let it go, assuming that they were two grooms coming home late, if he hadn't heard the word *filly*.

He stiffened. He knew the men could have been talking about any female horse at the track, but it seemed too coincidental that they were arguing about a filly while standing alongside the shedrow that housed Never Done Dreamin'. Quietly, he left the shelter of the barn and came around the corner.

The two men were so deep in conversation that they didn't hear him coming. The lights were dim out here, but even before he took two steps, Seth recognized one of them. He muttered a curse. He didn't know the other man—a tall, lean fellow who needed a haircut and a shave, but in one glance, he decided that he didn't like the guy's looks. There was something about him that raised the hackles at the back of Seth's neck, and he took a tighter grip on his cane. He couldn't be sure, but he wouldn't be surprised if the stranger was carrying some kind of weapon.

If they came to blows, he thought, he'd just have to deal with the stranger when the time came. Right now, he turned his attention to the man he knew.

"Well, Davey," he said conversationally, coming up behind him. "What're you doing out so late?"

Davey LaRue jumped a foot. Whirling around, he took one look at Seth and started off. Calmly, Seth reached out a hand, caught the little man by his jacket and jerked him to a halt.

"Not so fast," he said. "I want to know what you're still doing here."

Davey tried to squirm away; Seth held him fast. "You got no right to do this," Davey complained. "The last I looked, it was a free country. I can work where I want."

"You're still insisting that you've got a *job* here?"

"That's right. So, let go. I got things to do."

Since it was already nearly midnight, Seth snorted. "What things?"

"*Things.* I don't have to tell you. It's none of your business."

"All right, then. Since you won't say, maybe your friend here will enlighten me."

Seth turned to where Davey's companion had been standing, but the man was gone. Seth spied him half running toward another shadowed shedrow, and called, "Hey, you, wait!"

The man didn't even look back. With a burst of speed, he disappeared into the darkness. Frowning, Seth looked at Davey.

"Who was that guy?"

Davey wouldn't meet his eyes. "I don't know," he muttered. "Just some fellow I met the other day."

Seth didn't believe him. "Just some fellow," he repeated. "Why do I think there's more to it than that? Come on, Davey, spill it. What are you up to now?"

"Nothing! I told you. I just want to clean stalls and be left alone! Now, do you mind? It's late, and I—"

"I know. You've got things to do. Well, fine, Davey. But remember this. I'm going to be around for a while, and I've got my eye on you."

"You're going to...stay?" Davey stammered. For an instant, he looked scared. "But I thought—"

"You thought wrong. I mean it, Davey. I'll be watching you. And if anything happens to that filly in there—*anything at all*—you're the first one I'm going to look for."

"Me! Aw, come on. I'd never do anything to—"

Seth's eyes were hard. "Make sure you don't. And stay away from Honey, too. The last thing she needs is you showing your face at Dunleavy Farm."

"Are you telling me I can't see my own daughter?" Davey demanded indignantly.

"Naw, I'm just reminding you what will happen if you blow this for her."

"I'm her father!"

"Fine. Act like it for once, and think of her instead of yourself. Now, go on. Get out of here. And remember—"

"I know, I know. You made your point. But I'm telling you, Seth, you got me all wrong!"

"Good," Seth said uncompromisingly. "Prove it."

Davey gave him a wild look, and started off—in the opposite direction to the one that the stranger had taken. Seth watched him go, but even after Davey had been swallowed by the darkness, he just stood there. His leg was throbbing, and he needed to sit down, but still he didn't move.

What was going on here? he wondered. First it had been Done Driftin' and the stable accident that had ended the colt's racing career. Then Done Cryin' had vanished. The colt still hadn't been found, despite tremendous search efforts and the promise of a big reward even for information about the disappearance.

Now something strange had happened to Never Done Dreamin', right before a big race. The filly's bout with colic could have been coincidental, but Dwight didn't think so and neither did Seth. Whoever had given the horse access to that cold water had known what he was doing.

Seth frowned. He wasn't sure that even Davey was low enough to try to prevent the filly from racing, but he had to consider everything. Of course, the problems with the two colts had happened before Davey arrived on the scene, so maybe suspecting his father-in-law was stretching it. Still, Seth had caught the man in some underhanded schemes before, and he didn't trust Davey as far as he could throw him with one hand. If Davey was involved in something nefarious, he wanted to know what it was.

He began walking slowly back to Dwight's barn. He didn't like the looks of the scruffy character Davey had been talking to; it was obvious to him that that man, at least, was up to no good. Until he learned what connection they had, he couldn't rest.

CHAPTER ELEVEN

SOMEHOW, Honey managed to get through the Derby victory party. It had taken sheer determination to smile and talk and laugh as though her life hadn't just ended. By the time the party was over, her smile had felt permanently frozen into place.

Maintaining such a facade after her husband had just said he wanted a divorce was one of the hardest things she'd ever done. It became even more difficult throughout the evening, when people inevitably noticed Seth's absence and asked where he was. Because she didn't want to ruin the party for anyone else, she made up excuse after excuse, then quickly changed the subject. She even managed to fool Carla and Nan, who both looked at her strangely when she told them Seth's leg was bothering him.

She thought her ruse was successful until the following morning when Jamie sought her out and said, "Honey, we have to talk."

Honey was sitting on the swing at the end of the big front porch. It was a beautiful day, soft and warm, the hint of a breeze carrying with it the sweet smell of fresh grass. Lost in thought, Honey didn't notice Jamie until her mother-in-law was standing right in front of her.

"Talk?" she said blankly. "About what?"

Jamie smiled. "Oh, this and that."

Last night, Jamie had been in chiffon and sequins; today she was wearing another of her free-flowing outfits, this one a long dress in brilliant tie-dye colors. Her short blond hair was tousled; her face almost bare of makeup. She looked, Honey thought mournfully, much too young to have a grown son.

"May I sit down?" Jamie asked. Without waiting for an answer, she took a place beside Honey in the porch swing. "It's a lovely day, isn't it?"

"Yes, it is."

Jamie appeared not to notice her lack of enthusiasm. She commented, "You looked like you were enjoying the party last night."

"Did I?" Honey said. Hastily, she corrected herself. "I mean, yes, I did. Never Done Dreamin's Derby win was certainly something to celebrate."

"Indeed it was," Jamie agreed, glancing sideways at her daughter-in-law. "The question is, why wasn't Seth there to help us rejoice?"

"Oh, he...his leg was bothering him," Honey said, giving her stock excuse. She was sure she saw skepticism in Jamie's eyes, and went on quickly, "When it aches like that, the only thing he can do is elevate it and rest."

"I see," Jamie said. "Then I can assume he's still upstairs ... with his leg up?"

Honey didn't know how much longer she could keep up the pretense. She was perilously close to tears, and she was afraid that any second she was going to burst into sobs and spill the whole awful story. But she couldn't lie to her mother-in-law; it would be too easy for Jamie to go up to the empty bedroom, knock on the door and check. What would she say when she found that Seth was gone? Even worse, what would she think?

Swallowing hard, Honey said, "No, he isn't there, Jamie. He's ... gone."

"Gone? You mean, he already went somewhere this morning?"

"No, he ... he ..."

Her struggle was obvious, and Jamie was no fool. Softly, she said, "Is there something you want to tell me?"

Jamie's gentle tone was her undoing. She didn't mean to say it, but when she saw her mother-in-law's sympathetic expression, she started to cry.

"Oh, Jamie!" she said in sheer misery. "He didn't leave this morning, he left last night. We had a terrible fight, and ... and—"

The words clogged her throat. How could she admit it? To confess aloud that Seth had asked for a divorce would mean that it wasn't some awful scene she'd imagined. And once she admitted it, she'd have to confront the sad reality that her marriage had failed. That *she* had failed.

Oh, Seth! she thought. *What happened to us? What went so wrong that we couldn't fix it?*

She didn't know the answer. The only thing she knew this morning was that she should have done anything, said anything, *promised* anything, to keep him from walking out that door last night. Nothing was worth this misery, she thought: no amount of pride or dignity or self-respect. What did any of it matter if Seth left her? He was her *life*. How could she go on without him?

Jamie took her hand and gave her fingers a gentle squeeze. Quietly, she said, "I know we don't know each other very well, Honey, so if you'd rather not talk about it—"

The last thing in the world Honey wanted to tell her husband's mother was that she hadn't been woman enough, *wife* enough, to hold her marriage together. Oh, if only she had—

She stopped the thought. What could she have done that she didn't do, that she hadn't tried, over and over and over again? She would have changed the way she walked, or talked, or looked, if there had been the faintest hope that any of it might have worked.

Pain rose inside her like poison. She wanted to wrap her arms around herself and keen with unhappiness. But couldn't break down, not here, not now, when Jamie was sitting beside her. And soon the whole family would be up, wondering how Seth was, asking her if he was feeling better, questioning how long he was going to stay up in the guest room.

She felt desperate. How could she carry on as if nothing had happened? Sooner or later, everyone would have to know. She had to make plans, decide what to do.

She wanted to cry again. It seemed so hopeless. She remembered how cold Seth had been last night when he'd told her he wanted to end their marriage. His handsome face that she loved so much had been like a mask; even his body had seemed foreign to her. She had never seen him look or act like that. It was as if he... despised her.

Jamie was still holding her hand, and Honey unconsciously tightened her grip. She needed all the support she could get, for she felt as though she were standing at the edge of an abyss. She could feel herself leaning forward, almost wanting to fall. It would be so easy, she thought.

Fiercely, she got hold of herself. No matter what she felt, she had to think of the baby. The innocent life growing inside her was paramount. She would not allow her child to suffer because its parents had failed in their relationship.

It'll be all right, she told herself shakily. *Somehow, I'll work things out.*

Jamie had been silent. Now she asked, "What do you want to do, Honey?"

Honey's lip trembled, and she started crying once more. "I want him back! Oh, Jamie, I want him back!"

Jamie didn't hesitate. Gathering Honey into her arms, she held her and stroked her hair and murmured soothing nothings until Honey couldn't cry anymore. Then she lifted Honey's chin and said, "Don't worry. We'll work it out."

With all her heart, Honey wanted that to be true. But whenever she thought of Seth's expression last night, she doubted anything could heal the rift between them. She knew her husband; one of the most infuriating and strangely endearing things about him was that when he finally decided something, he wouldn't be swayed. She knew nothing was going to make him change his mind.

Not even the baby?

She wasn't going to think about that, or she might start crying again and not be able to stop. She didn't have a tissue, so she wiped her tearstained cheeks with the backs of her hands and sat up. Her crying fit had passed; now all she felt was drained—and embarrassed.

"I'm sorry," she muttered. "I didn't mean to break down like that."

Jamie pulled a delicate linen and lace handkerchief from the pocket of her voluminous skirt. As she pressed it into Honey's hand, she said, "There's no need for an apology. We all need a good cry at times."

"I guess so," Honey said, dabbing at her eyes. "And this time certainly seems as good as any."

Jamie waited a moment, then she said, "Seth doesn't know about the baby, does he?"

Honey jerked with surprise. She could feel her mouth dropping open as she turned to look at Jamie. "How . . . how did you know?"

Jamie smiled. "I didn't, until now." She hesitated again. But then, her eyes glimmering with a few tears of her own, she said, "I know this isn't the right time, but I want you to know how delighted I am for you."

Honey felt like crying again. Trying to control herself, she hiccuped, "Th-th-thank you. It was supposed to be such a h-h-h-happy occasion—"

"It still is," Jamie said, putting an arm around Honey's shoulders and drawing her close. "And when Seth finds out, everything is going to be all right. You'll see."

Honey pulled away. "He's not going to know—not for a while, anyway. And I don't want you to tell him."

"Not tell him! But why not?"

The reasons she had deemed so sensible last night suddenly seemed like the height of idiocy in the light of day. Why *didn't* she tell him? Honey asked herself. It would solve everything—or at least, it would make things so much easier. She and Seth would reconcile; they would pretend this had never happened, and all would be well. He'd love the baby, and they'd live happily ever after.

But would they? Hadn't she decided not to tell him in the first place because she didn't want him staying with her out of obligation? A sense of duty was a poor substitute for love, and eventually it would take its toll—on all three of them. She hadn't been so young when her mother had deserted her and Davey that she couldn't remember the tension between her parents, the resentment, the anger, the hostility and the tears.

In a way, it had almost been a relief when Amber LaRue had finally walked out. As much as she had missed her mother, Honey hadn't missed living a lie, trying to pretend that everything was all right when it wasn't.

Jamie put a hand on Honey's arm, dragging her back to the present. Tentatively, she said, "I know you're upset, Honey, but I wonder if you've really thought this through. This is Seth's child, too. Don't you think he has a right to know?"

"Yes, I do." She saw the relief in Jamie's face and hated to dash her hopes. But she added quickly, "But I won't use this baby as a lever to make him change his mind about leaving me. I won't do it!"

"But, Honey—"

"Please, Jamie," Honey said desperately, "I've thought about this a lot—you don't know how much. I can't allow you, or anyone else, to talk me out of a decision that was difficult enough to make."

"It's not my intention to try and talk you out of anything. I know you've made up your mind. And perhaps," Jamie added reluctantly, "you're right."

Now that Jamie had conceded her point of view, Honey felt perversely compelled to ask, "Why do you think that?"

Jamie glanced away for a moment as if collecting her thoughts, then she turned back to Honey. Her expression even more troubled than it had been before, she said, "I've never told this story to another living soul before, but..." She took a deep breath. "I do understand, Honey, more than you realize. You see, I was once in your position."

Honey gaped at her. "You were?"

Jamie smiled slightly, regretfully. "Well, there is a small difference. I wasn't married to my son's father."

"You mean—"

Her glance turning inward, Jamie said, "I met Russ McFarland not long after I left Dunleavy Farm. I was so angry in those days, so furious with my mother. I convinced myself at the time, and for a lot of years afterward, that I'd been cruelly banished from home. I felt so sorry for myself. I was the starving artist slaving away in my San Francisco garret, living on coffee and cigarettes, with no one to love me."

"How...sad."

"No, it wasn't. I enjoyed it. I wanted to suffer, you see. Childishly, I believed that in order to become great, an artist had to experience pain. And since I was determined to become one of the greatest, I set out to find as much pain as I could. That's when I met Russ."

"And he changed your life."

"He changed it, all right," Jamie said wryly. "Before I knew it, he'd moved in with me. But that was okay because I was in love. He was so handsome, Honey—just like Seth, tall and athletic and blond, but with blazing blue eyes instead of Seth's green. You had to love him, and everyone did. Especially women. Lots of women loved Russ, and who could blame them? I was crazy about him myself, too crazy to realize that he was just using me until someone better came along. It wasn't long before someone did."

"He left you for someone else?"

"Yes, a rich widow who lived on Telegraph Hill. She was twenty years older than he was, but I guess she wanted—what is it called now?—oh yes, a 'boy toy.' Russ was only too happy to oblige. In fact, the truth is, he was perfectly suited to the role."

"But what about you and Seth?"

Jamie sighed. "Ah, yes, me and Seth."

"Did you tell Russ about the baby?" Honey held her breath.

"Yes, I told him," Jamie said, looking down at her hands. "But I'm afraid my motives weren't as noble as yours. I wanted to do anything I could to hold Russ—even using our baby as bait."

Honey was almost afraid to ask. "What did he say when he found out?"

Jamie looked into the distance. "He told me to get rid of it," she said. "He was even magnanimous enough to offer to pay for the procedure."

Honey gasped. She couldn't imagine Seth saying that to her under any circumstances. She took her mother-in-law's hand. "Oh, Jamie, I'm so sorry."

Jamie squeezed her fingers. "Seth doesn't know," she said. "I told him that I didn't want to marry his father, that I kicked Russ out because I was too busy, too involved with my painting to worry about a husband."

Honey was shocked. "And he accepted that?"

"For a while, he did. What could he do? He was a child. But when he got older, and the time came for me to tell him the truth, I...just couldn't hurt him that way. I never wanted him to know that his father would rather have paid for an abortion than accept a role—any role—as a father."

"But Seth knew you loved him."

"Did he?" Jamie's expression was bleak. "Sometimes I wonder." She blinked quickly a few times, then tried to smile. "But he has you, my dear. And for that, I'm eternally grateful."

After Jamie's wrenching confession, Honey couldn't lie to her. "He has me, Jamie. But I don't have him. Last night, he told me he wanted...a divorce."

There. She'd said it, and the world hadn't come to a screeching halt. The sky hadn't fallen; the earth hadn't opened up. But why, then, did she feel as if something had pierced her heart? Tears welling up again, she turned away.

"I see," Jamie said after a moment. "And you intend to give him one, is that it?"

She closed her eyes. "What choice do I have?"

"You can fight for him. You can fight to save your marriage, and your...family."

"I want to, but it seems so—" She stopped, biting her lip. After a moment, she was able to go on. "I don't know what to do, Jamie. I had such high hopes that Seth would accept his family...." She stopped again. "I guess the only thing to do is for me to leave."

"Leave! Oh, no, you can't do that!"

She looked mournfully at Jamie. "But I don't belong here."

"Yes, you do," Jamie said fiercely. "And everyone else will say that, too. Why, it's been *years* since we've had a baby around here. I'm going to be a grandmother—" She stopped and winced comically. "Oh my, that *does* make me sound old, doesn't it? Well, never mind. It's worth it. And when Mother finds out that she's going to be a *great*-grandmother, she's going to be over the moon. Oh, my dear, surely you aren't thinking of depriving us of something so special!"

Honey was grateful for Jamie's support, but she had to ask, "But what about Seth?"

"I told you, we'll work something out. He'll come around." Jamie gave her a hug. "We'll make sure of that."

"I thought I heard voices out here," Meredith said just then. "Am I interrupting, or are you two having a private conversation?"

Honey jumped when she heard Meredith's voice. When she turned, Seth's aunt was coming toward them. In one hand was a cigarette, in the other, a coffee cup. Apparently, she'd just gotten out of bed. She was wearing a long peach-colored satin wrapper, and on her feet were matching mules with marabou trim. But not a hair was out of place, and her makeup was perfect.

"Put that damned cigarette out, Merry," Jamie said at once, with a quick glance at Honey. "You shouldn't be smoking at all—much less at this hour."

Meredith yawned. "It is rather early, isn't it? For a cigarette, or anything else. I can't imagine what I'm doing up."

Clearly, Jamie wasn't in the mood to deal with her older sister. "I can't, either. So why don't you go back to bed."

"My, my. What a sharp tongue you have, little sister. But then, as I recall, you always did."

"I'm not the only one. But now that I think of it—"

"What?" Meredith drawled, but suddenly her glance wasn't quite so lazy. "What are you going to be on about now?"

Honey didn't want to get in the middle of what seemed to be a developing quarrel. She started to say, "If you'll excuse me, I'll just—"

Meredith turned to her. "Please don't go on my account."

"*Will* you please put that damned cigarette out?" Jamie cried as the smoke wafted their way. "It's not good for pregnant—"

She stopped, too late.

Meredith raised an eloquent eyebrow. "Someone's pregnant?" she said as Honey turned bright red. Her glance went to Honey and she smiled. "Well, well. Since I doubt it's my sister, who is a little over the hill, it must be you, my dear."

Tossing the offending cigarette over the porch railing, Meredith came and gave Honey a kiss on the cheek. "Congratulations, dear. It's about time Jamie became a grandmother."

"Please don't tell anyone," Honey said quickly. "Not yet, I mean."

Meredith nodded conspiratorially. "Oh, I see. You haven't told Seth yet, is that it?"

"No, I haven't." Honey could feel Jamie look at her.

"Oh, how delicious. I'll bet he'll be delighted when he finds out."

Try as she might, Honey couldn't hold a level gaze. Weakly, she said, "I . . . hope so."

Before Meredith could pursue that strange remark, Jamie changed the subject. "Where have you been hiding, Merry? Ever since I came to visit, you've made yourself scarce. It couldn't, perhaps, have anything to do with wanting to avoid me, could it?"

"Don't be absurd," Meredith said. "And I haven't been *hiding*. Unlike you, I *do* have friends here, even after all these years. Visiting the farm is one thing. Hanging around like a lovesick cow is quite another. You do recall, I'm sure, that I'm easily bored."

"Yes, but even for you, you haven't seemed quite yourself. For instance, when you came in last night—"

"What about it?" Meredith demanded, too quickly.

Jamie looked surprised at the attack. "Why, nothing," she said. "It's just that you seemed agitated when you came in."

"I was in a hurry, that's all."

"And that's another thing," Jamie said. "Where *were* you yesterday? No one saw you at the races—"

As she followed the conversation, Honey thought she saw a gleam of fear in Meredith's eyes at Jamie's question. She told herself she was mistaken. Meredith Dunleavy was the last person in the world who should be afraid of anything.

Meredith put her coffee down on the porch railing. Her hand shook so badly that the cup clattered against the saucer. Honey looked at her in surprise again, and was even more startled to see that underneath the expertly applied makeup, Meredith had gone quite pale.

Apparently realizing that Honey was staring at her, Meredith pulled herself together. To Jamie, she said, "Not that it's any of your business, but I didn't go to the races yesterday. I had ... other things to do." She turned to Honey. "I'm sorry, my dear. It's just that I've never really been interested in racing."

"You could have fooled me," Jamie muttered.

Meredith turned to her sister. "Now I remember why I disliked you so much as a child. You always *were* one for obscure remarks. What are you mumbling about now?"

"Oh, nothing. It's just that I remember Dwight's mentioning that he'd seen you at the track several times since you came home."

Meredith looked angry. "Well, so what if I was? Do I need to check in and out with you?"

"No, you don't. But since you dislike racing so much, it seems strange that you visit the backside, anyway."

"For your information, I went to see Never Done Dreamin'. Naturally, I was curious. Is that a crime?"

"Not at all. It's just that, what with all the things that have been happening—"

"And you think any of that has something to do with *me?*"

"No, of course not." Jamie seemed to realize she'd gone a little too far. "The way you've been acting... Oh, hell, Merry, I guess what I'm asking is, is anything wrong?"

"Wrong?" Meredith laughed shortly. "What could possibly be wrong? It was a wonderful day yesterday, was it not? Never Done Dreamin' won the Derby. What could be better than that?"

"Well, in a couple of weeks, she could win the Preakness."

Again, Honey saw that flash of fear in Meredith's eyes. This time she was sure of it, even though Meredith immediately tried to hide it by asking, "Oh, is she going to run in Maryland?"

Jamie must have seen something in her sister's face, too. "That's the plan, I think." She turned to Honey. "Isn't it?"

"Yes, I believe so," Honey said, still preoccupied with Meredith's strange reactions. It was obvious that mention of the filly had disturbed her, but why? Involuntarily, Honey thought back to the day Never Done Dreamin' had come down with colic. Had Meredith arrived at the farm by that time?

She told herself she was being absurd—Meredith couldn't have had anything to do with the filly's illness. Suddenly, she remembered Carla telling her that Meredith had interrupted a trip back to England to watch Done Driftin' race. She'd been here when the colt had been involved in the accident that had ended his career.

And Nan had said that Meredith had surfaced again just before Done Cryin' disappeared.

Now she had arrived before Never Done Dreamin' took sick.

Shocked at herself, Honey tried to get a grip. She should be ashamed, she thought. It was ridiculous even to question if Meredith Dunleavy—*Meredith Dunleavy, of all people!*—had had anything to do with the problems the Dunleavy horses had been encountering this year. The things that had happened had just... happened. There was no plot, no conspiracy; it was absurd and paranoid even to think of such a thing.

Wasn't it?

Was it all some ghastly series of coincidences, or was Meredith involved in sinister goings-on regarding the people and the horses at Dunleavy Farm?

CHAPTER TWELVE

THREE DAYS BEFORE the running of the Preakness Stakes, Never Done Dreamin' left Churchill Downs in the dead of night for Pimlico Racetrack, in Baltimore, Maryland. The filly departed under the strictest secrecy, in a plain white four-horse trailer driven by Dwight Connor himself.

After what had happened to Done Driftin', and the still-missing Done Cryin', the trainer was taking no risks with the valuable filly. In fact, Dwight had waited until almost the last minute to transfer Never Done Dreamin' from Kentucky to Maryland; normally, he would have given a horse almost a week to get acclimated to a different track, especially before a major race.

But this race was different, and so was the horse. As Dwight had said repeatedly—and worriedly—nothing was going to happen to *this* filly, even if he had to stake his life on it.

So, with Seth along for company, and to help in case anything went wrong, they left the track about midnight and drove down the back roads at a snail's pace. Alone in the trailer, the filly seemed to be riding comfortably, and finally Dwight relaxed enough to chat.

"You want to hand me a cup of that coffee?" Dwight said to Seth after a long silence.

They'd brought provisions with them, so they wouldn't have to stop. Along with sandwiches and other edibles, the thermos was on the seat between them. Seth poured a cup of coffee and handed it across.

Dwight took a sip, then he said, "I appreciate your coming along, Seth. I trust my guys back at the track, but I think I trust you more." He glanced across with a grin. "You having a vested interest in the cargo, I mean."

Seth capped the thermos and put it back on the seat. "I told you a hundred times, Dwight, that filly isn't mine."

"I know what you told me, but the fact of the matter is that your name is right up there with your wife's on the registration papers."

"That doesn't mean a thing."

"Well, it would to me."

"Yeah, well, that's you. And you don't have to thank me for coming along. You know I was glad to do it."

"You've been a big help these past couple of weeks. I have to say I've rested a lot easier at night, knowing you were sleeping in the barn, guarding the filly."

"I'm just happy you gave me the chance to do it."

"There's just one thing—"

"What's that?"

"Well, I know it's none of my business, but when are you going to let that pretty wife of yours know what you've been up to?"

"You're right. It's none of your business, Dwight."

"Aw, now, don't go getting your back up, Seth. I know you're having troubles with your marriage. Hell, who hasn't? But the fact that you made me promise not to say anything makes me feel like a first-class fool when Honey comes around. She looks so sad sometimes, it just about breaks my heart."

"Don't start," Seth warned.

"Well, someone has to," Dwight insisted. "It's not fair, what you're doing. Honey thinks you've gone back to Arizona. You've even got that groom back there covering for you."

"And it's worked so far, so let me worry about it. Besides, I won't be around much longer. And in the meantime—"

"In the meantime," Dwight said stubbornly, "if you're sticking around to watch over this horse, then Honey should know it."

"I don't know why. Until you started bellyaching about it, everything was fine."

"That's what you think. If Honey finds out I've been hiding you all this time, how am I going to explain why I never said anything?"

Frowning, Seth slouched down in the seat. "If you don't tell her, how's she going to find out?"

"Oh, women have ways," Dwight said ominously. "I don't know how, but they do."

"Well, she hasn't found out yet, and the race is only three days away."

"Yes, and this filly's going to win."

Hiding a smile, Seth asked, "And if she doesn't?"

"If she doesn't, then there's no justice. But don't try to distract me. You know that if she's still sound after this race, we'll go to New York and she'll run the Belmont. Are you going to be skulking around until then, with Honey worried out of her mind?"

Frowning again, Seth grabbed the thermos and took the almost-empty cup from Dwight. "I don't know what I'm going to do," he said irritably as he poured another cup. "Right now, I'm just taking it one day at a time."

"Oh, that's just great," Dwight muttered.

"Yeah, well, that's the way it—" He stopped mid-sentence, realizing that Dwight wasn't listening, but was staring tensely into the truck's side mirror. A chill ran up Seth's back, and he asked, "What is it?"

"There's a car behind us," Dwight said.

Seth turned to look into the mirror on his side. He could see the other car's headlights clearly. He glanced at his watch. It was two in the morning. Whoever was out at this hour was obviously in no hurry. The vehicle kept their slow pace instead of speeding up and overtaking them. He frowned.

"How long has it been there?" he asked.

"Not long. I've been checking the mirror so often, I'm getting a crick in my neck. If it had been there even a mile or so back, I would have noticed it."

"Well, just keep driving. Maybe the driver will get impatient and pass."

But the driver of the other vehicle seemed content to stay tucked in behind them. Several more miles crawled by, both Seth and Dwight stiff and silent with tension. During that endless time, no other cars came up behind them or approached from the other direction. It was as though their rig, and whoever was with them, were the only vehicles on the road.

"Do you think I should pull over and let him go by?" Dwight asked finally.

Seth had already considered that possibility. "No. I don't think we should go any slower than we are. And if we stop..."

He didn't have to spell out that they'd be that much more vulnerable. Dwight understood, and he nodded grimly. "I'll just keep to this speed," he said. "And if that guy wants to follow us at forty miles an hour all the way to Baltimore, I guess that's his business."

Ten more miles crawled by. By this point, both Seth and Dwight were so edgy, they would have liked nothing more than to jump out to confront the guy behind them.

"Maybe it's a reporter," Dwight said at last. "We tried to be so careful about our plans, but things leak out all the same. Maybe he's just following us to get a story."

"It won't be much of a story," Seth said tersely. "All we're doing is—"

He never got a chance to finish the sentence. With a sudden surge of power, the driver behind them sped up and actually rammed the back of the trailer.

The entire rig shook violently, and as Dwight fought the wheel to keep them on the road, Never Done Dreamin' let out a frightened shriek. Holding on until Dwight got them back on course, Seth muttered angrily, "That son of a—"

He was interrupted by another hard hit that shot them forward.

Dwight was better prepared this time, but the truck still skittered toward the side of the road. It didn't help that the terrified horse had started kicking; with her frenzied plunging back and forth, the trailer was threatening to bounce off the hitch.

Dwight pressed down on the accelerator, and over the noise of the roaring engine, he shouted, "What do you think we should do?"

They shouldn't stop, Seth thought, and shouted, "Keep going!"

Because they hadn't wanted to alert any other drivers to the fact that they were on the road, they had agreed not to use the CB radio. But that was before the maniac behind them started bashing the trailer. They had to do something, Seth decided, and reached for the mike just as they were blindsided by another hard jolt. The microphone jumped out of his hand, and as he lunged for it, he banged his head on the dash.

"That guy's crazy!" Dwight yelled. "He's not just going to hurt the filly, he's going to kill us all!"

"Yeah, well, I hope he kills himself in the process!" Holding his bleeding forehead with one hand, Seth scrabbled around on the floor. When his fingers found the mike, he grabbed it.

"Mayday, Mayday, Mayday," he shouted into the speaker. "Anyone in the vicinity of—" He stopped and looked wildly across at Dwight. "Where the hell are we?"

"I...I don't know." Dwight's voice sounded strangled, and he jerked his head toward the back of the truck. "Look at that."

Seth turned to look. They'd kept one of the lights on in the trailer, and through the front window, he caught a horrifying glimpse of the filly trying to rear. His heart almost stopped. If she broke the tie that held her head and went up into the hay manger, they might have to cut her out.

"We have to stop," he said.

Dwight was trying to steer and keep an eye on the other driver at the same time. "Are you nuts? What about this madman behind us?"

"We'll just have to take our chances. Come on, Dwight, pull over. I think she just got loose."

That was all Dwight needed to hear. Few things were so dangerous as a maddened, terrified horse, loose in a confined trailer. With the instinct for flight taking over, a horse could do major damage to itself, not to mention the vehicle, all in a matter of seconds. Muttering a vivid, frightened curse, Dwight immediately pulled over to the side of the road.

Seth didn't wait until they came to a stop. Completely forgetting his cane, he was out and half running, half hopping toward the trailer before Dwight could put it in gear and jump out himself.

"Whoa!" Seth shouted. "Whoa, now, girl!"

For all the attention the horse paid him, he might as well have been shouting in the wind. Maybe she didn't even hear him; the noise from inside was earsplitting. The filly was still trying to kick her way out, and the entire trailer was bucking and shaking with her efforts. Bracing himself, Seth reached for the feed door by the manger. Trying not to think what each of those frenzied kicks might be doing to the filly's delicate legs, he jerked the door open.

"Whoa!" he said, trying to speak calmly, and yet be heard over the terrible noise. "Whoa, now, girl. It's all right, it's all right."

Already, the horse was covered with sweat. Drops of it flew off and hit Seth in the face when she reared back again. Her eyes rolled until the whites showed, and she was in such a state of panic that Seth was afraid she might make a bid for freedom by jumping out the small feed door. Reaching in, he grabbed the shredded end of the tie where she'd jerked loose, and held it.

"Come on, girl, come on, girl," he kept murmuring over and over. "It's all right, you're just fine."

Whether it was the sound of his voice, or his outwardly calm demeanor, or that after a while, she was simply exhausted, Never Done Dreamin' eventually quieted. She stopped kicking and stood trembling from head to foot.

Seth was shaking, himself. He had the horse calm now, but they still had to open the trailer and see what damage she might have done to herself. Finally remembering Dwight, he looked around.

The trainer was nowhere in sight.

"Dwight?" he called nervously. He didn't know what to expect.

To his relief, Dwight appeared from the back of the trailer. He said, "I was just making sure that maniac was gone."

"And is he?"

Appearing relieved and regretful at the same time, Dwight said angrily, "Yeah, and it's a good thing for him. If I got my hands on him right now—"

"I know what you mean. You didn't happen to get a license plate, did you?"

"Are you kidding? When I pulled over and pretended to be talking on the CB, he shot by like the hounds of hell were after him. He was gone before I could even see what he was driving."

"It was a Jeep with a winch on the front. I caught a glimpse of it when I got out of the truck."

"Did you—"

"No, I didn't get the plate, either. I was a little busy at the time."

Dwight handed him his cane. "Here," he said gruffly. "You forgot this."

He'd been so preoccupied with the horse that he'd completely forgotten about his leg, which was throbbing like the devil now. He took the cane with a muttered, "Thanks."

They'd stalled long enough. Although neither of them wanted to do it, they went around to the back of the trailer. The ramp was battered almost beyond recognition, but at least it had held. They had the dickens of a time unlocking it and forcing it down, but finally Seth stood back as Dwight went inside and coaxed the filly out. Perversely, now that the way to freedom was available, the horse stood like a rock. She was still shaking, and it took all Dwight's powers of persuasion to make her take even one step back.

During her frenzy, the trailering bandages had come half-undone; when the ends flapped against her legs and she gave a terrified kick, Seth told Dwight to wait.

"Hold it," he said, taking a knife from his pocket. He didn't want her to start up again, so with a few quick slices, he cut the bandage tails off. Then he saw the blood.

"Oh, jeez," he muttered.

"What is it?" Dwight asked anxiously.

Seth put a hand on the filly's trembling hide. It came away bloody from a gash on her side.

"I think she's hurt," he said.

Dwight was holding the horse's head. His voice mangled, he asked, "How bad?"

"I don't know. It's hard to see in this light."

"There's a flashlight in the truck."

The flashlight revealed more cuts and scrapes on the horse's head and flanks. But to their mutual relief, none were serious enough to warrant stitches. The filly's legs were a different story, and neither of them said a word when Dwight led her back and forth along the side of the road and they saw that she was already lame.

Finally, Seth said, "I guess we're lucky. The way she was kicking in there, she could have broken both hind legs. Or worse."

"Yeah," Dwight agreed morosely. He sounded near tears. They both knew that if she was off stride tonight, there was a good chance it would get worse before it got better. And the race was in three days. Not much time for her to get fit.

Trying not to think about it, Seth said, "Well, let's put her back in—if she'll go. We've still got a drive ahead of us."

"If this rig will make it," Dwight said, obviously trying to focus on something other than the filly's prospects for the Preakness. He dashed a quick hand across his eyes. "We'll get to the next town if we can, and I'll call for another truck and trailer."

"And while we're at it, we'd better call the police."

They looked at each other. Then Dwight said heavily, "Yeah, for all the good that will do."

"You never know."

"I know one thing."

"What's that?"

"Whoever the bastard is, he's probably going to try again."

WHOEVER THE BASTARD WAS, he didn't get a chance to try again—not before the Preakness, anyway. As soon as they got to the racetrack, Dwight hired round-the-clock guards for Never Done Dreamin'. She wasn't left alone for two seconds; her food and water, even her blankets and bandages, anything that touched her, was kept under lock and key.

Diligence, and the filly's seeming iron constitution, paid off. Three days later, Never Done Dreamin' went to the gate for the Preakness. Despite the trauma of the trailer incident and the stress of being in new surroundings, the filly took the lead as soon as she was on the track and never looked back.

Racing again with the best colts in the country, the only distaff runner in the field of twelve, Never Done

Dreamin' was so clearly in a class by herself that she was alone at the wire by a full two lengths.

In any circumstances, it was a stunning victory. Given the conditions the filly had overcome, it was a magnificent triumph. The racing crowd went wild; sports announcers and odds-makers alike were so ecstatic, they were practically incoherent.

And down in the winner's circle once again, Honey was radiant as Ian brought the filly in for the jockey's weighing and the presentation. The scrapes from her recent nightmarish experience on the road were still visible on the filly's gleaming hide, but such was her presence that few noticed the blemishes. In that moment, she seemed almost surrounded by a halo of light.

Or maybe, Honey thought, dizzy with delight, it was the flash from all the cameras. The band struck up the "Maryland, My Maryland" song, and Honey had to force herself to wait until Ian had jumped off the horse and weighed in with the saddle. But then, just before Dwight tossed him onto the horse again for the pictures and the presentation, she gave the jockey a jubilant hug.

"Oh, Ian, you were wonderful!" she exclaimed.

Grinning from ear to ear, he replied, "All I did was go along for the ride. She had command, just like always."

Never Done Dreamin' had command, all right. A growing, exultant racing crowd pressed around the winner's enclosure, eager to catch a close glimpse of the best distaff runner since the glorious Ruffian. They seemed undeterred by the increased security.

Uniformed men and women were ostentatiously on display; undercover officers scanned the throng for anyone or anything that looked remotely suspicious. Men and women with wires discreetly running from their ears into their collars roamed the grounds constantly, and the slightest element out of place received intense scrutiny.

Posing for pictures with Never Done Dreamin' before the awards presentation, Honey tried to forget the tension of the past few days and just concentrate on the filly's victory. But as she smiled again up at Ian, who was almost hidden by the magnificent blanket of black-eyed Susans, the Maryland state flower, she found it was a difficult task. She was all too aware that the man who had been assigned to be her bodyguard was standing close by, his hand resting casually inside his coat.

Honey wasn't the only Dunleavy with a personal guard. Octavia, Carla, Nan, Meredith and Jamie, who had delayed returning to San Francisco so she could see the last two legs of the Triple Crown, had been assigned protection today. Nervous track officials had agreed with the police that extra caution was necessary. Even though it seemed that Never Done Dreamin' was the target, no one could be sure that a member of the Dunleavy family wasn't the real quarry.

At Dunleavy Farm, no one had been certain of anything. Honey had almost fainted when Dwight called to report that someone had tried to ram him on the road; Carla and Nan had been white-faced and furious. Worried about the effect on Octavia, they'd all tried to keep the news from her, but of course that had been impossible. No matter what precautions were taken, the media services got hold of it, and before that day dawned, headlines were already trumpeting stories of the filly's brush with death. The only damage control anyone had been able to mount was to downplay the deliberateness of the act. So far as anyone outside the immediate family knew, the accident had been just that: an accident.

But Honey knew better, and as she smiled and posed for pictures, pretending that she hadn't a care in the world, inside she was terrified. There had been two attempts to keep the filly from racing. And both had taken place *before* Never Done Dreamin' had won today's Preakness. Could all the security in the world protect this horse from the person or persons who seemed determined to prevent her from trying for the Triple Crown?

Under the warm Maryland sun, Honey shivered.

Dwight had just signaled that he was going to take the filly back to the barn for a well-earned rest, when one of the photographers shouted, "Just one more, Honey! Look over here!"

Honey obliged, and turned to look—right into Seth's eyes. He was standing behind the photographer who had called out to her, and for a moment, she couldn't even breathe. She'd only talked to Seth one time by phone since the night he had asked for a divorce. The conversation had been stilted and awkward, as though they were strangers. She'd felt so awful that she hadn't wanted to talk to him again.

But now, here he was, not ten feet from her. As she stared into his eyes, it was as though the world re-

ceded and they were the only two people left on the
planet. The raucous sounds of celebration became
muted; the jostling of the crowd around her faded.
There was only Seth. She was so frozen with—what?
Anticipation? Dread? Fear? Delight?—that she
couldn't move. He had to come to her.

The excitement over, the winner's circle had emp-
tied around her. Another race—as though anything
could be more important than the Preakness on this
mild May day—was about to be called, and people
were already consulting their *Racing Forms* and sages.
Seth made his way through the departing crowd,
which was heading toward the paddocks and the bet-
ting cages, but Honey just stood there, drinking in the
sight of him, wondering what miracle had brought him
here.

"Hi," Seth said when he was about five feet from
her.

She tried to speak, but her throat felt constricted.
From the corner of her eye, she saw her bodyguard
moving closer, but she managed to lift a hand to signal him that it was all right. Seth saw her gesture and
smiled.

"It's okay, Harry," he said to the guard. "I won't
hurt her."

Harry put two fingers to an imaginary hat in salute
and moved off again—but not too far. Honey knew it
was ridiculous, but she couldn't think of anything to
say other than, "How do you know Harry?"

When he looked at her, Seth's eyes were that deep,
clear green that she had always loved. Her heart

lurched when he actually smiled at her. Offhandedly, he said, "Oh, we've met before."

She couldn't seem to act like anything other than an idiot. When she wanted to ask him where he'd been, *how* he'd been and what he was doing here, all she said was, "You have? Where?"

"Oh, here and there," Seth said.

After all this time apart, just the sound of his voice was like the gentlest of caresses. She wanted so badly to touch him, just to put her hand on his arm, but she didn't dare. Even now, she couldn't be sure that he wasn't a dream she'd conjured because she so desperately missed him.

But if he was real, she didn't want him to disappear. So she concentrated on something safe to say, something that wouldn't alarm him, or make him angry, or put that cold look back in his eyes. She'd die if she saw that iron door slamming shut on her.

"Did you…did you see the race?" she managed to ask.

He nodded. "Yeah, I was watching from the rail."

She hadn't seen him, she realized incredulously. How could she have missed him? Even with all the excitement, she should have *felt* him there. She felt him now, she thought. Even though he was standing slightly away from her, as if reluctant to come any closer, she felt the heat of his body all the way to her bones. It was awful, this terrible yearning for him, and she closed her eyes against the pain rising in her.

"What's the matter?" he asked quickly. "Are you all right?"

She opened her eyes. He had come closer. In his concern for her, he had his hand out, as though he expected her to fall. She did feel faint, she thought vaguely. Maybe it was the sun...or the excitement. She looked up at him, but suddenly the world spun dizzily. She didn't realize she'd swayed until he swooped her up.

"Honey?" he said worriedly.

She hardly heard him. The sensation of being in his arms, of resting her head against his chest, of feeling the beat of his heart, was pure bliss. She wanted to stay nestled like that forever, cuddled and protected and wrapped in his arms and his love.

Then she remembered his leg.

"You can put me down," she said. "I'm okay. Honest."

When he didn't move, she looked up at him. This time, their faces were only inches apart. His breath fanned her cheek; his arms tightened around her. Under her hand, still resting on his chest, his heart leapt— just as hers was doing.

"Seth?" she said unsteadily.

He wouldn't stop staring at her. A muscle jumped in his jaw as if he was trying to control himself, but he said, "I've missed you, Honey. *God,* how I've missed you."

Was this really happening? Did she dare to believe he'd really said that? Her lip trembled, and she raised her hand to touch his face.

"I've missed you, too," she whispered. She couldn't begin to tell him how much.

He closed his eyes. When he opened them again, their green color was brilliant with the glimmer of unshed tears. When she saw that, she said, "Oh, Seth!"

"So what do you want to do now?" he asked hoarsely.

She didn't even have to think about it. She knew she was expected back at the barn for the immediate celebration; people were waiting for her; another big party was planned for later. She didn't care about any of it. Never Done Dreamin' knew what she had done; that was the important thing. Right now, the only one who mattered was Seth.

Holding his eyes, she said, "I want to be alone with you. Will you take me back to my hotel?"

THANKFULLY, the hotel was nearby. Seth couldn't take his eyes off his wife. Honey had never looked more lovely to him; it was as though she were illuminated from within. Her eyes were brilliant; even her skin seemed to glow. His heart pounding, his groin already throbbing by the time they reached her room, he took her into his arms and kicked the door closed.

As she pressed against him and he held her tight, the thought flashed across his mind that she felt different. But then her lips met his, and he couldn't think about much of anything for a while. The needs of his body took over, and all he could do was drown himself in her. Her breasts were fuller and she seemed more rounded in places, but he didn't question it because passion was driving him. Her desire matched his, and as they pulled their clothes off and fell, clutching each other, onto the bed, Seth was so lost in sensation that he even forgot about the damned cast on his leg.

He never thought he could love Honey any more than he already did, but that afternoon, he buried his face in her sweet-smelling hair and wanted to shout with sheer joy. And when her long legs went around him, and he buried himself inside her, he couldn't stop the shudders that ran violently through him just at the feel of her. She took him to places he'd never been before, and before the climax overtook him, he looked down into her face and thought she was the most beautiful creature he'd ever seen. How could he ever have thought of leaving her?

Then he felt her tighten around him as her own climax shook her, and together they sailed over the edge of the world, locked in mutual pleasure.

"Oh, Seth!" she murmured when it was all over.

He was so exhausted that all he could do was lie, breathing deeply beside her.

CHAPTER THIRTEEN

THE DUNLEAVYS KNEW how to throw a party, there was no doubt about it. Champagne and wine flowed the night Never Done Dreamin' won the Preakness; there was an open bar, and the big buffet tables groaned from the weight of all the food. By the time Honey and Seth arrived, the celebration was in full swing with a four-piece combo providing background music. As Honey looked around the crowded ballroom, which was decorated in Dunleavy Farm's colors of royal blue and gold, she was amazed. She spotted Octavia at one end of the big room and tugged on Seth's arm.

"There's your grandmother," she said. "I think we should go and congratulate her."

Seth immediately looked uncomfortable. "You go ahead," he said. "I'll get us something to drink."

"I don't want anything, thanks. But don't you want to—"

"I'll talk to her later," he said, and headed in the direction of the bar.

Frowning slightly, Honey watched him go. Then she shrugged. They'd discuss it later, she thought—along with a host of other things. For now, it was enough that he'd agreed to stay for the Belmont.

Honey was just starting toward Octavia, when Nan materialized at her shoulder.

"Well, well," Nan said with a sly grin, "I see that you finally got here."

Honey blushed. "Oh, you noticed, did you?"

"Your conspicuous absence, you mean? Yes, it has been remarked upon."

"Oh dear. Is your grandmother upset?"

Nan's eyes sparkled. "Not in the slightest. But since this is a victory celebration, everyone was wondering where you were."

"Not that we couldn't guess," Carla said, coming up to Honey's other side. She, too, was smiling. "But don't worry. As good cousins should, we made excuses for you."

Honey knew she was bright red. "How did you know?"

"After that film-style reunion at the track?" Nan teased. "You've got to be kidding."

"So," Carla said, "I take it things are looking up?"

"I think they are," Honey said cautiously. "We...er...haven't talked about it yet, but at least he's here, so that means something. Doesn't it?" she added, needing reassurance.

"I'd say so," Carla said dryly.

"It's about time, too," Nan said.

"Well, we'll see," Honey said. "And in addition to that, I'm still concerned about how to get him and his mother together."

"One step at a time," Carla said. "At least he came back."

Honey smiled. "And he's going to stay through the Belmont—if the filly runs in New York, that is."

"She'll run," Nan said confidently.

"But even if she doesn't," Carla said, "that still gives you time to talk some sense into him. Maybe the win today will help change his mind."

"It's not so much his intractable stand about the filly," Honey said. "I just want him to acknowledge his family."

"It's hard when you realize that things aren't what they've always seemed," Carla said. "I can speak from experience on that score."

"I can, too," Nan said. She gave Honey a quick hug. "Don't worry. He'll come around." She glanced at Carla. "We did."

Honey sighed. "Yes, but sometimes I think women are so much more practical than men."

"Sometimes," Nan said, twinkling. "Not always."

"And she speaks from experience on that one, too," Carla teased. Then she laughed at herself. "For that matter, so can I."

"And I," Honey said ruefully. She noticed then that Octavia was making her way slowly, but deliberately, toward the door. Quickly, she excused herself and hurried to Octavia's side.

Octavia saw her coming and held out both hands. "Honey, I thought you weren't coming."

Honey took the proffered hands and gave Octavia a kiss on the cheek. "You know I wouldn't have missed this."

"It has been a fun day, hasn't it?" Octavia said with a sigh.

"You get no argument from me there. And you were certainly popular."

Octavia dismissed the compliment. "Nonsense. It's just that I've been around forever. People are still amazed that I'm alive."

"Oh, that's not true and you know it!"

Octavia had been the center of attention all day. As had happened during the Derby, the moment the head of Dunleavy Farm stepped on the grounds at Pimlico, she'd been surrounded by friends, well-wishers, admiring fans, sports announcers and just about anyone who could get close to her.

Honey had watched all the activity from a distance, pleased at the attention paid to the grande dame of racing. But she couldn't help thinking that, with the crush around Octavia, it would have been all too easy for anyone with motive to get too close. It was a horrible way to think, but she'd been glad that Octavia had been assigned a bodyguard.

"This is a wonderful party, Grandmother. How did you ever manage this on such short notice? It looks as if you've been planning it for weeks."

"For weeks?" Octavia's eyes sparkled. "Oh, my dear, I've been planning it for *years!*"

"But you couldn't be sure that Never Done Dreamin' would win."

"Well, it was a distinct possibility, you have to admit. But even if she hadn't, she still would have deserved a victory party, just for getting to the gate. After what happened—"

A shadow passed over Octavia's face, but then she smiled determinedly again. "But we won't dwell on that, at least not tonight, will we? Tonight is for cele-brating, and we certainly have enough to celebrate, don't you think?"

Honey saw Octavia's glance go to Seth, who was still at the bar, talking to someone now. When Octavia turned back to her with a knowing glance, Honey could feel herself blushing once more. Oh, yes, she did agree that tonight was indeed a night for celebration.

IT WAS LATE; Octavia had retired hours ago and so had the rest of the Dunleavys. The big ballroom was al-most empty. When the service personnel, who had been waiting to clean up, bustled in and proceeded to dismantle tables and clear away the clutter, Honey knew she and Seth should leave them to do their jobs.

It had been such an exciting day, one of the best; she wanted to prolong it until dawn. She didn't want this moment with Seth to end, so she took his arm and said, "Let's go for a walk."

He looked at her. "Now?"

She dismissed her sudden uneasy feeling that some-thing was wrong. After all, the day *had* been long, and Seth did look tired. His leg was probably bothering him, too.

"We won't go far," she said. "Just enough to get a little fresh air."

To her dismay, he pulled away from her. "I can't."

Again, she felt a stab of alarm and suppressed it. She was imagining things, she told herself. After what had happened this afternoon, surely nothing could be wrong.

"All right, then," she said, giving him an arch look. "Let's just go back to our room. I'm sure we can find something to do."

His voice sounded even more strange. "You go. I've got to get back to the track."

"The track? Why? Has something happened to Never Done Dreamin'?"

"No, no—not that I know of, anyway. I just want to make sure that nothing does."

She let out a relieved breath. For a moment there, she'd had nightmare visions of another attempt to hurt the horse. But Seth was just being his usual cautious self. "Aren't you worrying unnecessarily? Dwight has two men guarding the filly. Nothing's going to happen, so let's—"

"I told you, Honey, I can't."

She could no longer pretend that the atmosphere hadn't changed between them. But what had happened since they'd left the hotel room, wrapped in a warm, satisfied glow? She faced him. "Seth, what's wrong?"

"Nothing," he insisted, avoiding her eyes. "I told you. I've got to get to the track. It's my job."

"Your *job?* What do you mean?"

He finally looked at her. "Listen, Honey, I should have told you before. Dwight wanted me to, but I thought it was best that you didn't know."

"What are you talking about?"

He sighed. "I'm talking about the fact that ever since the Derby, I've been keeping watch over Never Done Dreamin' at night."

For a moment, she wasn't sure she'd heard right. Seth had been at Churchill Downs all this time and hadn't told her? Unsteadily, she said, "I don't understand. Do you mean you've been staying at the track? I thought you were in Arizona."

Seth was looking more and more uncomfortable by the minute. As well he should, Honey thought in a fit of temper. What kind of trick was he trying to pull here? If he'd been in Louisville, he should have told her.

Seth saw the flare of anger she couldn't hide and explained hastily, "I started out to go there, but...well, when I stopped in to see Never Done Dreamin' that night, Dwight and I got to talking, and before I knew it, I was volunteering to sleep in the tack room. We both wanted someone to be close in case anyone tried to get to her, and the logical choice seemed to be me. Dwight could watch her during the day, but he was running himself ragged. He was so worried about her that he wouldn't go home."

"So...you stayed to watch over the filly?"

"Well, yes."

She tried to see it from his point of view. "Look, Seth, I appreciate that you wanted to help guard her. But all this time, I thought you'd gone to be as far away from me as you could get. Now I realize that you've been in Louisville..."

She couldn't go on. As grateful as she was for what he'd done for the horse, she was hurt to the core that he'd been so close and hadn't told her.

Seth saw her face. Quickly, he said, "I thought it best if no one knew. Honey, please try to understand."

"Oh, I understand, all right," she said bitterly. "I've been to the track quite a few times since that horrible night you told me you wanted a divorce, but I never saw you. Why did you think you had to sneak around? If you didn't want to see me, all you had to do was say so."

"It wasn't like that," Seth said. "I told you. Dwight was sleeping at the track so he could guard the filly. He didn't trust anyone else, so what could I do?"

"You could have told me! I wouldn't have bothered you if you didn't want me to!"

"Aw, Honey, it wasn't that."

"Oh, no? Well, it sure seems like that to me."

"Come on, Honey—"

He reached for her, but she jerked away. "I don't know you anymore, Seth," she said, her voice trembling. "Maybe I never did. But we do agree on one thing, at last. This marriage is dead. Like you, I don't see any point in going on—not if you're so desperate to stay away from me that you'd rather I didn't know you were nearby."

She didn't trust herself to say any more. Without giving him a chance to speak, she turned and ran out of the ballroom without looking back. But once outside, standing alone on the sidewalk, she didn't know what to do. She didn't have any money with her, any credit cards, not even any identification.

She wasn't going to go back inside. She needed to walk off some of her anger, so she chose a direction and started off.

By the time she felt the first sharp stab of pain in her belly, she had walked so far, she could no longer see the hotel. Even then, she wasn't really afraid, for she was still on the main road; all she had to do was turn around and go back.

Then the pain hit her again—this time with such force that she gasped and bent over. For a horrible few seconds, when she wondered if she was going to pass out, she managed to stagger over to a street sign and hang on for dear life, gasping the whole time. It took longer for the cramp—if that's what it was—to pass, but it left as suddenly as it came. When she realized it was gone, she took a few shallow, experimental breaths. When nothing happened, she straightened. She didn't know what was going on, but she knew she'd better get back to the hotel in case it happened again.

"Whew," she muttered. "That was—"

The third time the pain hit her, it was as though someone had plunged a hot knife into her. The agony was so fierce and all-encompassing, she couldn't even hold on to the sign. Wrapping her arms around her waist, she sank onto the pavement. It felt as if someone were twisting a blade, tearing her apart inside.

Sweat broke out on her forehead. She thought she was going to be sick. The sidewalk seemed to tilt, and she knew she was going to faint.

"Are you all right?" someone said.

For a glorious instant, she thought it was Seth. He'd come after her! she thought. Now that he was here, everything would be all right.

But when she managed to look up through a haze of pain, she saw a concerned-looking older couple staring down at her. She tried to reach for them, but the slightest movement made her gasp.

"Please, call an...ambulance," she panted. "I'm...pregnant, and I think... Oh, God!" she cried as the pain overtook her, "that I'm losing my baby!"

The woman bent down. She had a kind face, Honey thought, before she doubled over again.

"We'll get help," the woman said. "Don't worry, dear. Just tell us your name...*your name...your name...*"

The words echoed in Honey's mind, and she tried to answer, but it was as if a hot flood had burst within her. All she could do was allow herself to be swept along by it—right into a dark tunnel that mercifully brought unconsciousness.

BACK AT THE HOTEL, Seth was pacing the lobby, cursing himself for letting Honey run out like that, when he looked up and saw his mother. He stopped midstep.

"What do you want?" he asked impatiently.

Jamie didn't blink an eye. "I thought it was time for us to talk."

The last thing he wanted to do right now was to have a discussion with his mother. "We don't have anything to talk about."

"I think we do."

"That's your privilege," he said. "I don't have anything to say to you."

"Well, I've got a few things to say to you."

"Not now. I have other things on my mind."

"I hope one of them is your wife."

He stiffened. "I always think of Honey."

"Do you? I thought you were too busy feeling sorry for yourself to think of anyone but Seth Dunleavy."

Too agitated to stand still, Seth had resumed his pacing. At that crack, he stopped dead again. "And what is that supposed to mean?"

Jamie sighed. "I don't want to fight. I just want to try to work things out."

"After all these years?"

Her gaze was direct. "Yes, after all these years. As the old saying goes, it's better late than never."

"That's not always the case."

"Look, Seth, I know I made mistakes, but I can't change the past. I can only try to explain how things were then. I'd appreciate it if you'd grant me the courtesy of listening."

"I'm sorry, Jamie. I stopped listening when you sent me to that hellhole of a military school. I knew then I was in the way. You didn't want me around."

"I sent you away because you needed discipline," she said. "You wouldn't listen to me. You wouldn't listen to anyone."

"You never had time for me. You were too involved in your painting!"

"I was trying to make a living! And you were spending too much time at the track."

"Speaking of the track, why didn't you ever tell me we were related to the Dunleavys of Dunleavy Farm? Did it just slip your mind?"

Her level gaze faltered. "I admit, that's one of the things I was wrong about. I should have told you—"

"Yes, you should have."

She met his eyes. "What can I do to make it up to you?"

He hadn't expected her to ask that, and he was silent. But she had opened an old wound, and it had to be drained. "You can tell me about my father," he said.

Jamie bit her lip. He could see a struggle going on inside her. Finally, she said, "I never wanted to tell you this, Seth. I thought it was better that you didn't know. But after all that's happened in this family, I'm beginning to realize it's never a good idea to withhold the truth."

"And the truth is . . . ?"

She took a deep breath. "The truth is, when I told your father I was pregnant, he. . .he offered to pay for an abortion."

It was as if she'd landed a hard one right in his gut. For a few seconds, he just stared at her. He wanted to believe she was lying to him, but the truth was there in her eyes, in her face, in every line of her body. He had to believe her.

But then, deep down, hadn't he always wondered? Even if she had sent his father away, refusing to marry him, why hadn't the man ever contacted him?

"I'm sorry, Seth," Jamie said. "I would have given anything not to tell you." She shook her head, obviously weighed down by regret. "In fact, I did give up everything—or at least the one thing most precious to me."

"And that was?"

"You," she said, her eyes filling with tears.

His lips stiff, he said, "The guy must have been a real bastard."

"No," Jamie said at once. "He was just . . . young. We both were. And we needed different things. I wanted acceptance. Russ wanted freedom. We both wanted love. I don't know, maybe those things are all part of a whole we just couldn't find together. But one thing—" She put her hand on his arm, her grip so fierce, he couldn't pull away. "Your father might have been driven by his own demons—as we all are—but he did one thing in his life for which I will always be grateful."

"And what's that?"

Her answer was simple. "He gave me you."

Seth couldn't let it go. "And I disappointed you, too. You always said I wouldn't amount to much if I followed the track, and you were right. I haven't."

Jamie was silent. Then she said, "Have you ever asked yourself why you stayed with the fair circuit, Seth? If you wanted to succeed so much in racing, why didn't you ever try to make it at the 'A' tracks? You could have, yet you didn't." She paused. Then, obviously deciding to take a chance, she said, "Could it be that you *wanted* to fail?"

He stiffened. "Don't be ridiculous. Why would anyone *want* to fail?"

She blinked back tears. "I can't blame you. It's our fault, mine and Russ's. You believed—rightly or wrongly—that neither of your parents wanted you. Your father never contacted you, and I sent you away. Perversity is in all of us at times, Seth. Maybe you were your own self-fulfilling prophecy. I think you believed that if no one wanted you, maybe you weren't worth anything. Therefore, you weren't entitled to succeed."

"What a bunch of hogwash," he scoffed, but uncertainly.

"Maybe you're right. Maybe I don't know what I'm talking about. It's just that... Oh, Seth, you have so much to offer. I know you love Honey, and she's so in love with you that it's almost painful to watch. But she thinks that if she tells you about the—"

Abruptly, she stopped. When her eyes slid away from his, he took her arm.

"What were you going to say?"

"Oh, Seth, I promised not to mention it."

He pulled her toward him. "I thought we were done with lies and evasions. If you know something about Honey, you'd better tell me."

She hesitated, then said reluctantly, "All right. You have to know, anyway. Honey is...pregnant."

He looked at her. "She is?" he said. "How do you know? I mean, are you sure?"

"Yes, I'm sure," Jamie said. "She told me herself."

"Oh, my God! I've got to find her!"

Alarmed, Jamie said, "What's wrong?"

Everything was wrong, he thought. He had to find Honey. This discussion with his mother had made him realize how much time he had wasted.

But no more, he thought. Nothing was worth losing Honey—nothing. *They'd work it out,* he told himself fiercely. Somehow, they'd get through this, and when they did, he'd be a different man—a different husband . . . a father.

"I've got to find Honey," he said. "When you came in just now, did you see her?"

"No, I didn't," Jamie said. "Why, what's the matter?"

It would take too long to explain, and he wasn't sure he wanted to go into it with his mother, anyway.

"We had a fight earlier, and she went out," he said. "I should have gone after her, but . . . I didn't. Are you sure you didn't see her?"

Jamie didn't get the chance to answer, for just then the hotel concierge rushed up to them. Hurriedly, the man asked, "Are you Seth Dunleavy?"

Seth nodded impatiently. "Yes. What is it?"

"I have a message for you."

"Well, what?"

The man looked even more anxious. "I'm sorry to tell you this, Mr. Dunleavy, but your wife has been taken to Baltimore General. They need you there immediately. If there's anything the hotel can do—"

Seth wasn't listening. He looked in a panic at Jamie and saw the same fear in her eyes. Had there been some kind of accident?

Jamie was apparently in better shape than he was. She immediately said, ''Go! I'll tell the others, and we'll follow you.''

His throat too constricted with fear to speak, he nodded jerkily. The concierge had already called a cab; it was waiting for him by the time he reached the curb. Throwing himself inside, he said, ''Baltimore General—and hurry!''

The driver took a look at Seth's face in the rear-view mirror. Without a word, he put up the flag and stomped down on the accelerator.

CHAPTER FOURTEEN

HONEY WAS so drowsy from the medication she'd been given that she didn't know someone had come into her hospital room until she looked up and saw Seth standing by the bed. She realized dimly that he must have been there for a while, for as soon as he saw her eyes open, he looked relieved. Leaning down, he kissed her forehead.

"Welcome back, sleepyhead," he said.

Weakly, she asked, "What time is it?"

He reached for her hand. Holding it carefully, as if afraid she might break, he said, "It's late. But you're safe and well. You gave us all quite a scare, Mrs. Dunleavy."

Honey couldn't remember what had happened. She didn't even recall how she'd gotten to the hospital. She supposed it had been in an ambulance, but by the time she'd come to, she was in a brightly lighted room and all sorts of people were rushing around her. Terrified that she'd miscarried, she'd grabbed the sleeve of the doctor who was listening to her chest with a stethoscope.

"The baby!" she'd whispered hoarsely. "Did I...?"

The doctor had smiled reassuringly. "No, you're fine, and so is the baby. As near as I can determine, this little episode was brought on by tension. Have you been under stress?"

Honey wanted to laugh hysterically. Stress? She almost told the doctor he had to be kidding, but she said, "Things have been a little...hectic lately."

The doctor patted her hand. "You're going to have to learn to relax, my dear. You don't want this baby coming into the world before it's ready, do you?"

Honey definitely didn't want that. With a shudder, she'd promised to take it easy. The next thing she remembered was waking up and seeing Seth.

"How long have I been here?" she asked.

"Just a few hours." He cradled her hand in both his own. "I'm so sorry, Honey. I didn't mean for this to happen. I swear to God, I didn't."

"It's my fault. I shouldn't have run out like that."

He looked down at their clasped hands for a moment. Then he asked, "Why didn't you tell me you were pregnant?"

She didn't feel strong enough right now to argue with Seth, or to try to explain her decision. And what difference did it make, anyway? she wondered wearily. What was done was done. She couldn't change it now.

So she said, "I don't know. I guess I...just never found the right time. How did you find out?"

"Mother told me."

"Mother?"

He smiled slightly at her surprise. "Jamie, then. We had quite a talk tonight. I learned a lot—most of it things about myself that I didn't really like."

"Such as?"

He rubbed a thumb along the back of her hand. "Such as what a fool I've been all these years."

"A . . . fool?" she said cautiously.

He grimaced. "Jamie said I was my own self-fulfilling prophecy, and she was right. I thought I was destined to fail, so I did. But that's all over now."

"It is?"

"I don't blame you for looking skeptical. But we can talk about it later. Right now, we have something more important to discuss."

"And that is?"

"Well, the baby changes everything, doesn't it?"

She'd been afraid of this. "I don't know what you mean."

"Well, it's obvious, isn't it? We're going to be parents. Things are different now."

"Are they?" She wanted to believe that Seth meant what he said about turning over a new leaf, but as the adage went, a leopard didn't change its spots overnight. He was just telling her what he thought she wanted to hear. Because she was pregnant. Pulling her hand away from him, she tried to sit up.

"Let me help—"

She pushed him away. "I can do it."

He stepped back, a hurt look on his face. "You're still angry with me, aren't you?"

"Angry?" she repeated, adjusting the pillow behind her so she could lean back and still see him. "No, I'm not angry anymore, Seth. I'm too tired to be angry."

"I know you've had a bad experience," he said worriedly. "But it's over now—"

"Is it?"

He looked even more anxious. "Isn't it? When I talked to the doctor, he said there was no reason to worry."

"I know. He told me the same thing. That's not what I'm talking about."

"Then what do you mean?" He tried to take her hand again, but she reached for the water glass by the bed. He watched in silence as she took a few sips, then he asked, "Honey, what's wrong?"

What's wrong? Everything is wrong. Didn't he know that?

"Why are you here, Seth?"

He looked startled. "I'm here because you're my wife and I love you."

"I thought you wanted a divorce."

He reddened. "That was a stupid thing to say. I never meant it."

"I see. Then you only said it to hurt me."

"I never wanted to hurt you. I just thought that, given the circumstances, it would be better—for you."

"And what circumstances were those?"

Puzzled by her manner, he said, "You know what they were. You wanted to stay at the farm, I wanted to go home. I didn't see how we could ever work things out. But Honey—" He reached for her hand again and this time succeeded in capturing her fingers. "It doesn't matter now, don't you see? Things have changed."

Her hand was quiet in his. "Nothing has changed, Seth," she said. "I knew that if you found out about the baby, you'd do this. But it's not necessary."

"Not...necessary?" He looked puzzled. "That's a strange choice of words."

"This is a strange situation," she said tiredly.

"Why are you acting this way? I thought you'd be glad—"

She lifted her head. "That you changed your mind?"

"I didn't change my mind. I told you. I never wanted a divorce in the first place."

"Oh, yes, that's right. You only said it to find out what my reaction would be."

Trying to hide his exasperation, he said carefully, "I'm not sure why you're acting like this, but believe me, I want to work it out. After all, we're going to have a baby." He grinned. "I'm going to be a father."

She didn't know why she felt so numb, but she did. "That changes nothing."

His smile faded. "Of course it does."

She looked away. She didn't know what was happening to her; she felt so distant and cold. Seth was finally saying the words she had longed to hear, but it was too late. Much too late.

Plucking absently at the thin hospital blanket, she said, "I think you were right after all. Maybe the best thing we can do for each other *is* to get a divorce."

"How can you say that? This should be one of the happiest moments of our lives. Instead, you're acting like a stranger. I know I've been stupid and childish—"

"Yes, you have been. But it doesn't matter. We're past that now."

"I know we've had our problems, Honey. But that's all in the past. From now on, it will be different."

"How?" she asked, looking him in the eye. "How will it be different, Seth? Are you saying that you're going to abandon this stubborn stand you've been on for the past few months and accept your grandmother's offer to stay at the farm? Do you intend to accept the filly, because Octavia—not me—wants you to? Just what does it mean, Seth?"

Beginning to look a little desperate, he said, "It means that I'm willing to do whatever it takes to keep you. I love you. I don't want to lose you—or the baby."

Oh, Seth! she thought miserably. *Why couldn't you have said this before, when it was just you and me? Why wasn't I enough for you? What went wrong?*

She didn't say it. Instead, she repeated, "You're only saying all this because I'm pregnant."

"No! I told you—"

She looked at him, and he stopped midsentence. "I'm sorry, but I don't believe you," she said. "You stood in front of me only a couple of weeks ago and told me you wanted a divorce."

"Honey—"

She turned her face to the wall. "I'd like you to leave now. I'm very tired, and the doctor said I need my rest."

She felt him standing there for the longest time; she knew he was looking at her with an expression that would break her heart if she looked. So she closed her eyes and willed him to go. After an endless while, he turned and went out. The door closed softly, and she was alone.

She had to make plans, she thought; she had to decide what to do now. She wouldn't think about Seth, so she thought about the farm. The idea of leaving those connected to it made her heart ache. Faces flashed through her mind. She saw Octavia, aged but indomitable, and Carla, so sharp and sophisticated—except where Wade was concerned. There was Nan, so quick and energetic, and so much in love with Trent, it almost hurt to see them together; Meredith, whose aloof manner hid a heart too easily injured; and Jamie, who, despite her exotic flair, was so down-to-earth and sensible.

And finally, there was Never Done Dreamin', who, against incredible odds, had just won the first two legs of the Triple Crown. She pictured the filly, her coat flashing in the sun, her long tail streaming behind her as she took to the air and ran. There never seemed to be any doubt in the filly's mind that she had been born to race.

But Honey had doubts. Was she wrong to send Seth away? No. She loved him too much to tie him to her out of a sense of duty. And she couldn't stay on here. From what little Seth had said about the conversation with his mother, it seemed there was a chance he might not leave the area—at least not for a while. No matter how welcome she felt at the farm, no matter how encouraging Octavia, Carla, Nan and Jamie had been, Honey couldn't stay on. It would be too awkward, too... painful. No, she thought, it was time to move on.

But move on to what? The idea of a future without Seth was not only empty but frightening, especially when she thought of having sole responsibility for a baby.

Her lip trembled, and she bit down hard. It didn't matter how scared she was, she told herself. She'd stay until the Belmont; she owed Octavia and the filly that much. But as soon as the race was over, she'd pack her things and leave Dunleavy Farm.

WHEN SETH CAME OUT of Honey's hospital room, the entire family was there waiting. In a glance, he took in his grandmother's face and realized with a pang that she seemed to have aged ten years since the party tonight. He looked at Meredith, pale and tense; and at his cousin, Carla, who had the same tight, worried look on her face. Nan jumped up when he appeared in the waiting area, but even she seemed subdued.

Then his mother approached. Jamie hadn't changed out of her party dress, but under the stark hospital lights, her sequined jacket seemed dull and lifeless. She put her hand lightly on his arm.

"How is she?" Jamie asked.

It was an effort to focus. "I...I'm not sure," he said. "The doctor said that physically she's fine, but..."

He couldn't tell them just how much Honey had changed. A light seemed to have gone out inside her. Right before his eyes, she had retreated to a place where he couldn't talk to her, much less touch her.

"But?" Jamie prodded.

He tried to answer. "I don't know, Mother. I guess...maybe—" He stopped. Unable to explain, he just shook his head.

Jamie seemed to understand. "Perhaps she only needs time."

He knew that all the time in the world wasn't going to change Honey's mind. He had seen it in her eyes, in her face, in the way she held herself...away from him.

I've lost her, he thought numbly. *And there's nothing I can do to get her back.*

His despair must have been obvious, for Jamie said in a low voice, "Come to the hotel, Seth. You can't do anything more tonight, and Honey needs her rest."

His eyes burned as he looked at her. "She wants to go through with the divorce. Even with the baby coming, she thinks our marriage is over."

"She's had a shock, Seth. She was in terrible pain, and she's probably woozy from medication. I don't think you should act on what she said until you can both discuss it away from here."

Oh, if only that were possible! he thought. But he knew Honey: once she'd made up her mind, nothing could sway her.

He didn't want to argue with his mother, not here, anyway, so he nodded. His eyes bleak, he said, "Maybe you're right."

"Of course I am," Jamie said. She wound her arm through his. "Let's go back to the hotel."

He couldn't go back there; he had to stay close to Honey. Shaking his head, he said, "No, I think I'd better stay here for a while. Just in case..."

"I'll stay with you, then," Jamie said.

He needed to be alone. "No, it's not necessary. You go back with the others. I'll call if there's any change."

Clearly worried, she searched his face. But finally she said, "All right, if that's what you want."

Nothing was as he wanted. He was about to lose the one thing in life that was most precious to him, and he was helpless to prevent it. Worse, he had only himself to blame.

He looked at his mother, and tried to smile at her. Perhaps he could start mending fences. He'd been wrong about Jamie. He could begin with her.

"Don't worry," he said. "Somehow, things will work out."

She searched his face again. Then, tentatively, she reached up and touched his cheek. "I know they will," she said softly.

He took her hand and held it between his. "Thanks."

"For what?"

It seemed so simple to him now. "For being here when I needed you."

She tried to respond, but tears filled her eyes, and she gave his hand a squeeze. "Promise you'll call me," she said. "Even if you just want someone to sit here with you."

He promised, and after coming up to him and offering various forms of assurance and comfort, the family left. He thought everyone had gone, until he looked up and realized his aunt Meredith had stayed behind. When she saw his consternation, she tried to smile. It turned into a grimace and he realized that she was nervous.

"I want to talk to you for a minute, if I can," she said.

He didn't want to talk to anyone else right now. But he forced himself to say, "What about?"

She began to answer, but then opened her purse. "This might take a while. Do you mind if I smoke?"

Instead of answering, he pointed to the No Smoking sign posted in the waiting room. She looked at it and sighed.

"Can we go outside?"

He didn't want to be that far away from Honey, but Meredith's tension was almost palpable. Remembering the other night when she'd been so agitated, he said, "If you like."

Outside the hospital, Meredith lit up with a relieved sigh. "Ah, that's better."

He didn't want to linger out here. "You said you wanted to talk to me about something."

She took another drag and looked at him. Even more tense than she'd been before, she said, "Yes, I did. I just don't know how to begin."

"What's it about?"

"It's about . . ." She took another nervous puff and finally said it. "It's about what's been happening to the Dunleavy horses."

"Maybe you'd better start at the beginning."

"I would, if I knew how far back it went. I can't prove it, but I'm beginning to think it started with Done Roamin's so-called accident."

Seth tensed. "Go on."

Meredith threw the cigarette down on the walkway and ground it into ashes with her heel. "I hope I'm wrong, but I believe a man named Alan Bradshaw is behind all this—the stallion's injury, Done Driftin's stable accident, Done Cryin's disappearance."

"Alan Bradshaw?"

"Yes. I'm sure he's also responsible for the things that have happened to the filly. And I don't think he's finished."

He couldn't believe it. "You're making this up—"

"You think I'd make up something like this?" she snapped.

Thinking he didn't know what she'd do, he said, "Let's go back a little. Who's Alan Bradshaw, and what would he have to do with the Dunleavy horses?"

"A long time ago, Alan Bradshaw was the manager for Dunleavy Farm." She barely paused before she added, "He was also once my husband."

Seth was speechless. By this time, he'd heard the story of how, long ago, Meredith had enraged and alienated her mother by eloping with the farm manager. He was hazy on the details—Honey had told him while they were lying in bed—but he vaguely remembered that Octavia had had the marriage annulled. Meredith had never forgiven her for interfering; in fact, after a thirty-five-year silence, it was only recently that the two women had begun to speak again.

"That's a serious accusation," he said finally. "Do you have any proof?"

She shook her head. "No proof, just motive."

"And that might be?"

"Alan is a bitter man. He's never forgiven Mother, or me, for what happened all those years ago." She laughed shortly. "It's so ironic. At the time, I thought

Mother was a monster for doing what she did. I hated her for years. Now I realize she was right all the time. Alan *was* an opportunist. He never loved me at all. He just married me for what I could give him.''

Seth could see how much the admission cost her. But he had to ask, "And that was ... ?''

"What do you think? Dunleavy Farm, of course.''

He was silent. If it was true, he thought, it made a weird kind of sense. But then he thought of something and asked, "This happened so long ago. If Bradshaw *is* responsible, why did he wait so long to take his revenge?''

"You'll have to ask him that.''

"I'd like to. Where can I find him?''

"I don't know. The last time I saw him—''

"You've been in contact with this guy?''

She winced at his tone. Defensively, she said, "How do you think I became suspicious?''

"Well, I don't know, Aunt Meredith,'' Seth said, trying to keep his anger under control. "Maybe you can tell me why you've kept this to yourself until now.''

For the first time, she glanced away. "You have to understand—''

"I'd like to,'' he said tersely.

She turned back to him in sudden fury. "What did you want me to do? I don't have any proof. I'm not even sure I'm right. But if I am, this man is my daughter's father. What was I going to say to Carla? How could I explain that her own father was responsible for such awful deeds? Have you heard how they found Done Roamin' that morning? It was not a pretty sight. It was as if someone had taken a lead pipe to his hock.''

Seth felt sick. ''Do you think that's what happened?''

''I don't know. But it's a possibility. And as for Done Driftin's so-called stable accident—Alan Bradshaw owns a motorcycle....''

Meredith took another cigarette out of her purse and lit it with a quick snap of her lighter. Seth didn't smoke, but he was almost tempted to grab it out of her hand and take a drag on it himself.

''What about Done Cryin'?'' he asked, wondering if he really wanted to know the answer to that. Thrusting aside a fleeting image of the horse being taken to the killers, he made himself say, ''Is he dead?''

''I don't know,'' Meredith said tensely. Her mouth tightened. ''I don't think even Alan is that depraved.''

''Do you know where the horse is?''

She shook her head.

Seth was silent a moment, then he asked grimly, ''And what about Never Done Dreamin'? Is she still in danger, or is Bradshaw satisfied with the trouble he's caused already?''

With an effort, Meredith held his gaze. ''I know Alan doesn't want Dunleavy Farm to win the Triple Crown,'' she said. ''I don't know how far he'll go to prevent it.''

Seth took a tighter grip on his cane. He had to make himself say, calmly, ''Before I try to find this guy, I'd like to know one thing. I can understand why you didn't want Carla to know, but why in the *hell* didn't you confide your suspicions to Trent or Wade—or even to Dwight, for that matter? If you had, you might have saved everyone a lot of misery."

"I know. And I won't make excuses even I wouldn't believe. But you must remember, Seth, I wasn't sure. I'm still not."

"That's another thing," Seth snapped. "Why *did* you continue meeting with this guy? Don't tell me you still have feelings for him!"

She flinched. "I guess I deserved that. And no, I'm not in love with him. The truth is, he was black-mailing me."

"What? How?"

"He said that if I didn't give him money, he'd contact Carla and get some from her. I didn't want Carla to know what kind of man her father was."

"I think you underestimate Carla."

Wearily, she said, "You don't understand. How could you? You're not a mother. As ridiculous as it sounds now, I wanted to protect Carla. I know she's a grown woman, but she'll always be my daughter. I'd robbed her of one aspect of her heritage by denying we had any connection to Dunleavy Farm. I couldn't deprive her of another. I thought it was better for her to have her own image of her father."

"But—"

"I'm sorry, Seth, but you're not qualified to judge me," she said. "Perhaps when you have your own child, you'll understand. Until then, let me deal with the fact of just how wrong I was about Alan all those years ago. It's difficult to admit what a fool I've been.''

Seth was silent again. Then he said, ''You're right. I've got no call to judge. I've done some things... Well, it doesn't matter. I guess the point is, how we go on from here. Can you tell me where to find Bradshaw before he tries something else. What does he look like? Maybe I've seen him around the track.''

''Maybe,'' she said doubtfully. ''He doesn't bear much resemblance to the man I was once foolish enough to marry—I guess too many years of bitterness, not to mention all that drinking, have taken its toll. But he's about six feet tall, with sandy-colored hair.''

''That description could fit hundreds of guys. Anything else?''

Meredith looked ashamed. ''I hate to say it, but most of the times I've seen him, he looks like a disreputable bum.'' She laughed painfully. ''It's a long story, but Nan saw him once, and she said he was 'scruffy-looking,' you know—unkempt and unshaven.''

An image of the guy he'd seen with Davey that night at the track flashed across Seth's mind. It couldn't be that easy, he thought, but he'd pursue it, anyway. He had to do something. Now that the Preakness was over, he and Dwight would be bringing Never Done Dreamin' back to Churchill Downs for a while before shipping her up to New York for the Belmont. If Bradshaw was going to do something, he'd probably try it in Kentucky.

Filled with a sense of urgency, he glanced at his aunt. She looked so forlorn and defeated that he felt sorry for her. Without thinking, he put a comforting arm around her shoulders.

"If he's the culprit, we'll get him," he said. "Don't worry."

Meredith shuddered. "I just hope that you find him before he gets to Never Done Dreamin'. After what she's been through, it would break Honey's heart if something happened to that filly."

Seth had been thinking the same thing, and he vowed that he'd get this guy if he had to move heaven and earth to do it. It might be the last thing he could do for his wife.

CHAPTER FIFTEEN

THE MINUTE Seth got back to Kentucky, he headed directly to the track to locate Davey. He found his father-in-law sitting on an upturned bucket outside a training barn, spinning stories to an appreciative audience.

"I want to talk to you," Seth said, his voice hard. "Now."

Davey took one look at Seth's face and excused himself. Seth took hold of the man's arm as they found a place where they could talk in private.

Obviously trying to postpone whatever it was that made his son-in-law look ready to kill, Davey beamed up at him and said, "Whew, that was some Preakness, wasn't it? I wish I could have been there in person to see—"

"Cut the small talk, Davey," Seth said. "I want information, and I want it now. You've got one answer, and it had better be the right one. How do I find Alan Bradshaw?"

"Alan who?"

Seth's grip tightened. "Don't mess around. I'm not in the mood."

Davey winced at the pressure on his arm. "But I don't—"

"Let me refresh your memory, then," Seth said. He was hanging on to his control by a thread. "You were talking to him outside Dwight's barn the night the filly won the Derby. Does that ring a bell?"

Davey looked frightened. "Oh, yeah, that guy," he said with bravado. "I know who you mean, but his name isn't Alan *Bradshaw*. At least, that's not what he told me when he wanted me to—"

Davey stopped, looking as if he wanted to bite off his tongue. Resisting the urge to shake the man senseless, Seth said ominously, "When he wanted you to what? You'd better tell me, Davey. We can do this the hard way or the easy way. And I guarantee you won't like the first option."

Swallowing hard, Davey said, "I was going to tell you, Seth, honest. As soon as you got back from Baltimore. I . . . I know how you feel about me, but I just couldn't have it on my conscience anymore."

"Spill it, Davey, and I mean now!"

"You have to believe I wasn't involved," he said anxiously. "I swear it. I admit I'm not much of a man nowadays, but I'd never do anything to hurt a horse. And you know that, too."

Unmoved, Seth said, "Yeah, that may be so. But you damned sure didn't tell anybody what was going on, either, did you?"

Davey had the grace to appear ashamed. "Well, no. But even you should understand that I had no choice. I mean, the guy threatened me if I told. And he was going to send the horse to the killers. You'd have done the same thing. I know it."

Seth frowned. "What are you talking about?"

"I'm talking about when I took that colt, Done Cryin', from the guy, of course. What did you think?"

Seth felt like someone had punched him hard in the gut. Slowly, he said, "Are you saying that you know what happened to Done Cryin'?"

"Not only that, I know where he is. Wasn't that what I was just telling you? I swear, Seth, sometimes it wouldn't hurt you to listen instead of going off half-cocked all the time."

Seth counted to ten. "I'll remember that," he said. "In the meantime, *tell me where I can find that horse.*"

"Gladly," Davey said, relieved. "Truth to tell, I was getting a little tired of the responsibility."

Seth couldn't allow himself to believe that the mystery of Done Cryin's disappearance could be solved so easily. Dragging Davey with him toward the parking lot, he said, "If you're lying to me, Davey, or jerking me around, you're going to be sorry. You got that?"

"Got it," Davey said meekly, climbing into the truck.

"Good," Seth said, and slammed the door, locking him in.

BACK HOME at Dunleavy Farm, two days after her ordeal, Honey was leafing through a magazine in the living room, when she heard the sound of a vehicle. Curious about who might be coming to visit, she went to the front window and peered out. It was a truck and trailer. She squinted to see the logo on the side. It was too far away to read, and when she didn't recognize the rig, she went to get Nan, who was working in the office down the hall.

Nan had been studying pedigrees and bloodlines ever since they got back from Baltimore. Euphoric over Never Done Dreamin's back-to-back victories in the Derby and Preakness, Nan had decided that Dunleavy Farm needed an infusion of new mares—especially since next season, Done Driftin' would be king of the breeding shed.

Although Honey tried to muster the same enthusiasm as everyone else about the changes taking place at the farm, she couldn't help thinking about Seth. With every hour that passed, she became less sure that she'd done the right thing by sending him away. People *can* change, she told herself, and she knew she had to—*wanted* to—give him another chance. But she hadn't seen or talked to him since she'd been released from the hospital, and when they returned to Kentucky, he was nowhere to be found.

She'd called Arizona so many times that Ed, the man who was taking care of the place in their absence, anticipated her now. As soon as he heard her voice, he immediately promised, as he had so often already, that he'd call if even a rumor about Seth turned up. Aside from that, he couldn't help her.

Nan looked up from her desk as Honey knocked lightly on the door. As always, Seth's cousin didn't mince words. "You look terrible," she said. "Are you *sure* you're feeling all right?"

Honey was tired of reassuring everyone that physically, at least, she felt fine. That frightening episode the night of the Preakness, when she thought she was losing the baby, seemed like a bad dream now.

"I'm fine, Nan. But there's a truck and trailer coming in, and I thought you would know something about it."

"A truck and trailer?" Looking surprised, Nan got up. I'm not expecting anyone, are you?"

"You have to ask?"

Nan flushed. "You're right. I'm sorry. Well, let's go see who it is."

But when they opened the front door, Nan didn't recognize the vehicles, either. "No, I don't know—" She stopped midsentence. Her eyes wide, she turned to Honey. "You're not going to believe this, but I think it's Seth."

"Seth! But he doesn't have a rig like that!"

"I know, but—"

The truck pulled up in front of the house. Honey caught a better glimpse of the driver and drew in a sharp breath. For a moment or two, it seemed that her heart stopped. Then it started again, pounding so hard, it almost hurt her ribs.

"It *is* Seth," she said, clutching Nan.

"Who's that with him?"

Honey hadn't even looked. Jerkily, she transferred her gaze to Seth's passenger. "Why, that's my... father! What's *he* doing here?"

They were about to find out. By the time Seth and Davey started to climb down from the cab, Nan had pulled Honey out to the front porch with her. Honey didn't want to go. She'd been worrying about Seth for days. Now that he was safe and sound, she didn't know what to say to him. Just the sight of him made her heart race, and she wanted to run down the steps and into his arms. Frozen with indecision, she stayed where she was.

Nan left Honey by the porch railing and ran down to Seth herself. "Hey!" she said excitedly. "What's this?"

Seth glanced in Honey's direction. Their eyes met for a second, then Honey looked away. A look of hurt flashing across his face, he transferred his gaze again to Nan.

"Hello, cousin," he said. "I brought you a present."

The horse in the trailer neighed shrilly. The sound was so loud that it alerted the entire farm, and before Nan could respond, answering calls came from the other horses, the most resonant, as always, from Done Roamin' himself. The noise drowned out what Seth said next.

Nan had been on her way to give Seth a welcome-back hug. But at the sound of that whinny, she stopped midstride. Her glance flew to the trailer and her face turned pale. From her position on the porch, Honey saw the change in Nan and straightened.

"Nan?" she called.

Nan didn't hear. Her eyes were on Seth, and she said in a strangled voice, "Is that Done Cryin'?"

He grinned. "Don't you recognize the whinny?"

Nan swallowed. "Oh, Seth, don't tease me. If you—"

He took her hand. "Come and see for yourself."

Davey went proudly before them, heading around to the back of the trailer and letting the ramp down. He went inside to unhook the lead, then had to skip nimbly out of the way when the horse came out of the trailer like a rocket. When Nan saw who it was, she gasped.

Honey was watching. When she saw Nan's reaction, her eyes went to the horse, but at first all she saw was a rather thin, definitely out-of-shape bay Thoroughbred. His coat wasn't even brushed.

Then from across the paddocks, Done Roamin' let out another of his shrill, commanding neighs, and the horse by the trailer lifted his head to stare imperiously across at the old stallion. When she saw that, Honey drew in a breath. *Could it be?* she wondered, astounded. Her glance went back to Nan and Seth.

Nan seemed to be doing her best not to break into tears. Her voice shaking, she said, "I'd know Done Cryin' anywhere, Seth. How...how did you...?"

Emotion overcame her, and she stopped with a helpless shake of her head. Smiling even more broadly, Seth gave her a little push forward.

"We'll talk about it later," he said. "For now, just go and say hello to your horse."

Nan didn't need a second invitation. Approaching the young stallion with reverence, she laid a hand on the colt's shoulder. Done Cryin's muscles rippled at her touch, and he lowered his head slightly and gave her a nudge. Obviously, that was all Nan needed. It was clear that she'd been holding on to her control by a thread; when Done Cryin' acknowledged her, she began to sob. Tears streaming down her face, she turned and threw her arms around Seth.

"I thought he was dead," she whispered. "I thought I'd never see him again. I thought..." She shook her head a second time; it was a moment before she could go on. "I don't know how you did it, Seth. But I want you to know that I'll never, *ever* forget this. I'm in your debt forever."

Honey had been so involved in the unfolding scene, she hadn't realized that Octavia and Jamie had come out onto the porch. With them were Carla and Meredith, and all were staring at Done Cryin' with almost identical expressions of amazement and disbelief.

As always, Octavia took charge. To disguise her own obvious emotion, she said briskly, "Well, it's about time you showed up, Seth Dunleavy. Another day or two and I would have sent the dogs out to get you."

Leaving Done Cryin' in Nan's care, Seth came up the steps to kiss his grandmother on the cheek. Then he turned to Jamie and did the same thing. He would have gone to Honey, but she had retreated to the other end of the porch, as far away from the group as possible. When he saw that, he stopped in his tracks.

Clearly intending to give Honey time to decide how she was going to handle Seth's reappearance, the old woman turned and gestured toward the blissful Nan and the young stallion they'd all thought was lost.

"I'm sure there's a story here," she said to Seth. "Would you like to tell us?"

With all her heart, Honey longed to go to Seth. But she wouldn't allow herself to do it, not even when he glanced her way and she saw the hurt in his eyes. Quickly, she averted her gaze and saw her father standing by the trailer. Davey was a welcome distraction and she went to talk to him. Behind her, Carla tactfully took up the slack.

"I for one would like to hear the story," Carla said, tucking her arm inside Seth's. "Come on, cousin. From the looks of things, you've got a lot to tell us."

As the rest of the family gathered around him, Honey turned to her father. Her voice low, she said, "Okay, Pop. What gives?"

Davey immediately looked wounded. "Why are you so suspicious?"

"Because I think it's just a little too convenient that you and Done Cryin' show up at the same time, that's why. You know how worried this family has been about that horse—you didn't have something to do with his disappearance, did you?"

"Aw, now, Puddin'—"

"Don't you *Puddin'* me. I mean it, Pop. If you had *anything* to do with—"

He drew himself up indignantly. "I'm not so sure I like your insinuations. Especially when I helped to save the horse in the first place."

"How did you do that?"

"Ah, now, *that's* a story."

Grimly, she said, "I'll just bet it is."

"You know I'd never hurt a horse!"

"I used to know that, Pop. For the past few years, I haven't been so sure."

He looked genuinely distressed. "What does that mean?"

"You know what it means, Pop," she said. "Now, you tell me how you came to be involved in bringing this horse back home. And it had better be the truth."

"Have I ever lied to you?" he asked plaintively.

When she just stared at him silently, he sighed. "All right. Maybe I have stretched the facts at times. But the *truth* now is that I deserve the reward that's being offered for the safe return of this particular horse. After all, *I* was the one who saved him." He saw her face and raised his voice. "Isn't that true, Seth?"

Interrupted during the telling of his version of the story, Seth turned to Davey. "What's that?"

Davey glanced sideways at his serious daughter. Quickly, he said, "Honey doesn't believe me, but I was the one who led you to this horse. Come on, you tell her now. The truth."

"That's true," Seth said. "As far as it goes."

"Aw, come on, now! Don't be so hard on an old man down on his luck." Obviously realizing he wasn't getting any further with his son-in-law than he had with his daughter, Davey appealed to Octavia. Snatching off his faded baseball cap, he said, "Mrs. Dunleavy, no one's seen fit to introduce us, but my name is Davey LaRue—"

"I know who you are, Mr. LaRue," Octavia said.

Davey looked at little startled at that. But he went on, "Well, then, beggin' your pardon, ma'am, but you just heard Seth here admit that I led him straight to where this horse was. So I think, all things being equal and all, that I deserve the reward. There is still a reward, isn't there?"

Before Octavia could answer, Nan stepped in. Ecstatic that her colt had been returned safe and sound, she hadn't left Done Cryin's side. "Oh, yes, there is indeed a reward, Mr. LaRue. And since it seems that you're the one who—"

"Hold on a minute, Nan," Seth interrupted. "Before you go canonizing Saint Davey here, perhaps you'd better listen to just *how* he led me to Done Cryin'." He fixed his father-in-law with a stern gaze. "Tell them, Davey."

"Yes, I'd be interested in hearing that story, too, Mr. LaRue," Octavia said.

"So would I," Honey muttered.

Twisting his cap in his hands, Davey looked from one family member to the other. "Well, it's not like you think—"

"Can it, Davey," Seth warned. "Are you going to tell them, or shall I?"

"I'll do it, I'll do it," Davey muttered. With a fierce glare in Seth's direction, he jammed his cap back on his head and pulled the brim down over his eyebrows. Then he said, "All right, some fellow approached me not long after I got here about did I know anyone who might want a racehorse—cheap."

"Some fellow," Honey repeated, her eyes hard on her father. "Who?"

"He said his name was Alan—that's all, I swear. And he told me he'd gotten this horse from a guy who was delinquent on his bills. You know how it goes at the track, people not paying their accounts sometimes, running out in the middle of the night with horses that could or couldn't belong to them. You never know. Why, a while ago—"

"Stick with the point, Pop," Honey said.

"All right, all right. The *point* is that he wanted to give the horse away. Said he couldn't use him, he was just taking up room in his own barn. So I said I'd take him."

"To sell yourself, right?" Honey said. She felt sick at the thought.

"Well, how was I to know who the horse was?" Davey demanded.

Too embarrassed to look anywhere else, Honey stared into her father's eyes. "You didn't know who this horse was?"

Davey's glance slid away from hers again. "Well, I couldn't be sure, me not having access to the papers, and all."

"But you had a good guess, right?"

Davey flinched. "Yeah, well, maybe I did," he acknowledged. Then he lifted his head again and looked defensively at the silent group. "But you all should be glad I did take him, right? Who knows what would have happened if someone had asked too many questions. He could have gone to the bush tracks, or been sold for a jumper, or even went to the knackers. Those people don't care—"

"We get the picture, Mr. LaRue," Octavia said. "Please, go on."

"Well, there's not much to go on with. I said I'd take the horse—had a hell of a time finding a place for him, too, you know. And say what you like, Honey, but someone here owes me some room and board for this colt. I had to put out my own stash.''

Nan still had her hand on Done Cryin's neck. She said, ''We'll take care of it, Mr. LaRue.''

''Well, now, that's better. That's all I want. Just a little compensation.'' He looked slyly at Octavia and added, ''Of course, the reward wouldn't be bad, either.''

Apparently, Octavia had heard enough. ''I agree that you should have a reward of some kind.''

Davey grinned at her. ''All right, then. Now, there's a lady, folks, no doubt about it. I thank you kindly, ma'am.''

Octavia said dryly, ''You won't be thanking me so kindly when I tell you that as far as I'm concerned, your reward, Mr. LaRue, is staying out of jail.''

''Oh, now—''

''I wasn't finished.''

Davey hung his head. ''I'm sorry, ma'am. Please, go on.''

''I was about to say that since you have done us a great service, Mr. LaRue, I think we should offer you a job at Dunleavy Farm. I'm sure that our barn manager will be able to keep you busy enough to stay out of trouble.''

Nan grinned. ''Oh, that won't be a problem at all!''

Davey didn't look so pleased, but he didn't dare argue with Octavia Dunleavy. Besides, Honey could tell from his face that he honestly believed that this time, at least, he'd gotten off lucky.

At least where the rest of the family was concerned. Embarrassed and angry and ashamed at what

he'd put these people through, she said, "I can't believe you, Pop. You must have known that everyone
here was worried to death—"

"I know, darlin', I know. And I was going to tell
you—when the heat died down." He shook his head.
"I don't know about that fellow, Alan. I've known
some pretty seedy, shady characters in my time, but
that guy..." His voice trailed off. "He's dangerous,
Honey. To tell the truth, he scared the spit out of me.
I didn't know what he'd do if he thought I'd ratted on
him." His eyes finally met hers. "I didn't want him to
hurt you so I kept quiet."

Honey looked into his face and knew he was finally
telling the truth. Sighing, she threw her arms around
him. "You exasperate the hell out of me, Pop, but I do
love you."

"I love you, too...Puddin'." He gave her a hug in
return, then pushed her gently toward the group on the
porch. "You go on now. This little lady—" he grinned
at Nan, who grinned back, apparently charmed, as so
many people were by Davey LaRue "—and I will take
care of the horse. You go and talk to your husband."

Now that the moment had come, Honey knew that,
if nothing else, she had to thank Seth. She met him at
the foot of the steps, and when everyone else went in,
she said, "I guess you know that you made Nan the
happiest woman on earth."

"I was glad to do it. I hoped it would make up a little for all the other things I've done wrong."

"You don't have to make up for anything, Seth."

"Yes, I do. I want you to know how much I love
you."

"I love you, too. But when I think of how it's been the past year or so..."

"I admit we've had some hard times—"

"It's not the *hard* times I'm talking about. I could have lived in a hovel with you and not cared. It's the way you've acted toward me, the way you've treated me. Sometimes I think you almost hated me."

He dared to take her hands. "I was a bastard, I don't deny it. But I hated being a burden to you—"

"You were never a burden!"

"Oh, yeah? After that damned horse fell on me, I couldn't do anything for myself. I couldn't do anything for you." His jaw tightened with the memory. "And when I saw how hard you were working, I—"

"But I've always worked hard. I never minded that."

"But I was supposed to change that, don't you see? When we got married, I wanted you to have everything. But I couldn't make it work out. I hated myself for not being able to give you what you deserved. And then, when you started going on and on about coming to Dunleavy Farm, it seemed like the last straw. Someone else was going to provide what I couldn't, and I hated that most of all."

"Oh, Seth!" she said mournfully. "I never meant for it to end like this."

Fiercely, he said, "It's not going to end—not if I have anything to say about it! I know I've made mistakes. I know I've hurt you. But damn it, Honey, I love you! If we try, we can work it out. I'll do anything for you."

She wanted to believe him. But she had to be sure of one thing. "Seth, are you sure you're not saying this because I'm pregnant?"

"Honey, I love *you*. Why do you think I stayed at the track to watch over Never Done Dreamin'? Why do you think I went to Baltimore? Why have I been gone these past couple of days to bring Done Cryin' back?"

"You did that for me?"

"Like I said, I'll do anything for you." Grasping her chin so she had to look up at him, he held her eyes as he said, "I know you wanted me to come here so I'd finally have a family of my own, like you and Davey do. And I have to say, I'm glad I did come...now. But the truth, my love, is that *you're* all the family I ever needed, and I'm lost without you."

Honey's eyes filled with tears. "And I'm lost without you."

Seth took her in his arms and kissed her like the husband he'd once been, and would be again.

For Honey, it was all she needed. With all her heart, she kissed him back.

CHAPTER SIXTEEN

"I'M SO EXCITED, I could die," Nan said on the day Never Done Dreamin' was scheduled to run in the Belmont Stakes. "Aren't you?"

Honey was too nervous to be excited. In a short while, Never Done Dreamin' could accomplish what no other filly in racing history had. *If* nothing happened to prevent her from trying.

Everyone in the family had come to New York to watch Never Done Dreamin' run in this last leg of the Triple Crown. Wade and Trent had accompanied Octavia, Meredith and Jamie to their reserved box, but Honey and Nan and Carla were down by the paddocks. The horses had been saddled a short time ago, the jockeys given last-minute instructions. Now the field of twelve was out on the track, warming up. The time was almost here, and Honey was so anxious, she felt faint.

Rubbing her cold hands together, she said, "Do you really think she can win?"

"The way she's been training? I don't think there's a three-year-old alive who can beat her," Nan said. She pretended to look around for eavesdroppers. "Don't tell Trent, but I think that includes his beloved Majnoon."

Honey smiled with lips that felt too stiff to bend. Even though Dwight had installed stringent security measures in his barn to protect Never Done Dreamin', and had carried them over when he and Seth moved the filly to New York for training, she couldn't stop worrying. There had been no sign of the elusive, mysterious Alan since the Maryland episode, but she couldn't rid herself of the feeling that he still had something awful planned.

"It is now post time!"

When the announcement came over the loudspeakers, Honey jumped a foot. The race was about to begin. If Alan had set anything sinister in motion, it was too late to stop it.

Carla took her arm. "Let's go. We have to get up to the grandstand with the others."

Trying to stop her teeth from chattering, Honey said, "You go ahead. I want to watch it down here."

"But you promised Seth you'd watch from the box."

"I know. But he'll understand. I can't explain it. I just have to stay here. It'll be okay, I promise." Summoning a bright—and completely false—smile, she made a little motion with her hand. "Go on now, or you won't make it."

They were reluctant to depart, but finally they hurried off. Left alone in an ocean of surging humanity, Honey found a place by the rail. From her position in front of the grandstand, near the finish line, she could see the horses and their outriders coming up to the gate. Her dread increased. In another minute or two, they'd all be inside, the doors would open—and history might be made. Despite her deep concern for the filly, she couldn't help marveling that Never Done Dreamin' could be the first filly in the sport of racing to take the Triple Crown.

She closed her eyes, and thought: *Oh, please, even if she doesn't win, just let her come back safe.*

FROM HIS POSITION near the starting gate, Seth was thinking the same thing. Dwight probably was, too, although he couldn't be sure. The trainer was hyperventilating so badly that Seth had forced the man to sit down. Seth had promised not to let the filly out of his sight, even for an instant.

Now, it was almost out of his hands, all the days and nights of worrying and wondering if Alan whatever-his-name was would try something again. Things had been quiet ever since they got back from the Preakness—ominously so. Seth knew that everyone wanted to believe Alan was gone, but he was sure it wasn't over.

Still, he thought as he turned to search the crowd—for what, he wasn't sure—what could Alan do now? It was post time, the horses were at the gate, soon they'd be out on the track and running. Unless the bastard intended to shoot the filly out from under Ian, what could he be planning?

Even so, his eyes restlessly scanned the stands, the apron before the grandstand, even the paddock area. He didn't see anything suspicious, but that didn't reassure him. He couldn't shake that feeling deep in his gut that something was wrong.

In fact, he'd been so worried, he'd insisted that Honey watch the race with the rest of the family, instead of here with him. She hadn't liked it, but she'd agreed.

Glad he didn't have to be concerned about her—for the moment, at least—he turned toward the track again. Ian and the filly were just coming up to the gate, and despite his worry, Seth had to admit that Never Done Dreamin' had never looked better. Her head was up, her ears pricked, her eyes alert. Her blood-bay coat shone in the afternoon sun, and she looked ready—eager—to run.

Someone joined him at the rail. When Seth saw his father-in-law, he frowned. "What are you doing here?" he asked.

"Aw, now, let's call a truce for the moment—at least until after the race, all right?" Davey said. His eyes found the filly and he grinned. "She's looking just fine, isn't she?"

Seth was about to agree, when suddenly Davey's face changed. His eyes widened and he looked so scared that Seth grabbed his father-in-law's arm. Quickly, he asked, "What is it?"

When Davey's mouth opened and closed like a fish, no words coming out, Seth looked toward the gate, but he didn't see anything that ought to concern him—or so he thought. Turning back to Davey, he gave the man a hard shake. "Talk to me, Davey," he warned.

These past couple of weeks, Davey had been turning himself inside out to be helpful. Davey's portion of the reward money had something to do with his attitude, Seth was sure. Seth hadn't wanted to take the

reward, but Trent and Nan had insisted. They had
pointed out that he could use it to set up a trust fund
for his coming child. He couldn't argue with that;
then, in a spurt of generosity that surprised even him,
he'd given Davey a share. After all, he'd rationalized,
no matter what Davey had done, he *had* helped to find
Done Cryin' and bring him safely home. The colt was
now at Dunleavy Farm, getting fat and fit and enjoying a well-earned rest. Nan hadn't decided if she'd race
him again this year, but there had been a gleam in her
eye when she recalled the Breeder's Cup races that
took place in the fall.

Davey pulled himself together. With a shaking finger, he pointed toward the gate, where the last of the
horses were being loaded. Everything was as it should
be.

Or was it?

"There he is," Davey gasped.

Seth didn't have to ask who Davey meant. Whirling around, he searched the area again. This time, with
Davey's help, he spotted Alan. Never Done Dreamin'
was in post position five; she had already been loaded
into the gate. As with all the horses, an assistant starter
was inside with her and Ian. His job was to stand on
the narrow ledge by the horse's head and be ready to
help in case something happened. Seth took one look
and knew the man was the one he'd been looking for.

He didn't have time to wonder how Alan had talked
his way into such a position. Time seemed to slow until it was barely in motion. In the background of his
mind, Seth heard the raucous noise of the big racing
crowd falter and then hush as everyone waited for the

horses to leave the gate; he saw the jockeys crouch low and the horses lean back on their haunches. Even the air seemed to grow still.

With vision that seemed suddenly much too acute, Seth also saw Alan's hand move in the split second before the gate opened. He wanted to shout a warning, but already it was too late. Alan slapped something on the filly's neck, then the gate doors flew open and eleven of the twelve horses inside thundered onto the track.

Never Done Dreamin' wasn't with them. Transfixed with horror, Seth saw the filly rear. For a terrified moment, he thought she would go right over backward.

But Never Done Dreamin' was too much the champion for that. In a move that Seth knew he would never forget, the gallant filly fought for her balance, and won. She had barely come down on all four feet again, before she was out of the slot and racing after the field. Her takeoff was so violent that Ian was nearly unseated. Grimly, the jockey clung to her mane, and they were off.

So was Alan. By the time Seth jerked his glance away from the sight of the filly back to the gate, Alan had jumped off and was walking briskly toward the opening in the rail that would let him onto the backside—and away from the track.

Without a thought for his cane or his cast, Seth took off after Alan. He thought he heard Davey's alarmed cry, but he couldn't take the time to look back. He ducked under the rail and headed after Bradshaw.

As he half hopped, half ran, he dimly heard the announcer calling the race, but he couldn't listen. It seemed a forgone conclusion that, no matter how fast she was, Never Done Dreamin' was out of the race. She'd been lengths behind when she finally hit the track, and she was racing against the best colts in the country. All he could do was hope that she wouldn't burst her heart trying to catch the rest of the field; knowing how competitive she was, how determined to win, anything could happen. No matter what, he knew she wouldn't give up.

Alan hadn't slowed down. In fact, he was walking faster, and Seth knew he was going to lose him. "Hey, you!" he yelled. "Stop!"

Alan actually turned around to see who was shouting at him. Seth realized that it was now or never, and in a burst of speed, he hurled himself forward in a flying tackle. He and Alan collided violently, and as they crashed to the ground, Seth grabbed what he could. This guy was *not* going to get away.

"Get off me, get off me!" Alan snarled, trying to get out from under. He punched and kicked in all directions, but Seth clung tenaciously. Locked together in combat, they rolled around on the ground. Seth freed one hand long enough to get in a few hard punches of his own.

"You...sorry...bastard," he panted, pummeling the man to make him stay still. "I'm going to—*oof!*"

Alan had managed to get free. The kick he aimed at Seth's head went a little awry, catching him in the chest instead. Gasping, Seth reached wildly for the guy's shoe, wrenched as hard as he could, and was rewarded by a howl of pain.

"How do you like that?" he growled.

But victory was short-lived. With a savage cry, Alan turned on him again with windmilling arms, trying to land any blow he could. Seth took one on the side of the jaw that made him see stars, and another to the gut that knocked the breath out of him. The thought flitted through his mind that he was definitely getting the worst of this match, and that spurred him on.

"Let me go," Alan shouted as Seth renewed the attack. "You got nothing on me!"

"Oh no? I saw what you just did to the filly! You've got a lot of questions to answer."

Seth was so enraged that he managed to get the upper hand. After a flurry of punches that drove Alan backward, Seth pushed him over a hay bale and rammed his good knee down hard on the man's chest, pinning him down—and for the first time, saw his face clearly. When he thought of how much misery this man had caused everyone at Dunleavy Farm, he drew back his arm. His expression was murderous, his fist was clenched, and in that moment, he was prepared to beat Alan Bradshaw senseless. His arm swung down.

"Seth! Seth!" someone called. "Oh, my God, please stop!"

Seth barely had time to register that the voice belonged to Honey before she was grabbing his arm and trying to pull him away.

"Stop, stop!" she cried. "You're going to kill him!"

Seth *wanted* to kill him. He drew back his arm again. It wasn't until then that he realized the man had fainted.

"Oh no you don't!" he shouted. "You're not going to get off that easy!"

Honey was still clinging to him. Dimly, Seth heard the blaring of the loudspeakers positioned around the backside. Amazed, he realized that all this had happened in the space of a minute or less: the race was still on.

The announcer was shouting. The excitement in his voice penetrated Seth's fury. With Honey holding him back, he lifted his head to listen.

The crowd was going crazy; even from this distance, the cheering and yelling was so loud and frenzied, it was hard to hear what was going on.

Then the announcer screamed over the noise: *"And it's Never Done Dreamin' making her move, Never Done Dreamin' in... fifth place... in fourth... in THIRD place now!"*

Honey and Seth looked at each other. The same thought was on both their faces: How was it possible? She'd been so far back. No filly, no *colt,* could have caught the field after a start like that.

Over their heads, the loudspeaker howled: *"And it's Never Done Dreamin' and Glory Snatcher fighting it out! Never Done Dreamin' and Glory Snatcher, down to the wire now! Never Done Dreamin'... Glory... And it's...!"*

The announcer gasped to a stop. When Seth heard the collective moan of the crowd, he knew it was a photo finish. Blankly, he looked at Honey.

"Do you think . . . ?" Seth couldn't say it.

Honey was more concerned with him. She cried, "Oh, Seth, look at your leg!"

He followed her glance. As if from a distance, he saw that on the leg with the cast, blood was seeping through his jeans. *Funny,* he thought. *I don't feel a thing.*

Honey tried to pull him away. "We have to get you to a doctor! Can you get up? No, wait! I don't think you should try to walk. Stay here. Don't move! I'll find someone and—"

"Wait—" Seth reached for her hand. "Don't you want to hear the results of the race?"

Honey's face crumpled. "I don't care about the race. You're more important! Seth, you're the most important thing in my life!"

And with that, she threw herself into his arms. Her cheeks tearstained, her face blotched from crying, Honey had never seemed more beautiful to Seth than at that moment.

Just then, Alan groaned, and Seth came grimly back to earth. "I guess we'd better call someone before he wakes up."

Honey got up. "You sit still. I'll go find a—"

She stopped. Nan was running toward them, shouting, "Where have you been? Everybody's looking all over for you! Didn't you see what happened? Didn't you hear?"

By the time Nan rushed up, Seth was on his feet. Nan was too excited to give more than a cursory glance to the prostrate Alan. Grabbing them both, she said,

"She caught him right at the wire. It was the most thrilling thing I've ever seen!"

Honey and Seth looked at each other. Then they both looked at Nan. Honey said, her voice choked, "Are you saying—"

"It was almost a dead heat," Nan crowed. "Can you believe it? She came from so far behind, but she did it! *Never Done Dreamin' just won the Triple Crown!*"

EPILOGUE

THERE WAS an air of excitement at Dunleavy Farm this spring evening. A very special event was about to happen. The double wedding would have occurred sooner, but the two brides had waited until their matron of honor was her slim self and their best man was out of his cast and on his own two feet again.

And everyone had wanted to wait until the newest addition to the family was old enough to attend. David James Dunleavy, or D.J. as he was affectionately called, had been a Christmas baby, one of the best presents the proud parents had ever received. A beautiful child, he had blond hair so pale it was almost white, and even as an infant, his eyes already held a hint of the Dunleavy green. He was a good baby, but as his smug grandfather commented more than once, on occasion there was nothing wrong with his lungs.

The wedding service was scheduled for early evening, one of the most beautiful times of the day at the farm. The gazebo where the ceremony was to take place was almost hidden under masses of cascading flowers and greenery; the scent of roses and carnations permeated the soft air.

The sun was already going down as Octavia slipped away from the house and made her way to the paddock area to give Done Roamin' his nightly carrot. Tonight her step was light, and as she walked along, she thought: *Everything had worked out. She couldn't have asked for a better ending.*

Then she thought of Carla, and her smile faltered slightly. Carla hid it well, but Octavia knew that her granddaughter was horrified at what her father, Alan Bradshaw, had done. Guilt-stricken, Meredith had tried to convince Carla that the man was only her biological sire, and that the one who really counted was Phillip, the stepfather who had raised her. Octavia knew that Carla would eventually be fine. She just needed time to adjust to the fact that her own father had been behind every one of the attacks on Dunleavy horses—including the so-called barn accident Done Roamin' had sustained.

Alan Bradshaw had planned his revenge for a long time, Octavia mused sadly, even going so far as to insinuate himself into the Belmont as a dependable assistant starter. The day of the race, he had switched with another man at the last minute so he could be in the gate slot five, which the filly had drawn. Once there, it had been a simple matter to palm the electric buzzer he'd used to scare Never Done Dreamin'.

Now Alan Bradshaw was in jail, where he should have been all along, and Octavia could afford the tiniest bit of pity for the man. How awful it must be, she thought, to be so embittered that it was acceptable to wreak vengeance on defenseless creatures. In addition to trying to ruin Never Done Dreamin's chances at winning, Alan had also confessed to injuring Done

Driftin', abducting Done Cryin', and to trying to run Nan off the road.

Still, Octavia decided more cheerfully, she always believed that most things happened for the best, and that was certainly true of this family. The experience had so changed Meredith that she was considering moving back to the States from England. Of course, Octavia thought with a secret smile, that could be because she wanted to be near Carla and Wade.

Nan, Trent and Derry would soon be a family, Octavia thought happily. She wanted Nan to take Done Cryin' with her to ChangeOver Farm, but Nan had refused.

"He belongs here, at Dunleavy Farm," Nan had said gently. Then, typical Nan, she had added with a twinkle, "But don't worry, as barn manager, I'll see him every day."

Another piece of news, Octavia thought as she walked along, concerned Seth. She still shuddered when she remembered the day of the Belmont, and how they'd all thought that he had done some permanent damage to his leg by chasing Alan down. But Trent had called his friend, the orthopedic surgeon, and she'd put Seth's leg back together as though it had never been broken. When the last cast came off, he hadn't even walked with a limp.

They'd all been celebrating, when a representative from a Fortune 500 company showed up at the farm to talk to him. Apparently, Seth had submitted an idea some time ago for what he called a "horse elevator"—a hydraulic device that raised or lowered horses, front or back, for purposes of breeding and medical treatment. The company wanted to buy Seth's patent and manufacture the device, and they were eager to pay him a princely sum for the right to do it.

Octavia had told Seth that she was willing to pay a handsome amount herself when the device came out. But Seth, who had changed so much since coming here, had laughed and told her she was one person who could take anything he had. After all, he'd said with eyes that sparkled, she was family.

Thinking about it, Octavia laughed. But wouldn't it be wonderful, she thought, if Done Roamin' could go back to the breeding shed again? She hugged herself at the idea. He'd give those hotshot sons of his, Done Driftin' and Done Cryin', a run for their money, wouldn't he?

As always, Done Roamin' was standing sentry on the hill when she approached the paddock. When he saw her, he uttered his shrill whinny and started toward her. Tonight as she watched him approach with that awkward, shambling gait Octavia thought of his magnificent daughter, Never Done Dreamin'.

Oh, what a race the Belmont had been! It still gave her chills to think about it. To start from so far back and to be first under the wire was a feat for the record books. If that filly had had wings on her heels, she couldn't have run a better race. They were all so proud of her, they could burst.

With all that had happened, Octavia had believed—mistakenly, as it turned out—that she'd be able to rest. But the farm was busier than ever now. Both her daughters were staying a while, and her grandchildren had big ideas. True, Never Done

Dreamin' had won her bid to become the first filly in racing to win the Triple Crown, but that wasn't stopping the younger Dunleavys. Carla was helping Wade with his training barn. Seth and Honey were working with the new additions to Dunleavy Farm. Nan was still manager and all four were combining their knowledge, talent and experience, to produce the best distaff runners in history.

They could do it, too, Octavia thought fondly, when Done Roamin' came to the fence and put his head over in their nightly ritual. As she stroked his nose and he chewed contentedly on his carrot, Octavia recalled all the outstanding horses Dunleavy Farm had produced. One of the greatest was standing here beside her.

The only thing she regretted now was that she hadn't been able to reconcile with Gary. She missed her handsome, difficult son at times, more than she could say, and she wanted to tell him—

Just then, the musical sound of a chime interrupted her thoughts. Sure she'd imagined the noise, she turned and looked in the direction of the barn. The sound came again, wafted along by a gentle breeze that seemed to have sprung up out of nowhere. Her glance went to the weather vane atop the barn's roof, and when she realized the chime was coming from that, she put a hand to her throat.

Gary mounted that weather vane, she remembered. He'd done it for her birthday one year before he left, because he knew she loved the chimes. But she hadn't heard the sound of it for years, and as she stared at it, it chimed a third time.

Gary, she thought—and then laughed at herself. Oh, she *was* getting to be a senile old woman if she believed that the chime was somehow a sign from him.

No, the answer was undoubtedly much less imaginative, and a great deal more practical. With all the sprucing up that had been going on around here, Seth had probably sent one of the men up to the roof to give the old weather vane a swipe with a polishing rag. There was nothing mystical about it.

But still ...

Smiling to herself as she turned away, Octavia decided that if she wanted to take it as a sign that Gary had forgiven her, that's what she'd do. Heaven knew, she was certainly old enough to believe what she wished.

Done Roamin' had almost finished his carrot; soon it would be time for her to go back to the house. But Octavia didn't want to leave just yet, and as she and the horse stood together by the fence, as they had so often, she felt excited, almost young again.

And why not? she thought. She'd done what she set out to do all those months ago when she'd written the letters to her grandchildren. After so many years of misunderstandings and bitterness and anger, she'd finally put the past to rest.

"We did ourselves proud, Roamy," she murmured, her hand on the old stallion's glossy neck. She thought of D.J. and the great-grandchildren she might have yet, and her heart swelled in her chest. "We've passed the torch to a new generation. Because of us, the Dunleavy legacy will live on."

As though he understood what she meant, Done Roamin' snorted. Then he lifted his head and let out a shrill blast of a whinny, as if to say that, whatever the future held, he would always be king at Dunleavy Farm.

Octavia smiled indulgently. And king he would be, she knew. But now it was time to go back to the house. It was a special day, and she couldn't be late.

AT THE GAZEBO, the nervous grooms, Wade and Trent, with their best man, Seth, took their places and tried to smile at their guests. In the audience, Dwight Connor grinned at them while Davey LaRue, looking both proud and uncomfortable in his tuxedo, showed Octavia to a place of honor on a chair in front. Then, to the lilting strains of a harp, Meredith came down the makeshift aisle. Dressed in a cameo-tinted silk suit, she was escorted to her chair by a beaming Derry, who was also wearing his first tux. As Meredith sat down next to Octavia, she patted her mother's hand, then winked at Jamie, who was sitting on Octavia's other side.

Jamie had toned down her appearance in deference to the two brides. But she couldn't help exhibiting her flair for the dramatic in another of her floating creations, and she was wearing tiers of chiffon that shaded from the palest pink to the deepest rose. Completing the ensemble was a wide-brimmed hat that evoked memories of days gone by. When she saw Meredith winking at her, she winked back.

Also in the audience was D.J., who began to comment on the delay by starting to fuss. Up at the front, his handsome father, resplendent in white tie and tails, gave his son a quick look. But Yolanda, who had flown in from Montana a few weeks before to be with Nan on her special day, and who had been easily persuaded that the youngest Dunleavy needed a nanny, saw Seth looking at them and indicated with a nod that all would be well. She and Teresa, who was sitting beside her, smiled down at the baby, and the child stopped fussing and bubbled back sounds of contentment.

The background music changed just then, and as the time-honored strains heralding the bride's arrival wafted through the air, everyone turned. Wearing a dress of royal blue satin and carrying yellow roses, Honey came down the flower-strewn aisle. With her blond hair pulled up and pinned with more roses, she looked much too young to be the matron of honor. She passed Yolanda and D.J., and when she looked down at the baby, he gurgled. Her eyes met Seth's, and at the adoring expression on his face, she blushed and glanced away.

The music changed to the wedding march and everyone stood as Carla and Nan, both radiant in their bridal gowns, came down the aisle together. Carla's dress of ivory satin and Belgian lace was breathtaking. With puffed sleeves, it was almost sheathlike, fitting her slender body like a glove. Instead of a veil, she had opted for a smart little hat tipped over one eye.

Nan, on the other hand, had chosen a more traditional gown. Off-the-shoulder, it was also ivory-colored, and the fitted lace bodice ended in a V below her waist, at which point the bouffant skirt billowed down to the ground, making her seem to float. In lieu of a hat or veil, she had chosen a headpiece made of tulle and pearls. It was difficult to decide who was more beautiful.

As Carla and Nan joined Wade and Trent at the altar, Honey stepped to one side, Seth to the other. Their eyes met again, and they smiled at each other. Then the minister came forward and began solemnly, ''We are gathered together today to join . . .''

In the audience, claiming his Dunleavy legacy right from the start, D.J. clapped his tiny hands together and crowed with delight. Despite the solemn moment, everyone laughed. The minister was just starting again when, from the paddocks, came the clarion call of old Done Roamin'. It was immediately answered by his three magnificent offspring. It seemed even the horses approved of this momentous occasion.

HARLEQUIN SUPERROMANCE

COMING NEXT MONTH

#666 AS YEARS GO BY • Margaret Chittenden
Showcase
The past: Englishwoman Bliss Turner falls in love with American
airman Paul Carmichael. But when the war intrudes, he leaves her,
unmarried and pregnant. She never sees him again. *The present:*
Simon Flynn is searching for "Bliss," the woman his grandfather
had loved during the war. He never dreamed he'd fall in love with
her granddaughter, Rebecca…or that he'd get caught up in the web
of deceit that had shaped the past—and threatened the future.…

#667 FATHERS & OTHER STRANGERS • Evelyn A. Crowe
Family Man
Matt Bolt. A top homicide detective before he made one, almost
fatal, mistake and ended up with a bullet in his chest, another in his
leg. Then the final blow. His ex-wife dies, and his son—a child
he's seen only *twice*—is now in his care. Worse, the boy seems to
hate him. Enter Virginia Carney, a woman running from her past,
running for her life. And Bolt thought he had problems *before!*

#668 THE KEEPER • Margot Early
Reunited
Zachary Key married Grace Sutter for love—and for a Green Card.
When Grace found that out, she went home devastated. She
returned to Moab, Utah, to take over her father's Colorado River
outfitting company. Now, more than a year later, Zac reenters her
life. Something strange happened to him after she left—something
he doesn't remember. Grace is still in love with him, but does their
marriage stand a chance?

#669 A MOTHER'S LOVE • Janice Kaiser
Women Who Dare
Anne Leighton's ex-husband, an air force flyboy, has refused to
return her son after his "holiday" in England. His childless new
wife wants someone to mother. But not Anne's son! RAF Base
Commander Grant Sarver becomes an unlikely ally, yet it may
come down to a choice of loyalties—for both of them.

AVAILABLE NOW:

#662 NEVER DONE DREAMIN'
Janis Flores

#663 THE SECRET CHILD
Jamie Ann Denton

#664 MAN OF MY DREAMS
Margot Dalton

#665 KATE
Patricia Armstrong